LOWCOUNTRY BOMBSHELL (#2)

"Boyer delivers big time with a witty mystery that is fun, radiant, and impossible to put down. I love this book!"

– Darynda Jones,
New York Times Bestselling Author

"*Lowcountry Bombshell* is that rare combination of suspense, humor, seduction, and mayhem, an absolute must-read not only for mystery enthusiasts but for anyone who loves a fast-paced, well-written story."

– Cassandra King,
Author of *The Same Sweet Girls* and *Moonrise*

"A complicated story that's rich and juicy with plenty of twists and turns. It has lots of peril and romance—something for every cozy mystery fan."

– New York Journal of Books

LOWCOUNTRY BOIL (#1)

"Imaginative, empathetic, genuine, and fun, *Lowcountry Boil* is a lowcountry delight."

– Carolyn Hart,
Author of *What the Cat Saw*

"*Lowcountry Boil* pulls the reader in like the draw of a riptide with a keeps-you-guessing mystery full of romance, family intrigue, and the smell of salt marsh on the Charleston coast."

– Cathy Pickens,
Author of the *Southern Fried Mysteries* and *Charleston Mysteries*

"Plenty of secrets, long-simmering feuds, and greedy ventures make for a captivating read...Boyer's chick lit PI debut charmingly showcases South Carolina island culture."

— Library Journal

Lowcountry
BORDELLO

**The Liz Talbot Mystery Series
by Susan M. Boyer**

Lowcountry
BORDELLO

A Liz Talbot Mystery

Susan M. Boyer

HENERY PRESS

LOWCOUNTRY BORDELLO
A Liz Talbot Mystery
Part of the Henery Press Mystery Collection

First Edition
Trade paperback edition | November 2015

Henery Press
www.henerypress.com

ISBN-13: 978-1-943390-17-5

Printed in the United States of America

For my son,
Brandon Thomas Washington,
with much love
and gratitude for all the joy you brought with you into my life.
I could've done without the premature grey hair.

ACKNOWLEDGMENTS

I'm deeply grateful to each and every reader who has connected with Liz Talbot and her sprawling network of family, friends, and clients. If you've recommended the books to a friend or your book club, I'm forever in your debt. If you are a bookseller who stocks the Liz Talbot Mysteries and recommends them to your customers, please let me know if you ever need a kidney.

To Jim Boyer, my wonderful husband, best friend, and fiercest advocate, thank you could never cover it; nevertheless, thank you for everything you do to help me live my dream.

To everyone at Henery Press—Kendel Lynn, Art Molinares, Erin George, Rachel Jackson, Anna Davis, and Stephanie Chontos, this book is better because of all of you. Thank you for all you do. I count myself as very fortunate to be a Henery Press author, and cherish the friendship of the other authors in the Hen House.

For everything, always, heartfelt thanks to the fabulous Hank Phillippi Ryan.

To my dear friends Martha and Mary Rudisill, eleventh and twelfth-generation Charlestonians, respectively, thank you for your continued enthusiastic assistance.

To my cousin, Linda Ketner, thank you for answering a million questions, and for the use of your former home in this book.

Thank you, Annalise and Jack Simmons, for lending me your bed and breakfast and answering my questions when I called out of the blue, even though you suspected I might be crazy.

Special thanks to all the members of Books & Wine with Wendi, a book club near and dear to my heart. The following members guest star in this book: Dana Clark, Wendi Hill, Amber McDonald, Lori Stowe, and Heather Wilder. None of these wonderful young women have ever worked in a bordello to the best of my knowledge.

To Ginger and Rut Jacks, thank you for a wonderful evening and for sharing such fabulous fodder. I hope you enjoy what I did with it.

As always, unending thanks to Kathie Bennett, Susan Zurenda, Rowe Copeland, and Liz Bemis. I have no idea what I'd do without y'all.

Thank you Jill Hendrix, owner of Fiction Addiction bookstore, for your continued advice and support.

I'm terrified I've forgotten someone. If I have, please know it was unintentional and in part due to sleep deprivation. I am truly grateful to everyone who has helped me along this journey.

ONE

The dead are not altogether reliable. Colleen, my best friend, calls herself a Guardian Spirit. I can't argue with the facts at hand: She's been dead seventeen years, and she watches my back. I'm a private investigator, so situations arise from time to time wherein my back needs watching. Technically, Colleen's afterlife mission is to protect Stella Maris, our island home near Charleston, South Carolina, from developers and all such as that. Since I'm on the town council and can't abide the notion of condos and time-shares on our pristine beaches, protecting me falls under her purview.

Solving my cases, however, does not. She'll tell me that in a skinny minute should I happen to mention how she could be more helpful. But she has been known to toss me the occasional insight from beyond that provokes a train of thought, which, upon reflection, proves useful. Here's the thing: Colleen shows up when she detects I'm in danger. Sometimes she warns me in advance. Occasionally she drops by just to chat. But she doesn't come whenever I think of her or call her name. It rarely works like that.

One Monday in December, I really could've used Colleen's perspective. We were closing in on Christmas, and I was getting married on the twentieth—in five days. I was a teensy bit distracted, is what I'm saying.

It was a little after ten in the morning, and I was at my desk in the living room of my beachfront house, which doubles as my office. I was deep into research on a criminal case Nate, my partner and fiancé, and I were working for Andy Savage. Andy was a high-profile Charleston attorney, and while this case didn't amount to much more than fact-checking, we hoped it would lead to a lucrative relationship for Talbot and Andrews, our agency.

I stared at my computer screen and reached for one of Mamma's Christmas cookies. My phone trilled out the ringtone named Old Phone. Old Phone was reserved for old friends. I grabbed my phone instead of the cookie.

Robert Pearson. He'd been a year ahead of me in high school, the same age as my brother, Blake. He'd married one of my best friends. Robert was also our family attorney, and he and I were both on the Stella Maris town council.

I tapped the green "accept" button.

After we exchanged the usual pleasantries, he said, "I wondered, if you're not too busy, could you drop by this afternoon? There's something I want to run by you."

"I have an appointment at one that's going to take most of the afternoon."

Multi-toned highlights are a maintenance issue, especially with hair as long as mine. My natural sandy blond would turn Tweety Bird yellow if Dori looked at it wrong. She always took her time, but five days before my wedding she'd be excruciatingly meticulous. I couldn't walk down the aisle with yellow hair.

"Noon?" he asked.

"Sure. See you then."

"Thanks, Liz. I really appreciate it." He sounded way too grateful for such an ordinary request. This is what should've tipped me off that something was up.

Stella Maris has a lovely park right in the middle of town. Main Street and Palmetto Boulevard, the island's two main thoroughfares, both spill into a traffic circle that borders the park. Robert's office was in the professional building on one side of the traffic circle, next to the courthouse. It was unusual for both his receptionist and his paralegal to be out, but when I walked into the reception area, no one was there except the three-foot-tall Santa Claus by the Christmas tree. LeAnn Rimes's remake of "Hard Candy Christmas" played through the office sound system.

"Robert?" I walked towards his private office. The door was closed.

"Coming." Footsteps. The door swung open. "Sorry about that. Everyone's at lunch. Come in. Have a seat." He made his way back to the other side of his massive desk, settled into his chair, and leaned forward, hands clasped on his desk. Robert was a good-looking man—chiseled face, brown hair, blue eyes, and a movie star smile. The smile was absent today.

I made myself comfortable in one of his guest chairs. "What's up?"

His eyes closed for a moment, then popped open and locked onto mine. "I need to retain you." The words tumbled quickly out of his mouth, like they had to escape before he lost his nerve.

A thousand things went through my head. I'd known for years that Robert, who was probably in the dictionary under "upstanding citizen," was hiding something contrary to everything I knew about him. Something that might've made him vulnerable to blackmail. I'd dug into his affairs back when I was working my Gram's murder but had never found anything. I was all atingle with excitement.

I held his gaze. "Tell me what's going on."

"This is confidential, right?"

I tilted my head. "Of course. Assuming you haven't committed a crime, aren't planning one, have no knowledge of one, et cetera."

It was his turn to raise his eyebrows and give me a look that said, *Really?*

"Robert, how long have we known each other?"

"You see?" He gestured dramatically with both hands, a thing he was not prone to doing. "That's the point."

"What's the point?"

"We've known each other most of our lives. In some ways, that makes this easier. In other ways it makes it harder."

"I'm listening."

He sat back in his chair. "Olivia's up to something."

"Olivia?" Olivia Tess Beauthorpe Pearson would stand as one of my four bridesmaids on Saturday. "What do you mean?"

"She's behaving oddly."

Exercising considerable restraint, I refrained from guffawing. I loved Olivia like a sister. But she'd never lived a commonplace day in her entire life. She thrived on high drama. She was a force of nature—a very well-bred one. "What do you mean, exactly?"

"She's going out more at night. She'll say it's to do with the wedding or book club or the Christmas program at church, but it's something all the time. And she stays out far too late. The kids ask me when Mommy's coming home and I don't know what to tell them half the time."

"Is that all?"

He screwed his face up into a powerful scowl. "No, that's not all."

I waited.

"She's on the phone all the damn time. Talking real low. When I come in, she'll raise her voice and say, 'Bye-bye now,' and hang up."

Gently I asked, "Do you suspect she's having an affair, is that it?"

The scowl got tighter. "No, of course not...hell, I don't know." He propped his elbows on his desk and rested his forehead on his clasped hands. "I don't want to ask a stranger to do this. Will you please just follow her for a few nights when she leaves the house and see where she goes? Who she sees? She's going out again tonight. Claims it's a committee meeting for the Charleston Library Society."

I pondered this for a few minutes. I cared deeply about both Robert and Olivia. As a general rule, I'd do anything to help a friend. But I was not about to put myself between two friends in the midst of marital discord.

"Robert, I'm really sorry, but I couldn't possibly."

He looked perplexed.

"Why not? Isn't this what you do for a living?"

"We do accept a fair number of domestic cases. But think this through. Heaven forbid, but what if I find out she's involved in something illegal? Or that she is having an affair? I'd maybe end up having to testify against one of my oldest friends in court. I just can't get in the middle of this. I think you should talk to Olivia."

"Don't you think I've tried that?"

"Well, what does she have to allow?"

"Everything's fine. I'm imagining things." His scowl melted into a crushed look.

I could read the pain on my friend's face. Damnation. I stood. I had to get out of there before my sympathy for him outsmarted my common sense. "Robert, I'll be praying that you are, in fact, imagining things. I'm so sorry. Please try talking to her again."

I walked over, reached out and placed a hand on his shoulder, and patted it. Then I got the heck out of there.

TWO

After dinner that night, in my favorite pajamas, I curled up in the oversized chair in the sunroom with a glass of pinot noir and a Harlan Coben novel. White lights twinkled on the Christmas tree, illuminating crystal and clear glass ornaments collected over the years, many of them angels. Gold mesh ribbon spiraled from the bow on top all the way down. Here and there, magnolia blossoms rested on the branches. A pile of wrapped gifts waited for me to put on ribbons and bows. I'd been waiting until I finished my Christmas shopping, and I had yet to think of something for Daddy.

Nate had built a fire in the fireplace before heading out for a bit of surveillance related to the Andy Savage case. I snuggled under my favorite quilt. Rhett, my golden retriever, snoozed by my side. I was settled in for the night, is what I'm saying.

Naturally, the phone rang. Nicolette, the wedding planner. I sent her to voicemail. I'd spoken to her five times that day already, and Mamma six. I picked up my book.

The phone rang again. Sweet reason. I needed a few minutes' peace. I reached for my iPhone and glanced at the screen. Olivia Pearson. *Hell's bells.* Maybe she had additional outrageous ideas for my bachelorette party.

Or maybe she'd found out her husband had tried to hire me that afternoon to suss out what was behind her recent behavior. If so, even though I'd turned down the job, knowing Olivia, she would have an earful for me on the subject. She was notoriously high-strung.

I gulped down a long drink of wine and tapped the green button. "Hey, Olivia."

"*Liz.* Oh, thank God. Come quick." She was in high-drama mode.

"Where are you?" I was on my feet. Rhett hopped up, immediately on alert.

"On lower Church Street in Charleston. Near the end. A few houses up from White Point Gardens. You'll see my car. I'll be waiting inside it. *Hurry.*"

I moved towards the mudroom with Rhett fast on my heels. "I'm on my way. Tell me what's wrong."

"I...oh sweet Lord." Her voice broke with a sob. "I'm in trouble. Bad, bad trouble. Robert...I'll explain when you get here. Just please come. Alone. Don't tell a soul. Not even Nate."

"Are you hurt? Did you call 911?" My adrenaline kicked in. I shoved my feet inside the only shoes in the mudroom—my Crocs—and grabbed a trench coat to cover my pajamas.

"No. And don't you dare either. Promise me on your mamma's life."

"Are you crazy? What—"

"I *trusted* you," she sobbed again. "Please come. I can't do this alone."

"I'm on my way. Stay put."

Rhett barked once, as if demanding to know what was up.

"Stay. I'll be back as soon as I can."

He huffed his displeasure.

"Colleen!" I glared at the ceiling and headed down the steps to the garage.

I made the eight o'clock ferry by the skin of my teeth, only because the captain saw me speed into the parking lot and held the gate. I put the car in park, cut the engine, and took a few deep breaths, tried to clear my head. Curiosity and guilt battled for the upper hand. What in this world had Olivia gotten herself into? Should I have taken the case Robert practically begged me to take earlier that day? If I'd been following Olivia, could whatever this was have been avoided? During the interminable ferry ride to Isle of Palms, through Mt. Pleasant, and over the Cooper River Bridge, these thoughts swirled through my mind.

I pushed my luck and sped through Charleston, zipping around traffic where I could. I took East Bay all the way down the peninsula to Atlantic Street. I made a right, and half a block later turned left on lower Church, a narrow, one-way brick lane. Olivia's red Lexus crossover sat in front of a Charleston single house on what appeared to be a double lot. The house was dark.

I pulled my green hybrid Escape in behind her and got out of the car, easing the door closed as I scanned the street. It was eight forty-five, but owing to the cold, stiff breeze and the off-and-on rain, not even a dog-walker was in sight. The sprawling live oak in the backyard, its gnarled limbs overhanging the street, heightened the eerie quality of the evening. My Escape blocked the gated drive, but I didn't aim to be there long.

I stepped around to the passenger side of Olivia's car. She unlocked the door and I climbed in. She didn't look at me. Arms wrapped around herself, she rocked back and forth. Even in the dim light from a streetlamp, I could see her shivering. Several locks of blond hair had escaped her French twist. She was disheveled and appeared to be in shock.

"Olivia?" I spoke softly. "Honey, tell me what's happened."

She turned towards the house, then looked at me. "It's Robert."

"Robert is here?"

"He's in there." Her voice was a whispery stutter. "He's dead."

"*What?*" A jolt of electricity stunned me to the core. "Oh my God, Olivia—what happened? Did you call 911? How do you know he's dead—for sure?"

"He doesn't have a pulse."

I pulled out my phone.

"I'm calling 911."

Quick as a snake strike, she snatched my phone right out of my hand. "You can't do that." She stared at me all wild-eyed, like maybe she was on the brink of full-on crazy.

"What is wrong with you? We have to do precisely that. Right this second. Give me my damn phone."

She shook her head. "No. Absolutely not. You don't understand." Her voice rose with each word. She put my phone in the left pocket of her blazer.

I had to check on Robert one way or another.

"Do you know who lives in that house?"

She seemed to deflate, then nodded, subdued.

"My Aunt Willowdean. She's my great aunt."

"Let's go see about Robert. Then you can tell me what happened."

"O-okay," she said. But she didn't move.

I got out of the car, dashed around to the driver's side, and yanked open the door. "Will you come on, Olivia? We've got to see if we can help him."

"We can't help him. I told you. He's dead."

After a moment, she swung her legs around, and I pulled her out. She guarded her pocket with her left elbow.

I linked my left arm through her right and dragged her towards the street-side door. Charleston single houses were situated on a lot with the side of the house towards the street. The door in front of us would lead to the end of the front porch.

Olivia pulled out a set of keys, fumbled for a minute, then inserted a large, ornate key into the lock.

"You have keys to your great aunt's house?"

She shuddered. "I own half of it. Great Aunt Mary Leona left it to me a few years back."

I squinted at her. We climbed the steps to the front porch. During my extensive research into Robert and Olivia's affairs back when Gram passed, I hadn't uncovered anything about this property.

"Long story," she said. We passed a pair of large windows to our left and stopped by the front door. She held a finger to her lips, then opened the door.

We crossed into a wide foyer. My eyes were adjusting to the dark. I made out a staircase on the far side.

"In here."

Olivia nudged me left. She was shaking so hard I was afraid she was going to fall.

The parlor we entered was pitch dark. I couldn't see a thing except large lumps I took for furniture. "This is ridiculous. Where's the light switch?" I felt around on the wall with my left hand.

"*No.* Do you want to wind up dead, too?"

I pushed the dimmer switch up and light gradually flooded the room.

Olivia gasped. She covered her mouth with both hands.

The parlor doubled as a library. It was tastefully decorated in neutrals. Heavy gold and cream drapes framed the windows and pooled artfully on the heart pine floors. The furniture looked expensive but comfortable. The Christmas tree by the front window was at least twelve feet tall and appeared to be designer-decorated. Bookcases lined the wall on either side of the fireplace.

I turned to Olivia. Neither Robert, nor anyone else dead or alive, occupied the room.

"He was right there!" she whispered, pointing to a spot on an ivory and taupe rug.

I looked closer. That rug looked to me like no one had ever walked on it, much less dropped a body on it.

"Olivia, you said you knew he was dead. How could you tell?"

"I felt for a pulse, on both sides of his neck."

"I don't understand why you didn't call 911 right then."

She crossed the room to the fireplace. A large, carved wooden pineapple sat on the end. She picked it up with both hands. "This was on the floor beside his head. It had blood on it. There was blood on the rug. I am telling you, someone hit Robert with this and killed him."

What in the name of sweet reason was going on? I studied her for a long moment. Her eyes were a bit crazed, but to be honest, that wasn't all that unusual for Olivia.

A board creaked. Then another. Someone was coming slowly down the stairs.

Olivia froze, a terrified look on her face. Her eyes dropped to the pineapple. She returned it to the mantel and stepped away.

"Who's they-ah?" a woman's voice called out.

Olivia took a deep breath, seemed to compose herself. She crossed the room quickly and stood by me. "It's me, Aunt Dean."

"Olivia? I thought you'd left dahlin'."

"I decided to sit a spell in the parlor. The Christmas tree is so lovely, I was just enjoying it. Have you finished your shopping?" She crossed back into the foyer, tugging me along.

I stopped at the doorway to the parlor, disentangled my arm from Olivia's, and grabbed my iPhone from her pocket. I snapped a series of photos, making sure to get overlapping images. Then I videoed a panorama for good measure before sliding into the foyer behind Olivia.

Aunt Dean descended the last three steps slowly, holding the banister. I pegged her at mid-eighties. Her snowy hair was in a single braid that lay across her shoulder. A long, thick gold robe covered whatever she wore underneath all the way up to her chin. Her monogrammed slippers matched the robe. When she reached the floor, she looked up at us.

Olivia said, "Aunt Dean, do you remember my friend, Liz Talbot?"

"I can't say that I do." Aunt Dean studied me.

I could only imagine what she thought, with me in a trench coat cinched tightly over pink and grey polka dot pajamas, with lime green Crocs. But Aunt Dean was clearly a lady. Her face betrayed no dismay.

"I'm certain you've met," Olivia said. "Several times, in fact. Don't you remember chatting at the Poinsett wedding last summer?"

I marveled at Olivia's flair for improvisation under stress. Not only had I never met her Aunt Dean, I didn't have the first idea which of the Poinsetts had gotten married last summer.

"Now you know, my dear, my memory isn't what it once was. So nice to see you, Liz," she said, as if nothing whatsoever was amiss.

"Nice to see you too, Miss Dean." I offered her a sunny smile. Whatever Olivia was into, this sweet old lady couldn't be involved. My protective instincts stirred.

"Would you girls like a sip of something? I had a mind to pour myself a glass of sherry."

"No ma'am, none for me—thank you," I said. "I'm driving."

"We need to be heading on out." Olivia crossed the floor and hugged her aunt. "Good night, Aunt Dean."

"Good night, dahlin'. Good night, Liz. Y'all be careful out there now. The streets are a dangerous place for young ladies. Nothing good happens this time of night."

I glanced at my watch. Nine twenty. Surely Miss Dean had been out past nine. Perhaps owing to the early dark this time of year and the weather it seemed later.

"Yes ma'am," Olivia said.

"Good night, Miss Dean," I managed to get out while Olivia pulled me out the front door and closed it behind us.

Once outside she fell apart all over again, rocking and shaking. I put my arm around her waist and guided her into the passenger seat of my car. Once I had her settled, I climbed into the driver's seat.

"What have they done with Robert?" Olivia said. "Oh my God. Oh my God. Oh my God." She seemed to be praying. It wasn't like her to take the Lord's name in vain.

Being an Occam's Razor enthusiast, I liked to eliminate the most obvious answers first. I pulled out my iPhone and dialed Robert Pearson.

He answered on the first ring. "Liz?"

I went weak with relief. "Robert? Are you all right?"

Olivia gaped at me.

"Of course I'm all right."

"Where are you?"

He sputtered. "At home, of course, with the children. But I have no idea where Olivia is. If you had only listened to me this afternoon, at least—"

"All right, all right, all right. I'll take the case. But only with Olivia's full knowledge and cooperation."

"How the hell is that going to work?" His frustration erupted through the phone.

"I'll explain it when I see you. And Olivia is fine—physically, at least. She's with me. We're in Charleston. We'll be on the ten-thirty ferry back to Stella Maris. See you shortly." I ended the call and turned to Olivia.

"Robert is fine. He's at home with Campbell and Shelby."

Relief battled disbelief on her face. "But whose body was on the parlor floor?"

Just then I was thinking Olivia was likely having some sort of psychotic break involving hallucinations. "Is your aunt safe in that house tonight?"

Olivia laughed harshly. "Of course she is."

"How can you be sure of that if you think someone was killed in there? That doesn't make a lick of sense."

"Trust me. No one is going to hurt Aunt Dean. She is well-defended. She'll likely never even have to use the twenty-two she carries in her robe, or whatever else she happens to be wearing. She sleeps with it under her pillow. Has for years."

I felt like I was missing too many pieces to this puzzle. "Olivia, who do you think killed *some*body in the parlor with the pineapple?"

"Well, it sure as hell wasn't Professor Plum."

I closed my eyes and drew a breath for strength. "Olivia."

"It had to've been Seth."

"Who is Seth?"

"Seth Quinlan. He's my second cousin on Daddy's side. We don't talk about him much. He's illegitimate."

"Did you see him here tonight?"

"No, but he lives in the guesthouse. It had to be him."

"Why is that?"

"Liz, you have to promise me you won't breathe a word of any of this."

"I can't promise you any such of a thing. What I can and do promise you is that I will do everything in my power to help you. You know I will."

She grabbed my hand and squeezed, then nodded. "Seth has been blackmailing me for years."

I squinched my face at her. "We'll come back to that in a minute. Who would he have killed, and why?"

"It could've been anyone."

My frustration was building. "Olivia. What do you mean by that? Clearly, it couldn't have been *anyone*."

"Well it damn sure could've been a lot of people. That..." she gestured towards the house, "...is the classiest bordello in town. Patronized by gentlemen from some of the most prominent families in Charleston. And Aunt Willowdean is the madam."

I took a moment to process that information. "It's time for us to go home. Give me your keys. I'm going to move your car over to South Battery. You can pick it up tomorrow."

THREE

We were both quiet on the trip from downtown Charleston to the ferry dock on Isle of Palms. I didn't want to hear any more until Robert was part of the conversation. And Nate. As soon as I parked the car in the ferry parking lot, I called Nate.

"Hey, Slugger," he said. "Where are you? I was just about to call you."

"Are you finished for the night?"

"Yeah. I just got home. I didn't think you were going out."

"Neither did I. Can you meet me at Robert and Olivia Pearson's house at eleven? I'm waiting for the ten-thirty ferry."

"Is everything all right?"

"We have a new case."

"*Now*? How are we supposed to—"

"Sweetheart, please. Humor me."

He sighed. "That is my usual custom. Drive safe."

As soon as I ended the call, Olivia flew into a hissy fit. "You *cannot* tell Robert about any of this."

"I won't have to if you will."

"I will *never* tell him. And if you were my friend, you wouldn't either. I *trusted* you. You just think you're so much smarter than everyone else—like you know what's best. You don't have any idea what I've been through."

"And whose fault is that? If you'd told me you were being blackmailed, I could've helped."

"I don't need you to solve my problems. I can take care of myself just fine."

"I can see how well that's working out."

"Oooh! You just drop me off at the end of my driveway and go straight on home and forget every single thing about tonight."

"Not a chance. Didn't you hear? Robert hired me."

She screeched at me. "How could you betray me like that?"

"I don't see it as a betrayal." I kept my voice calm and soothing. "I'm trying to help two friends, both of whom asked for my help."

"Exactly when did Robert ask you for help?"

"Like I told you, he hired me. He *tried* to hire me earlier this afternoon, and I turned him down flat, out of loyalty to you."

"Why didn't you call me right that very second and tell me? That's what a true friend would've done."

"Honestly, Olivia, I figured the best thing I could do was stay out of it all together. That was before you told me Robert was dead on the floor of a whorehouse, which, if I understand you correctly, you own half of."

That shut her up, but I could feel her seething. Another eruption was imminent. While I could get a word in, I said, "And you abdicated the right to tell me to mind my own business when you called and asked me to come to the scene of an imaginary crime."

"I didn't imagine a damn thing. *Someone* was lying facedown on the floor of that parlor with his head smashed in."

I held up my hands for her to stop. "Let's just hold off on all that until we get to your house."

She looked at me with so much venom I was momentarily afraid she might claw my eyes out.

"There is one thing I want to know right now," I said, "and you owe me this much. Was someone other than Seth blackmailing you and Robert regarding this...brothel...a couple years back? Around the time Gram was killed?"

At the mention of Gram, she looked away. After a minute she

said, "Because Robert is on the town council. That demon tried to blackmail me into getting Robert to vote in favor of a certain development project. I never told Robert. He knows nothing about any of this." The meanness crept back into her voice. "And I'd prefer to keep it that way."

I knew exactly which demon she referred to, my suspicions confirmed. The final piece to the puzzle surrounding Gram's murder fell into place. But that's a whole nother story.

Finally, the ferry docked. Cars trickled off. As soon as I could, I pulled onboard, parked, and opened the car door. "I'm going to get some fresh air."

Before long, we were underway. The ferry glided through the night air, whipping the brisk wind into a freezing frenzy. I shivered, even with my trench coat over my pajamas, but the cold air blowing all around and through me had a cleansing effect, cleared my head. Thankfully, my car was the only one on the next-to-last trip of the night. No one could see me and report my attire to Mamma, who would not have been amused.

Also thankfully, Olivia stayed in the car.

Robert and Olivia lived in the closest thing Stella Maris had to a subdivision: Sea Farm. It was situated on the southeast corner of the island, Pearson's Point. At one time, the land that now held roughly two hundred homes, a golf course, a clubhouse, Olympic pool, and tennis courts, had been Pearson family land. Robert and Olivia had a prime lot in the back of the neighborhood with the Atlantic just across the dunes.

Nate's brand-new Ford Explorer was in the drive. This one was a color Ford called Kodiak Brown, on account of the bad luck we'd had with two of the Metallic Grey versions. He got out of the car as I pulled in and parked beside him. The porch light on the traditional Charleston-style home came on and Robert opened the front door and stepped out onto the lower piazza.

Olivia had ruined my sunny disposition with her tirades. Nevertheless, I tried the gentle approach. "Come on, let's go get us a glass of wine and we'll figure this whole thing out."

She sat rigidly, eyes front, with one arm on the console, the other on the armrest. Her right hand gripped the door pull. She didn't say a word, but her posture shouted, *You can't pry me out of this car.*

I climbed out and called to Robert. "Would you help Olivia, please? She's a bit shook up."

Robert hot-footed it down the steps.

Nate and I met at the front of my car.

"Short version?" Nate said under his breath.

"She's either delusional or a witness in a murder case. Robert tried to hire me this afternoon to follow her. I turned him down, thought it was a domestic. Clearly it's something else and they need help."

Nate nodded, glanced at my attire. "You must've left the house in a powerful hurry."

I blushed, mortified at how I knew I looked. I combed my fingers through my hair.

"Now you know I didn't mean to criticize," Nate said. "In fact, you look quite appealing. That's just not your normal attire for a trip into Charleston."

Robert said, "She's locked the car door. Liz, can you help me out?"

I reached into my purse, grabbed the key fob, and unlocked the door. Before Robert could open it, Olivia pressed the lock button again.

"For Pete's sake," Robert said. "Olivia, you can't take up residence in Liz's car."

I walked over and grabbed the driver's door handle. The car automatically unlocked and I opened the driver's door in the same instant. "Sooner or later you're going to have to go to the bathroom, you know."

Olivia gave me a bonus hateful look, then opened the passenger door, sprung out, threw herself into Robert's arms and commenced theatrical wailing. "I thought you were dead," she managed to sob.

"Why on earth would you think that?" Robert hugged her reassuringly. After a moment, his eyes sought out mine.

I cocked my head towards the house.

To Olivia, Robert said, "I'm fine, sweetheart. Everything's fine. Let's get you inside."

"Everything is *far* from fine," she said. "You're going to divorce me, and Mamma and Daddy will disown me because of the scandal."

Robert gentled her towards the house. "This is all nonsense. Here we go now."

Nate and I followed them up the steps. Olivia babbled. Robert shushed her and rubbed her back, murmured soothing things. That man was a saint.

Colleen's voice came from the front porch. "For the first time in forever, she's probably not overreacting."

My chin snapped up. There she sat, in a wicker chair. Flowing red hair, bright green eyes, in a long white flouncy dress, with a ring of flowers in her hair. She looked like a fairy princess. No one could see her but me, of course. I'm her sole human point of contact. She can materialize when she wants to, but she only does that in extenuating circumstances. Colleen can also read my mind.

Where the hell have you been? I thought hard, and glared at her. *I need to know if anyone died at 12 Church Street tonight.*

"I had business to tend to. And to answer your question, I don't keep track of all the departures in the county."

Can you find out?

"I can try, but it's a long shot. If I'd been there at the time I could've told you."

Exactly.

She gave me a mulish look and vanished. But when our procession finally reached the keeping room that opened to the kitchen in the Pearson home, Colleen waited, sprawled across the granite island, her head propped in her hand, elbow on the counter. "I know she's nutty, but I miss Olivia."

Robert settled Olivia in a club chair near the fireplace, pulled her feet up onto the matching ottoman, and tucked a throw around her. He skipped the wine and poured her two fingers of bourbon. "What can I get y'all?"

Nate and I both declined his offer. I needed to keep a clear head.

Robert perched on the end of a sofa to Olivia's right. I took the other end of the sofa, and Nate grabbed a chair next to me. Olivia had gone quiet, save for an occasional hitched sob. Robert studied her carefully.

Gently, I said, "Olivia, honey, we're all here for you. But we have to know what's going on before we can help you."

"I told you what was going on." Her voice was subdued, which was a blessing.

"Well, you told me part of the story," I said. "But I have a lot of questions. And we need to bring Robert and Nate up to speed."

I looked at Nate, then Robert. "Olivia called and asked me to meet her at 12 Church Street this evening. She was quite upset, so of course I went straightaway. Olivia, tell us about the house on Church Street."

Her shoulders rose and fell with a sigh. "Fine." She studied a spot on the rug beside the ottoman. "Granddaddy Beauthorpe inherited the family homeplace here on Stella Maris. He had three sisters. The oldest girl married a Quinlan. The younger two girls, Willowdean and Mary Leona, never married. Great Granddaddy left the family home in Charleston—12 Church Street—to them, so they'd never have to worry. Or at least that's what he thought. He left them money, too, of course.

"But property values in Charleston have skyrocketed. The taxes, upkeep, insurance, and utilities on that house are insane. But it's been in the family ever since it was built in 1810. Aunt Mary and Aunt Dean couldn't bring themselves to sell it. When the money ran low, they started taking in boarders. It was a very word-of-mouth kind of thing. Friends of friends. Only young ladies from proper Charleston families, or with references from one. That was their idea, anyway. There were several College of Charleston students, a young nurse who worked at MUSC—like that. Things were working out. Or so I thought.

"Aunt Mary passed a few years back. She left me her half of the house, and I'm in Aunt Dean's will to inherit the other half. I suspect they thought I would be more understanding of their affairs than anyone else in the family. Mamma would've lit the match herself and burned the house to the ground."

A confused look slid over Robert's face. "Why on earth would she do that? And why didn't you tell me you'd inherited the property? That house must be worth millions."

Olivia dropped her chin and widened her eyes. "The money wasn't my first concern. Literally on the way out of the attorney's office, my second cousin, Seth Quinlan, was waiting for me. He's been blackmailing me ever since."

"Blackmailing you?" Robert's voice was incredulous.

"Yes," said Olivia. "It seems the proper young ladies who now occupy the guest rooms are actually mistresses—perhaps exclusive, high-dollar call girls is a better description—of several of the pillars of Charleston society. One of them—possibly more—has other clients on the side, I'm told."

Robert looked like he'd swallowed a live fish and was trying not to choke, but being real mannerly about it.

Olivia continued. "I could just hear Mamma saying, 'Olivia, Beauthorpe women simply do not own bordellos.'" She reached for Robert's hand. "I was afraid of what it would do to your career, our reputation."

He grabbed her hand and wrapped it inside both of his. "But why didn't you tell me? I'm an attorney, for Pete's sake. I could've had your cousin arrested and we could've evicted the prostitutes."

"And then we'd've had a financial millstone around our necks," Olivia said. "We couldn't sell that house out from under Aunt Dean. She's lived there her entire life. And she still owns half. But without the money coming in, the expenses would've fallen on us. Robert, that's an *eight-thousand-square-foot*, two-hundred-year-old house. And the scandal. We have our children to think of."

Robert closed his eyes, pinched the bridge of his nose.

I said, "Olivia, why did you go to the house tonight?"

"I finally worked up the nerve last week to tell Aunt Dean that Seth was blackmailing me. Seth lives in the guesthouse. He's the handyman, has been since he was a teenager. He thought they should've left the house to him. He was mad as fire that it was coming to me. Anyway, Aunt Dean and I have been trying to come up with a plan. She knows he's a problem, but he is family after all, and she depends on him for a great many things."

"That's one way to put it," said Colleen. "Get her to elaborate on what all Seth does around the house."

"Exactly where does he hang in the family tree?" I asked.

"Granddaddy Beauthorpe's oldest sister, Frances, had a daughter. She got pregnant as a teenager. It was quite the scandal. She never married and she died in childbirth. Aunt Frances and Uncle John raised Seth. He was always in trouble. Mamma never let me have much to do with him and that was fine by me. Aunt Mary and Aunt Dean felt like he just needed more love and attention. He spent a lot of time with them, helped out. Eventually he moved into the guesthouse and went to work for them full-time."

"And exactly what are his duties?" I asked.

"I told you. He's the handyman. He fixes things and runs errands. What do handymen normally do?"

Colleen shook her head. I took that to mean there was more to the story.

"And tonight?" Nate asked.

"Aunt Dean called me this morning. She wanted to talk, but not on the phone. When I got there, she told me about an idea she had to enlist the aid of some of the gentlemen who pay for rooms for their 'nieces.' She figured they could take care of Seth. They'd have a vested interest."

Nate's voice was casual. "In what sense do you suppose she meant they could 'take care' of Seth? Do you think she planned to have him evicted?"

"We didn't get into details," Olivia said. "Aunt Dean is often vague about unpleasantries."

Colleen snorted.

I ignored her. "So, Olivia, tell us exactly what happened from the time you parked your car in front of the house until I arrived."

She sipped her bourbon, drew a ragged breath. "I got there at seven and let myself in. The entire downstairs was dark. I didn't turn on any lights. I didn't want to see anyone, and I didn't want anyone to see me. I went straight upstairs to Aunt Dean's room. It has a sitting area. That's where she asked me to come. We talked for a while, thirty minutes or so. Then I told her goodnight and came back downstairs.

"The light was on in the front parlor." Her voice grew louder, anxious. She looked at Robert. "I swear on our children there was a body, facedown on the floor." She went to sobbing again. "I thought it was *you*."

"What in the world would I be doing there?" Robert asked. Something in his voice caught my attention.

"I don't know. I guess I thought maybe you followed me. Because it looked like you. I mean, I couldn't see his face. But his hair, his build...and he was wearing khakis and a checked button-down shirt, just like you are right this very minute."

I pondered that for a few seconds. Khakis and button-down shirts were common attire for men in our part of the world. Still. "Robert, just so we have all the facts, you haven't left the house this evening, is that right?"

"Well, yes. I mean, no...I did go out for a while. I had a dinner meeting with a client over in Charleston. Had to get a babysitter for a couple hours since Olivia wasn't home."

My BS alarm went off. "Robert, we can't help you if you are less than forthcoming. You of all people should know what it's like to have a client hold things back."

He heaved a deep sigh. "Dammit to hell. You wouldn't follow her. After you left my office, I arranged for a babysitter, then I tailed Olivia myself when she went out. Fortunately the ferry had a full load on the six o'clock trip. I was afraid she'd see my car. When she parked in front of that house, I pulled to the curb half a block away. I sat outside for fifteen minutes after she went in. Then I followed her. She'd left the doors unlocked. But I didn't see a soul. I couldn't find Olivia. I didn't want to go shouting through the house, get arrested for trespassing."

"What the hell, Robert? Why didn't you tell us that to begin with?" I asked.

Olivia gaped at him.

"You were there?"

"Well, yes, and I'm not proud of it. Skulking around strangers' houses...But as you can see, I'm quite alive."

This was getting messier by the minute.

"This just keeps getting better," said Colleen. "What we need is popcorn."

"Did you go into the front parlor?" I asked.

"Yes. But I most certainly did not see a body."

"So you turned on the light?" I asked.

"No. I had a flashlight."

"You didn't see anyone else?" I asked.

"No, but I heard doors opening and closing, footsteps, creaking floorboards, when I was in the back of the house. Other people were there. I just didn't see who."

"How much of the house did you go through?" Nate asked.

"Just the downstairs. I wasn't in there more than fifteen minutes, tops. I started to go upstairs. But then I felt ridiculous, following my wife around, going uninvited into someone's home." He reddened. "And I guess I was afraid of what I'd find upstairs. Usually that's where the bedrooms are."

"Robert Pearson." Olivia mustered indignation. "How could you think such a thing?"

"Well, what was I supposed to think?"

I said, "So Olivia went in and headed straight upstairs. You came in fifteen minutes later and looked around downstairs. You came back out at roughly seven thirty. Then what did you do?"

"I was aggravated at myself. Mad at Olivia. I drove back to Isle of Palms and waited for the eight-thirty ferry. The babysitter couldn't stay past nine."

"Getting back to the body," I said. "Olivia, when you saw it, why didn't you call 911 right then?"

Mean Olivia reared her head. "Because then my children would've read in the paper that their daddy died in a whorehouse and their mamma owned it."

Colleen said, "You mortals would be so much happier if you would get over your obsession with what other people think. What other people do. What other people have. Like my granny always said, 'Mind your own biscuits and life will be gravy.'"

Why, oh why had I said "no thank you" to that wine?

"Olivia," I said, "Campbell and Shelby are six and four if memory serves. I'm guessing they don't read *The Post and Courier* much."

Olivia straightened, nostrils flared, all puffed up like a cobra ready to strike. "Oh, you know exactly what I mean."

I would've argued the point further, how somebody needed medical help, could maybe have been saved, except I remained unconvinced there'd been a body. I'd seen no evidence of it. I kept my voice calm. "What happened next?"

She cut me with a nasty look, then turned to Robert. "I checked for a pulse. Several times. On his neck, his wrist. There. Was. No. Pulse. Whoever that was is as dead as a doornail. There was a gash in the back of his head. A big ole wooden pineapple with blood on it was on the floor beside him. I panicked. I ran out to the car and called Liz. A decision I deeply regret at this moment."

"Why didn't you go get your Aunt Dean?" I asked. "And why didn't you tell her about all of this afterwards, when we went back into the house?"

"Aunt Dean has a bad heart." Something about her tone did not have the pure ring of truth.

"I can check on that, you know," I said.

"Why are you not on my side here?" she practically screamed at me. "You're supposed to be my friend."

"Is she drinking that bourbon?" Colleen asked. "She needs a little more."

Robert said, "Olivia. Get ahold of yourself. You'll wake the children. Besides that, if Liz wasn't on your side, she wouldn't have come and gotten you."

Nate's easygoing tone had an edge. "I believe Liz has gone above and beyond the duties of friendship this evening."

I knew Olivia well. She was hiding something. Something else. "Why didn't you tell your aunt?"

She looked at Robert, then Nate, then me. I could feel the heat from how fast the wheels were spinning in her head. Finally, she said, "Because I wasn't sure she wasn't a party to whatever was going on."

My eyes locked on hers. "Come again?"

"Now we're getting somewhere," said Colleen.

"She was upstairs with me, yes," Olivia said. "But I've heard things...from a few of the residents I've spent time with since Aunt Mary passed. Aunt Dean insisted I get to know them. At first I flat refused. But then I thought maybe I'd find out something I could use against Seth. And I guess I did, but I've been too afraid to do anything about it. I'm told occasionally a 'suitor' gets out of hand. Over the years other...situations have come up. Aunt Dean relies on Seth to deal with any problems."

"And by dealing with these problems, you mean Seth has what..." Nate spread his hands, "bounced someone out of there? Or are we talking about something more serious here?"

"I'm not certain," Olivia said.

"Are you afraid of your Aunt Dean?" I asked.

"No, of course not," Olivia said. "But if she let on to Seth I'd seen something I wasn't supposed to..."

"Let's back up a minute," Nate said. "So you saw the body. You felt for a pulse. Then you went outside to your car and called Liz?"

"That's right," said Olivia.

"That was at seven forty-five," I said. "Olivia, think. How long did you stay in the parlor? More than five minutes?"

She shook her head.

"No. I was scared out of my mind. After I checked for a pulse, I got out of there quick."

"So you came back downstairs at seven forty, which explains how Robert missed you. He left ten minutes earlier."

Robert said, "Again, I did not see a body. And the parlor—the entire downstairs was dark the whole time I was there. If something happened, it happened within that ten minutes."

"It took me an hour to get there," I said. "But when I went inside with Olivia, there was no body in the parlor, and no sign that one ever had been. No blood, no signs of a struggle. The room was immaculate."

"A lot can happen in an hour," Nate said. "That's plenty of time for someone to move a body and clean up the mess."

Skepticism painted Robert's face.

Nate looked at Robert. "Bottom line. If you believe anything is going on here other than your wife being under a great deal of strain that maybe caused a momentary...vision, something along those lines, then we should call the authorities in Charleston and let them sort this out."

"No," said Colleen. "Not just yet."

"*No*," Olivia said. "I will not have all this dirty laundry aired. I have nothing to do with any of it, but that's not the way it will look."

"Liz..." Robert's eyes traded on years of friendship.

"What exactly do you want us to do?" I asked.

"Just look into it. The house, the aunts, this Seth character. See what you come up with."

"Is there anything else you haven't told me?" I asked.

"No," he said with a firm shake of his head. "I give you my word. And I apologize. I don't know what I was thinking."

I looked at Nate.

He looked at Robert. "Have you forgotten that Liz and I are getting married Saturday? The morning after, we leave for two weeks in St. John. We already have one case to finish, in addition to all the wedding preparations. Our hands are full right now."

"Just give it a day," Robert said. "One day. You can spare that, right, Liz?"

I had already said I'd help my friends. But Nate was clearly not happy with the situation.

Colleen said, "I don't have a good feeling about this. I don't know what happened there tonight, but that house has a long history of trouble. On the other hand, if Robert's no longer vulnerable—because Olivia's no longer being blackmailed—the town council, and ultimately the island, is less vulnerable. It seems clear this falls under my mission."

Nate's eyes met mine and saw the silent request. He glanced away, then back. After a long moment, he said, "All right then."

Even for friends—maybe especially for friends—we didn't open a case file without a contract. I pulled my iPad from my purse, opened a contract, and made some case specific notes. Then I emailed the contract to the address Robert gave me.

A few moments later, he stepped into his office and retrieved the printed document. Standing at the kitchen island, inches from Colleen, he checked boxes and filled in the blanks. Then he handed it to me with a check. "Thank you."

"You're welcome," I said. "I'm sorry I didn't accept this earlier."

"*Oh*," said Olivia. "Just exactly what do you mean trying to hire one of my very best friends to spy on me?"

Nate and I stood and made for the door.

FOUR

The next morning, we put on several layers of clothes and went for a run. In the pre-dawn hour, it was cold, but at least the rain had quit. Between the wedding, Christmas, and now this new case involving some of my oldest friends, I was on edge. The rhythm of the surf soothed my frayed nerves.

Nate, Rhett, and I made our usual loop around the north point of the island, past the bed and breakfast and the marina, to Heron Creek. There we turned around and ran back past the house, all the way to where Main Street dead-ends into the sand dunes, then home. It was a five-mile loop. Nate and I were quiet, lost in our own thoughts as we ran. For my part, I was noodling over what could possibly have happened on Church Street the night before.

As we headed up the steps to the walkway across the sand dunes, I said, "What are you thinking about?"

Nate shrugged. "Mostly I'm wondering how it is that you and Olivia are such good friends. You and she are very different women."

I watched where I was stepping, so I had somewhere to look besides at Nate. "Have I ever told you about my friend Colleen?"

"The one who died when you were in high school?"

Colleen appeared. She walked on top of the walkway rail like it was a balance beam. "Be very careful what you say."

I shot her a look. I wasn't going to tell him she was still hanging around. I knew that was against the rules, or so she told me.

"Yes," I said to Nate. "Colleen was my best friend since kindergarten. But she went through a bad time—an awkward phase, Mamma would call it—starting when we were about thirteen. She'd never been on a date. Lots of girls were mean to her. Olivia never was. She went out of her way to stand up for Colleen. And after Colleen died, Olivia was there for me. I know she can be impossible sometimes. But she has a good heart."

Nate said, "I'd bet good money any qualified psychiatrist would diagnose her with something requiring a prescription."

"Nate." I tossed him a quelling look. "She's my friend."

"Friends don't usually speak to one another in the tone she was addressing you last night."

"He makes a good point," Colleen said. "I would've thought Olivia would've outgrown her mean streak."

"She was overwrought," I said. "She's not usually like that. She lashes out when she feels like she's under attack. Her impulse control hasn't fully developed."

"If she verbally attacks you again, we're dropping this case and Robert can figure this out for himself. He's an attorney."

"Come on now—"

"What? You think I should just sit there while she spews venom at you?"

"I think we should take into account that she's under a great deal of stress."

"And you're not? With our wedding coming up in four days? Aren't brides always stressed?"

"Yes, and I have some knots in my neck maybe you wouldn't mind rubbing after I shower."

"Do you now?" His voice dropped an octave.

I gave him a slow grin and took off running towards the house.

"Really?" Colleen called after us. "Y'all don't have time for that stuff this morning."

But we made time for a long soapy shower, with lots of rubbing on each other's tense spots.

Later, after breakfast, we settled into the office to figure out the best approach to our new case. I was at my desk, Nate in a leather chair across from me.

At seven fifteen, Mamma called. "Liz, Nicolette has been trying to reach you. Is everything all right?"

"Everything's fine, Mamma. We're just busy wrapping up a couple cases."

She sighed.

"You've taken on entirely too much."

I was hard-pressed to argue with her. "What did Nicolette need? Do you know?" She'd left me a voicemail, but with all the drama, I'd forgotten to call her back.

"She needs the final count for the caterer for the reception."

"Unless Daddy has invited any more random folks from the flea market, we're at three hundred and four."

Nate looked up from his laptop, his face frozen in stunned panic.

I flashed him my best *Oh please* look. This was not news to him.

"There are always a few folks who can't come last minute," Mamma said. "And the caterer always plans for a few extra. I think we should tell her an even three hundred."

"Whatever you think, Mamma."

She said she'd call Nicolette back, gave me a litany of admonishments, most of which didn't register, and we said our goodbyes.

"Have you finished with the research you were doing on the Savage case?" Nate asked.

"All done. I emailed you everything I found."

He nodded. "Thanks. All I need to do now is pull the report together and get it to them. But that doesn't have to be done today."

"As for the Pearsons," I said, "the first thing we need to do is determine if there was a body in that house last night. If there was, and we don't report it, we have an exposure."

"But you didn't see a body. All you could report is hearsay, and you had evidence it was unreliable—there was no body when you arrived."

"True. And I took photos of the room. The date, time, and location is part of the files." I weighed that for a moment. "I think I'll call Sonny." Sonny Ravenel was an old friend—my brother, Blake's, best friend. He was also a detective with Charleston PD.

"And tell him what?"

"Who said I was going to tell him anything?" I grinned as I tapped Sonny's name in my favorites list.

"Ravenel." He answered on the second ring, sounding distracted.

"Sonny, it's Liz."

"I'm in the middle of something."

"I'm so sorry to interrupt. I just have a quick question. Any missing person reports in the last twenty-four hours?"

"Only one. An eighty-nine-year-old white female missing from the dementia unit at Ashley River Plantation. Look, I can't talk right now. Someone killed Thurston Middleton and left him propped straight up on a park bench at White Point Gardens. Has a newspaper in his lap, like maybe he just finished it. Damnedest thing I've seen in a while."

The back of my neck tingled. "Killed him how?"

Nate frowned.

"Blunt force trauma to the back of the head. Gotta go."

"Sonny, *Sonny*, wait. What's he wearing?"

"What?" His tone implied unkind things regarding my mental health.

"I'll explain later. I promise. Just tell me what he's wearing."

"Khaki pants and a checked button-down. No coat." He ended the call.

FIVE

Nate drove, and Colleen rode with us into Charleston.

"I tried to tell you there was no time for all that frolicking." Colleen's head poked between our seats. Today's outfit was a Christmas sweater with a jeweled angel, skinny jeans, and a Santa hat. Since her death, Colleen could wear whatever she liked simply by thinking about it. She was working my last nerve.

Hush up. Thinking my side of the conversation wasn't nearly as satisfying as talking. I purely hated it when she put me in a position where I had no choice and then baited me.

I called Olivia. "Have you picked up your car?" I asked the second she picked up. I'd left the car on South Battery, which bordered White Point Gardens.

"Robert sent his secretary over with a friend to drive it back. She called me just a second ago to let me know they found it. Why?"

"Call her back right now and tell her not to move that car until we get there. We're in a brown Explorer. Call me back." I ended the call before she could ask questions. Between the media and the looky-loos we'd never find a place to park.

A minute later my phone rang. Olivia said, "Something big is going on over there. They're holding the spot."

"What did she say, exactly?"

"Something happened in the park. There's crime scene tape and—" She made a godawful noise, somewhere between choking and yodeling.

"Listen to me. We do not know there's a connection. Do. Not.

Say. A. Single. Solitary. Word. To. A. Soul. Understand? *Tell me* you understand."

"Yes, of course. Ohmygod. Ohmygod."

"Olivia, do not panic. Go on about your day, just like any other Tuesday, hear?"

But for ragged breathing and muffled sobs, she was silent.

"I've got to go. I'll call as soon as I can." I ended the call.

Nate pulled onto the ferry. At eight a.m., even on a Tuesday, it was crowded. Along with regular commuters, this close to Christmas, lots of folks were headed to Mt. Pleasant and Charleston to shop. We stayed in the car.

"What was the victim's name again?" Nate asked.

"Thurston Middleton..." There'd been Middletons in Charleston forever. Something tickled the back of my brain. I pulled out my iPad and commenced Googling.

"*Damnation*," I said, after reading the first article that came up.

"What'd you find?" asked Nate.

"I thought that name sounded familiar. He's a local real estate developer. Into green technologies. Comes from money. He was gearing up to make a run in the Republican primary for the First Congressional District next year."

"Now right there's exactly what this mess needed. A politician. He was going to challenge Mark Sanford?"

"That was the plan. Assuming Sanford runs again, I guess. I don't follow politics beyond Stella Maris. Too depressing."

During the ferry ride and trip through Isle of Palms and Mt. Pleasant, I picked up as many details as I could from the internet, sharing salient points as I found them. From all appearances, Thurston Middleton appeared to be a Boy Scout. He'd served in the Air Force, was active in local efforts to assist the homeless, married to Julia Bennett Middleton for eighteen years, four sons.

"This is so sad," I said. "Looks like he was one of the good guys."

Nate drove onto the Cooper River Bridge. "Maybe he was. But

he was sure in the wrong place last night. Sonny's going to have fun with this one."

Scrambling, I said, "We don't know for sure his was the body Olivia saw."

"Are you kidding me?" Nate asked. "You are not seriously advocating the notion that two men who strongly resembled each other were killed last night, in the same manner, within a block of each other, wearing the same clothes, with one of their bodies unaccounted for. Are you?" He glanced at me long enough for me to read his incredulous expression before turning back to the road.

"It's possible," I said with a straight face. I stared at the photo of Thurston with his wife and sons in the newspaper article on the screen. "Though I can see the resemblance to Robert. Looks to be about the same height and build. Same hair color. Their facial features are very different, but from behind...The point is, all of this is conjecture."

Nate shook his head.

"You're too close to this case. Clearly you are incapable of being objective."

"Listen," said Colleen. "You can*not* turn this over to Sonny yet. As soon as Charleston PD goes into that house with a search warrant, the people they need to talk to are going to cover their tracks. One of them will do that by killing more innocents. Okay, innocents may not be the exact right word. But it's not their time."

"Alternate scenario?" I closed my eyes as soon as I spoke.

"I can't think of a single one," said Nate.

"Exactly," said Colleen. One of her gifts was to see what would happen if people made different choices. She called these alternate scenarios.

Nate took the East Bay Street exit off the end of the Cooper River Bridge. "We need to find Sonny and tell him everything that happened last night and wash our hands of this entire affair forthwith. We haven't cashed the check. Give it back to Robert."

"Nate, please. Let's just dig a little further. I have a feeling there's more going on here than we know."

"Oh, I'm dead certain you're right about that. But we are flirting with an obstruction charge."

"Not until we know the cases are connected. We have no evidence of that. You know how fertile Olivia's imagination is. She probably hallucinated that body in the parlor. I have photos, remember? Olivia must've recalled what Robert was wearing. She was nervous being in that house. It was dark...You and I are working a blackmail case."

"What are you not telling me?" Nate asked. "It's not like you to be irrational."

It killed me not to tell him. But I couldn't. The consequences would be losing Colleen for the rest of my mortal life. "Nothing," I said. "We just need time. My fear is, the second the police start investigating that bordello, everyone connected to it is going to do whatever is necessary to protect themselves. I want to know who all are involved—and I want as much information on them as possible—before they have a chance to hide evidence. And I don't want one of my bridesmaids dragged into a high-profile murder investigation right before our wedding. Mamma would have a stroke."

Nate fell silent.

"Turn right on Atlantic," I said. "Left on Church. Then make a right on South Battery."

He followed my directions and within a few minutes, I spotted Olivia's car.

"There." I pointed.

Nate tapped the horn twice as he rolled close. The red Lexus pulled away and Nate slid the Explorer right into the parking space. He turned off the car and turned to me. "In deference to your mamma's health, I'll give this case the day we promised Robert. That's it."

"Thank you."

"It's against my better judgement." He climbed out of the car and waited for me on the packed dirt pathway that bordered the north side of the park.

"Mine, too," I said. But he couldn't hear me.

"Good job," said Colleen. Then she vanished.

I got out and joined Nate. For a moment, we both just stood there taking in the pandemonium. Emergency vehicles lined Murrary Boulevard on the other side of White Point Gardens. A stiff December wind battered the crime scene tape that formed a perimeter around the middle of the park. Beyond that, uniformed police officers kept the press and the public at bay. Eager young reporters were broadcasting live.

Inside the yellow tape, a white tent had been set up between the Moultrie Monument and the bandstand. The tent served two purposes. It shielded the victim from public view, and protected the immediate area from the thick, low hanging clouds that threatened more rain. No doubt the body, the coroner, and the detectives were inside. Crime scene techs combed the surrounding area.

Nate said, "Whoever moved that body certainly wasn't concerned with hiding it. Just wanted it out of the house."

"We need to talk to Sonny. If Thurston Middleton was killed where they found his body and they know that, then there's no connection. The problem is, if Sonny verifies the body was moved, we'll have no choice but to tell him everything. Damnation. We can't talk to Sonny. Not yet."

"And with that in mind, we should probably leave before he pops his head out of that tent, sees us, and wonders what our interest in his case could possibly be."

"We need to get inside that house. We need to learn everything we possibly can, as fast as we can."

"Let's get you out of this chilly wind. We can sit in the car and plot how best to commit breaking and entering on a whorehouse."

"It's not breaking and entering if one of the owners gives us a key," I said.

We got back into the car, both of us still watching the circus in the park. "All right," said Nate. "Suppose Olivia gives us the key and the alarm codes. How do we get the other occupants out of the house? Stage a fake gas leak?"

"No, that's too risky. The handyman might not go very far. Seems like he'd stick close for something like that. What we need is a spa day."

"And you think that will get the handyman—what's his name? Seth—to leave?"

I pondered that for a moment.

"Yes, I do. He'll absolutely go if Olivia tells him he can't." I called Olivia using the Bluetooth system in the car so Nate could listen. I put a finger to my lips, asking him not to speak. "I need you to give every female in that house a spa day slash shopping outing for Christmas, Aunt Dean included. An expensive one. One no woman would turn down. I need you to go with them. And I need it to commence at noon. Today."

"I'll call Charleston Place and book every available time slot for every available service," said Olivia. "Aunt Dean can smooth things over with the...sponsors. You know, if they have appointments scheduled."

"Perfect," I said. I'd gotten Mamma and Merry each spa packages at Charleston Place for Christmas. "Now listen, this is important. I want you to rent a limo. Make as big a splash as you can. And tell Seth that he's not invited."

"If I tell him that, he'll go or die trying."

"Exactly. Make a scene about it."

"Ooooh." I could hear the smile in Olivia's voice. "Smart."

"Thank you. Just make sure you keep them all out of the house until I call you and tell you it's okay to bring them back. If you run out of spa appointments, go shopping, go out for drinks—or an early dinner.

"If anyone takes a notion to leave early, you have to insist they stay. Order a lot of champagne. If Seth starts to leave, encourage him. Tell him you have things to discuss with Aunt Dean privately anyway."

"Reverse psychology. I can handle this," said Olivia.

"I know," I said. "This is right up your alley. But if someone does leave, text or call me right away. And if you haven't heard from me, give me a heads up when you're on your way back."

"Okay. I'd better start making phone calls. I'll need to get Mamma to stay with the kids."

"Wait—does your Aunt Dean have a landline? And does she use it, or does she have a cellphone?"

"She wants nothing to do with cellphones. She has a landline. She's just very careful about what she says on it."

"And how many girls live there?"

"Five, plus Aunt Dean."

"Do you know their names?"

"That's complicated."

"I don't understand. You either know their names, or you don't."

Olivia sighed.

"Every 'guest' room is named for the family who sponsors the guest. Because these are 'nieces,' you understand, their last names are the same."

"So their last names are aliases."

"I guess you'd call them that. I can tell you the names they go by, but I'm not sure how much help that'll be."

"It's a start. Does your Aunt Dean know their real names? I mean, she pays them, right?"

"Heavens, no. Here's how this works. If there's an open room, through word-of-mouth, a gentleman will refer a young lady. Usually he says it's a cousin or a niece. Then he pays her rent to Aunt Dean—strictly a family obligation, you understand."

"Very slick."

"It is, isn't it? Of course the gentlemen in question pay exorbitant rent, even for South of Broad. I'm told they also give their 'nieces' or whatever allowances to 'tide them over.'"

I pondered all of that for a minute. "You said the rooms were named for the gentleman paying the bill. Are you saying the rooms stay in the same families?"

"No. Aunt Dean just has a new doorplate made when she needs to. Over time there've been a few repeats."

"Is one of the current names Middleton?"

"No. Why do you ask?"

She'd hear it on the news or through the grapevine soon enough. "Thurston Middleton was found dead this morning in White Point Gardens."

She drew in a sharp breath. "But that doesn't make the first bit of sense."

"We'll figure it out. I just need you to play your part. What's the alarm code?"

"Five nine two five. J-W-B-J. Jackson Wayne Beauthorpe, Jr."

"We need your keys. Nate will pass you on the street just after you get out of the limo. He'll bump into you and apologize. In case anyone is watching, act like you don't know him. Slip him the keys."

"Got it."

"And we need your written request that we set up security surveillance and monitoring over the entire property. I'm emailing you the document. Just sign it and send it back. Do you know the first names of the men involved?" I switched gears quickly so as not to allow her too much time to ponder the words "security surveillance."

Best not to call her attention to the fact she would also be on camera if she went inside. If she behaved differently, it might give us away.

"No. Aunt Dean keeps the business end of things very close to the vest. She's given me bits and pieces over time. Some things I've figured out for myself. It's like she wants to gradually initiate me. I imagine she thought it would be less of a shock that way."

"Is there any chance whatsoever your Aunt Dean doesn't know what really goes on there?"

"None. But no one could ever prove it."

"Then why on earth are you so worried about this coming out? If no one could prove it's anything but a boardinghouse, run by a sweet little old lady trying to hang on to her family home?"

"Because no one has to prove a damn thing to ruin all of our reputations. All the talk will do that. We'll never live it down."

Just then I was thinking how with a dead politician involved, this was likely going to be national news. I couldn't think of any scenario that would prevent that from happening. "All right, look. Just email me the names you have. And get everyone out of the house by noon." I ended the call.

Nate nodded towards the park.

"Clock's ticking."

I looked over my shoulder and saw Sonny emerge from the tent. He was talking to another detective, not looking our way.

Nate started the car. He negotiated the Explorer into traffic, which was moving at a crawl.

I said, "The first question on my mind is what exactly was Thurston Middleton doing inside 12 Church Street last night?"

"Hold on now. I thought your theory for the events of last evening involved Olivia hallucinating the body in the parlor."

"That's true," I said, "but I'm trying to be fair here. Give you a chance to prove *your* theory, all the while proving how I'm right."

"So you're planning to prove a negative."

"Exactly."

Finally, Nate turned left on East Bay. "You go to the liquor store to buy liquor. There's no other logical reason to open the door and walk inside. Same principle holds, regardless of the product."

"But you heard Olivia. There is no Middleton room. If he isn't a patron, what was his business there? He's a politician. You'd think he'd avoid going anywhere near the place."

"Well, Slugger, this is South Carolina. We're heavy into redemption here. All you have to do is confess your sins publicly and ask for forgiveness. Mark Sanford survived the Argentinian mistress scandal."

"If Middleton was trying to get the place shut down, he'd go in broad daylight, with protesters and the media. I need to dig deeper on Thurston Middleton's background, first thing."

"Just because there's no Middleton room currently doesn't mean there never was one."

"Good point," I said. "He may have been somehow trying to

cover his tracks before he formally launches his campaign."

"Makes sense. So, we've got a lot of ground to cover—a tall order for so little time. Where do you want to set up shop? It's nine thirty. We've got two and a half hours until we can get inside the house."

"We can't be running back and forth to Stella Maris, that's for sure. And we can't park on Church Street to watch who goes in and out after the ladies get back from their spa day." I did a quick search of local bed and breakfasts on my iPad. "I thought so. The house diagonally across the street, number 15, is a B and B. And they have third floor rooms. If we can get the room on the front of the house, we can see most of what we need to see without being seen."

Nate grinned. "We're going to get an unsavory reputation among local inns if we're not careful."

"We didn't even give our names at John Rutledge House Inn." I grinned at the memory of a pretext from a case back in the fall as I tapped in the phone number. Moments later we had a reservation for the Rose Room at fifteen Church Street, The Phillips-Yates-Snowden house.

SIX

Fifteen Church Street was a lovely brick English side-hall house. Similar to Charleston single houses, the narrow end of the house faced the street, but with the front door leading to a hall that ran the length of the house. According to BedandBreakfast.com, it was built circa 1842 and was currently owned by Jack and Annelise Simmons. Nate pulled through the gate, as we'd been instructed, and down the narrow drive all the way to the back. The car would be hidden from all but the most inquiring eyes.

Thankfully, we kept essential equipment, a change of clothes, and overnight necessities in each of our cars for emergencies such as this. We walked back around front and climbed the steps. On the landing, we looked at each other.

"I always wonder whether to knock on the door at a bed and breakfast. It's a business—"

"And it's also someone's home." I shook my head at him and knocked.

"They're certainly in the holiday spirit," said Nate.

The stair railing and every window were festooned with pine boughs, gold ribbon, magnolia blossoms, and white lights. Poinsettias lined the steps. The wreath on the door was a work of art.

Mrs. Simmons welcomed us into the hall, which ran down the right side of the house. She was a lovely woman, with a chin-length blond bob.

"Thank you for letting us check in so early, Mrs. Simmons," I said.

"Please, call me Annelise. No problem at all. We're happy to have you with us."

"You have a lovely home," said Nate.

The buttery yellow walls with white trim, gleaming floors, and gilded accents spoke of good taste and regular maintenance. The scents of the season—pine, cinnamon, and cookies baking—enveloped us. LeAnne Rimes crooned "Hard Candy Christmas." Annelise needed some happy Christmas music.

"Thank you so much." She went about the business of getting us checked in. "So y'all are locals, then?" she asked as she handed us our key.

"That's right." Nate smiled. Sometimes I wondered if he knew the effect that smile had on women. "From time to time we just like staying over downtown. Walk to dinner. It's nice."

"Well, you won't be needing my overview of the area, then. But I do hope you'll join us for our social hour at six. We'll have wine and cheese. We can get better acquainted then. I'm afraid the weather's too bad for us to be on the verandah. We'll gather in the living room."

I leaned in closer, spoke in a soft voice. "To be perfectly honest, Annelise, Nate and I are getting married Saturday. We desperately need some alone time. All the wedding preparations—you know how hectic that can get."

She returned my smile. "Congratulations. I understand completely. Well, if you feel like company, we'll be here. Breakfast is served between eight and nine thirty."

We thanked her and carried our things to the third floor. The Rose Room was aptly named. The walls were a lovely shade of pinkish red—it's easy for red wall paint to lean towards tacky, but this room was anything but. A black iron queen-size bed with a shelf of sweetgrass baskets above sat between two windows. A day bed and an armchair would give us room to spread out and work. The remaining décor was a mix of period pieces and wicker.

I crossed the room and checked out the view. From either side of the bed I could see rooftops, treetops, and beyond those, the harbor. On a clear day, this would be a beautiful vista. Looking down, I could see part of the south end of Church Street. Far more important to us were the windows on the front of the house.

I moved to the right front window. Diagonally across the street was the bordello.

"This was a stroke of brilliance." Nate peered out the left front window. "I need to walk around the block to be sure, but it would appear the only way to leave the property without resorting to going over or through some mighty thick shrubbery is to pass by these windows. I suppose one could hop the fence and slip through the yard to the left, but why would they? They don't know we're watching."

I stepped into the adjoining bath. A third window there offered another view.

"Only the killer—and the person who moved the body, assuming that's not the same person—would connect the body in the park to that house. The rest of the benefactors will have no reason to suspect anyone would be watching. And we need to keep it that way. If one of the clients is our guy, he may not be bold enough to come back in the next twenty-four hours, but the process of elimination may point us in the right direction."

"So what we need is for all the other patrons to be horny this evening. Then we can focus on whoever doesn't show up." Nate stepped away from the window. "I'm going to walk around the immediate neighborhood. I'll grab the binoculars, the camera and tripod, and the mobile hotspot from the car on my way back in. Anything else you think we'll need?"

"How many webcams do we have in the Explorer?"

Nate rolled his lips in, looked thoughtful. "A dozen of the air purifiers."

"That should do it. But no need to bring them up. We need some snacks. Cheerwine and Dove Dark Chocolate Promises. Something salty. Bottled water. Other than that I think we're good."

Nate shook his head and silently chuckled. "I'll be back shortly."

I called my sister, Merry, and asked her to swing by and see about Rhett. "I'm not going to make it back to Stella Maris until tomorrow, probably late in the day. Play with him for a while, will you?"

"Of course," she said. "I'll go by this afternoon when I get home. I need some quality time with my 'nephew.' We'll go for a walk on the beach. Do you want me to take him home with me?"

"Why don't you just stay in one of the guest rooms at my house like you're going to do while we're in St. John? You pack lighter than Rhett does."

"Okay. Are you getting nervous?"

I smiled. "Not really. I got it right this time. I'm excited. Mamma's nervous enough for both of us."

Merry laughed. "That's for sure. See you in a bit." She ended the call.

I squinched my face at the phone. She wasn't going to see me until late tomorrow, if then. I shrugged it off as Merry being at work, eager to get off the phone, distracted.

After checking the view from both front bedroom windows again, I moved the upholstered armchair over to the corner between the right front window and the window facing south on Church Street. Then I grabbed a couple pillows from the daybed and fashioned a lap-desk. So much had happened so fast. I hadn't had a chance to process everything.

My instincts were to dig straight into deep background on Thurston Middleton. But I needed to organize my thoughts. Like evidence, I needed to log and tag each fact. This case felt like a bowl of spaghetti in my brain. So many pieces already piled on top of each other and twisted together. I needed to sort what we knew into possibilities—feasible theories, or narratives of the crime. I pulled out my laptop and started a case file.

Because I had no proof there'd been a body in 12 Church Street the night before, and I had unequivocally witnessed—and documented—a body-free parlor, I started with what I knew: Seth Quinlan was blackmailing my client's wife. Olivia had gone to the house the night before to meet with her aunt. While there, she'd seen what she believed to be a body in the parlor. With excruciating detail, I documented the lack of evidence indicating a murder had been committed on the premises.

Then I created a profile on Seth Quinlan. I logged into a subscription database and located his birth certificate. No father was listed. He was roughly twelve years older than us. I checked public records. He owned no property I could locate except a 2010 Dodge truck. He had no adult criminal record, and no civil suits had been filed against him.

I was able to pull a copy of his driver's license from another database. At six feet three inches tall, two hundred twenty pounds, with long, unruly, medium brown hair, and hazel eyes, he was a nice enough looking man in an outdoorsy kind of way. I wondered why he'd never married, moved away from his aunts.

A quick property search told me The Willow-Mary Trust owned the house at 12 Church Street. It didn't take long to verify that Willowdean Beauthorpe owned half interest in the trust, and Olivia Beauthorpe Pearson had inherited the other half. This kind of information is only available if you know what to look for, which accounted for why I'd missed it a couple years back.

Only after I'd documented all the facts did I allow myself to create a sub-file labeled "Speculation." Here is where I would list all the possibilities. Speculation and possibilities were not admissible in court.

I heard Nate on the stairs before the door opened.

"Annelise sent up cookies." He set down the camera equipment, then crossed the room and bent to give me a kiss that made me lose every thought in my head. When he stood, his smoky blue eyes held mine. "I missed you."

"I missed you too."

"We need to wrap up this sordid business so we can go back to dreaming about our honeymoon." He handed me a napkin with two iced Christmas tree cookies.

"That gets my vote." I refocused, with great effort. "If you want to put the camera here, I can move. I thought the angle was better from the left window."

"This will work just fine." He went about setting up the tripod and camera.

"I've documented thoroughly how I don't think there was a body in the house across the street last night."

"That might well come in handy later. We can hope neither of us ends up on a witness stand, but I wouldn't put money on it."

"Purely as a hypothetical exercise, if there was a body, the only person who couldn't've been responsible is Aunt Dean. She was upstairs with Olivia while Robert was wandering around downstairs in the dark with a flashlight. At that point, there was no body. Aunt Dean was still upstairs when Olivia came down and found the body."

Nate canted his head towards his shoulder, looked skeptical. "If we believe everything our clients have told us thus far. They have both been less than forthcoming."

"Right." I inhaled deeply. "So for the moment, I see Seth as suspect number one."

"Agreed. He had the means and the opportunity. But what was his motive?"

"Based on the information we have right now, the only thing I can come up with is mistaken identity. He could've seen Robert come into the house and mistaken Thurston for Robert. If Olivia could confuse the two, surely Seth could."

"And he'd be thinking if Robert showed up at the house it was to put a stop to the blackmail."

"Exactly," I said. "But what would Thurston Middleton have been doing in that house to begin with? I'm going to have to talk to Aunt Dean as soon as the ladies are back from their outing."

"Talking to her is just as likely to send rats scattering as Sonny going in there with a search warrant. If she's an accessory to whatever Seth has done in his bouncer capacity over the years, she'll tip him off. And surely she's protective of her paying customers."

"But she'll be more protective of Olivia. Olivia is her partner, unwilling though she may be, and her heir. If I can convince her my only agenda is to protect Olivia, she might talk to me and keep it quiet."

Nate was quiet for a moment. "That will work better if Olivia goes with you."

I winced, shook my head. "That's too risky. She's too much of a loose cannon. But by then we'll have cameras live and the landline tapped. With Olivia's consent, it's like putting the whole house on a nanny cam. What Miss Dean does after I leave will tell us a great deal."

Nate pulled the binoculars out of a black duffle bag, adjusted the focus, and scanned every angle available from the window. "So if Seth is suspect number one, who do you make for suspect number two?"

"As much as I wish we could, we can't exclude Olivia."

"No, we cannot. She had means and opportunity. It's possible she killed Thurston for some unknown motive, but if it was her, it's more likely that she mistook him for Robert, even when he was upright."

"I just can't see that. Olivia is volatile, no doubt. But she seems crazy about Robert, and vice versa. She was nearly catatonic when she thought he was dead."

He raised both eyebrows, then pulled a chair up to the camera so he could sit and look at the flip out screen. He adjusted the camera. "I can get shots of the license plate from any car turning into the drive. If someone street parks, I may have to go downstairs to get the right angle. Bring me up to speed. What else've you come up with so far?"

I filled him in on Seth and the house, how Olivia's story held up that far. "I got Olivia's email with the girls' first names and the last names they go by—those of their benefactors. Suspects three through seven are Amber Calhoun, Wendi Gibbes, Dana Huger, Heather Prioleau, and Lori Russell."

"And there are five other men, patrons of the establishment

all, with last names of Calhoun, Gibbes, Huger, Prioleau, and Russell, who may also have had a motive to kill either Thurston or Robert."

"When you say it like that I get queasy." I turned back to my laptop.

"So first we need to figure out if Mr. Middleton expired inside that house. The next two questions: *If* he did, was he the intended victim, or was he in the wrong place at the wrong time; and who had a motive to kill him or Robert."

"What a godawful mess."

"My thoughts exactly."

Scanning my notes, I said, "In addition to the previously mentioned twelve suspects, it's possible one of the residents had an old boyfriend or other family member who was on a mission to get her out of there and somehow had an altercation with Thurston. You can never rule out the spouse, of course. And then there's the final possibility, an unidentified third party was in the house for reasons unknown, with intent to kill one of the two men, or who possibly fell into a misunderstanding."

Nate stared at the camera screen. "And then there's Raylan."

"Olivia's brother? How did he get involved in all this?"

"Well, he's just gotten out of the passenger side of your brother's car across the street. Do you want to go ask him, or shall I?"

"*Blake?* Sonavabitch. Blake is out there?" I sat the pillows and my laptop on the floor and scrambled out of the chair, searching the street from my window. I grabbed my phone and tapped Blake's name in my favorites list. On the street below, he reached into his pocket, glanced at the screen of his phone, then returned it to his pocket. On my end of the line, I heard his voicemail greeting.

"*Ooooh!* I cannot believe he just sent me to voicemail. I'm going down there."

"Probably best. I've only met Raylan that once, at our engagement party. And I really don't want to get between you and Blake this close to the wedding if you don't mind."

I headed for the door. "Open the window. Get his attention. Keep them on the street."

I flew down the stairs and through the foyer, catching a glimpse of Annelise and several other people in the living room. I had no time to worry about what they thought.

From the front porch, I saw Blake and Raylan Beauthorpe looking up at the third-floor windows of the bed and breakfast. Thank heaven. Nate must've gotten their attention.

I raised my hand and waved. "Merry Christmas, y'all." I hurried down the steps.

Blake squinted. Then his face broke out in disbelief. Raylan, a study in bewilderment, looked to Blake for guidance.

Blake started across the street. Raylan followed.

"Liz. What in the hell are you doing?" My brother's heart clearly was not filled with the joy of the season.

"I'm working a case. You're out of your jurisdiction." Blake was the Stella Maris Chief of Police. "What are *you* doing? Hey, Raylan."

"Hey, Liz." Raylan looked worried, and a little scared.

"Walk with me." Blake nodded north on Church Street.

I grabbed his arm. "This way." I pulled him towards the walk-thru gate into the side yard of the bed and breakfast. "Let's get off the street."

He retrieved his arm, cast me a look brothers reserved for younger sisters, and followed, muttering something under his breath Mamma would not have approved of.

Raylan tagged behind him, casting nervous looks all around.

When we were shielded by masonry fence columns and trees, I repeated, "What are you doing here?"

"You first." I recognized Blake's mule look. His eyes, the same cobalt blue as mine, held a challenge.

I blew out a breath. "I'm working a case, for heaven's sake."

Raylan said, "Did Olivia come to you? I tried to get her to do that weeks ago and she wouldn't."

"Yes, she did." I looked at Blake.

"I came with Raylan to try to reason with the blackmailer. He's here as Olivia's brother. I'm here as his friend, not in an official capacity. Safety in numbers."

I turned to Raylan. "When did Olivia tell you Seth was blackmailing her?"

"About a month ago. She's been hiding this from Robert for years, but it's getting harder to conceal. The money's adding up. Lately she's been...distraught. I just wanted to help." I couldn't help noticing how much Raylan favored Olivia. He was a good bit older—closer to Seth's age. But his blond hair and aristocratic features were classic Beauthorpe.

"Have you tried talking to Seth before? Alone?"

Raylan looked away. "Yeah. I came by last night."

"Aw, hell, Raylan," Blake said.

Hell's bells. Was everyone in Charleston County in the whorehouse last night? "What time?"

"About seven twenty."

My stomach clenched. "Seriously? Where did you park?"

"Over on Murray. I didn't want my car seen in front of that house."

"Why not? Your aunt lives there. The house has been in your family for years."

Raylan flushed. "You must know what goes on in there."

I nodded. Of course I knew. I was just verifying that he knew why Olivia was being blackmailed. "So did you talk to Seth?"

"I did. He and I used to be close, when we were little. He spent a lot of time at my grandparents' house. My grandfather and his grandmother were brother and sister. I thought I could reason with him. Appeal to his family loyalty. Apparently, he has none. He can't get past our aunts not leaving the house to him."

"Where did you talk to him?" I asked.

"In the guesthouse out back. That's where he lives."

"How long were you there?" I asked.

Raylan shrugged. "Twenty minutes. It was a short, ugly conversation."

I felt my face squinch up in confusion.

"And when you left, you didn't see Olivia's car out front, with her in it?"

"Her car was there when I arrived. I thought that was odd. It crossed my mind she might've gone to see Seth. Maybe she was trying to handle him on her own. That scared me. I hurried on back to the guesthouse. Thankfully, Olivia wasn't there. I figured she was visiting Aunt Dean, maybe trying to talk to her about Seth. When I came out, her car was still there. I didn't see Olivia, but it was dark."

"Other than last night, have you ever been inside that house?" I asked.

"Naturally. Like you said, it's been in our family for generations. It only became...what it is now over the last fifteen to twenty years."

"Have you tried to talk to Seth before last night about blackmailing your sister?"

"No."

I nodded, mulled. "Blake, if a Stella Maris citizen is being blackmailed by a Charlestonian, you could arrest him, right?"

"Sure. I'd ask a Charleston PD officer to accompany me to make the arrest."

"But if the suspect was in Stella Maris, you could just arrest him, right?"

"Of course. But I thought Olivia didn't want to file a complaint."

"She may change her mind. Listen, Nate's upstairs. We have the house under surveillance. There are extenuating circumstances."

Blake said, "There always are with you. Do they involve the body over in White Point Gardens?"

"You don't want me to answer that."

He nodded rapidly, managing to look both satisfied and seriously pissed off. "You need to give whatever you have to Sonny and step away. Olivia is going to have to put on her big girl...shoes...and face this. She hasn't broken any laws." He looked away. "That I know of."

Raylan's voice held a plea. "Blake, that's my baby sister. You have two of those. You understand. If there's anything we can do to protect her..."

Blake hitched up one side of his mouth. "Therein lies the problem, Raylan. That," he jabbed a finger at me, "is *my* little sister. And I can't have her breaking the law, maybe going to jail, to save Olivia a little embarrassment."

"Hold on, both of y'all," I said. "I have a plan. Blake, I'm not breaking any laws. Just give me until the end of the day tomorrow, then I'll turn everything over to Sonny. I promise." I neglected to mention the wiretapping thing. If we planned to listen to Olivia's calls, we were covered by her request form. Aunt Dean's calls were another matter.

He looked at me skeptically.

"In the meantime," I said, "y'all please go back to Stella Maris. I'll keep you updated."

Blake sighed. "Nate's here?"

"Yes."

"And you're working this together?"

"Yes," I said. "And we may need your help, so if I call, please do not send me straight to voicemail." I raised an eyebrow at him.

He gave me that mulish look one more time for good measure. "Come on, Raylan. We don't need to be in the middle of this."

They headed towards the car and I climbed the steps to the bed and breakfast. With a quick, "Hey y'all, Merry Christmas," to whoever was in the living room, I dashed up the stairs.

"They're leaving." Nate's eyes were on the screen.

"That's the good news," I said.

"There's bad?"

"Unfortunately, Raylan just gave our number one suspect an alibi. Though I doubt he'd've done it if he'd known that's what he was doing." I filled Nate in.

"That's an awfully tight timeline."

"Tell me about it." I typed it into a spreadsheet. "If everyone is telling the truth, someone was killed in the parlor between seven thirty and seven forty. It still *could've* been Seth. Barely."

"And if everyone is *not* telling us the truth, it could've been Raylan, Robert, or Olivia."

Something soured in my stomach and crept toward the back of my throat. "Or all three of them could've been a party to it."

I dug into public records and subscription databases for background on Thurston Middleton. Nate watched out the window, sometimes through the binoculars, sometimes through the camera screen.

Occasionally he went into the bathroom for a different vantage point. We were preparing for battle.

"Yes, you are." Colleen popped in. She sat cross-legged on thin air right in front of me, her back to the window.

I looked up at her. *Have you learned anything helpful?*

"Long-term," said Colleen, "the best way to protect Robert and Olivia is for her to convince Miss Dean to evict all the tenants and sell that house and move over to Bishop Gadsden. It's a lovely retirement village over on James Island."

I know where Bishop Gadsden is. I meant did you learn anything about what went on in that house last night?

"Nothing common sense hasn't already told you. Thurston Middleton departed for the next life from that parlor at seven thirty-five last night."

Was he the intended victim? Can you at least tell me that much?

"I can tell you this. Because he's on the Stella Maris town council, and therefore important to my mission, I would've known if Robert were in mortal danger. No one intended to kill him."

That helps, thanks.

"Liz?" Nate looked at me quizzically. "Everything all right? You're staring at that window awfully hard."

"Just thinking." I gave him my best imitation of a reassuring smile.

Make sure you get all the girls out of harm's way before you turn this over to Sonny. And know that I'll be with Olivia when she needs me. And then she was gone.

What had I been thinking about? Something important hid from me in a dark corner of my mind. The pineapple. I called Olivia. "I need you to think back to last night. Close your eyes and visualize what you saw."

"All right," she said, subdued.

"That wooden pineapple was on the fireplace mantel near the far right-hand side of the room when you and I went into the parlor last night."

"Someone must've cleaned it off and put it back while I was waiting for you," she said.

"Is that where it belongs? On the mantel?" I asked.

"That's right," she said.

"And the body on the rug, how was it positioned? Which way was his head pointing?" I asked.

"Towards the door," she said.

"Thanks, Olivia." I ended the call and told Nate what she'd said.

Nate said, "He was on his way out when he was struck from behind with an object from the other side of the room."

"Which implies several things," I said. "He wasn't attacked by someone who tiptoed into the room behind him. He had to have known someone else was in the room. They would've interacted, maybe argued."

"The light would've likely been on when the murder occurred—not turned on after the fact. Hard to imagine one of them wouldn't have turned on the light."

"Exactly. I've been in that room in the dark. For someone to locate the murder weapon and strike with accuracy as the victim was leaving without stumbling over the coffee table...that's highly implausible. Our culprit knew exactly who he or she was killing."

SEVEN

At five 'til twelve, Olivia texted me: *Almost there.*

"Nate," I said.

"I'm headed down. Video's rolling." He hustled across the room and out the door.

I moved to the left-front window and cracked it a few inches. Then I slipped an amplifier in my right ear and grabbed the binoculars.

Moments later, a black limousine negotiated the turn onto lower Church Street. It crawled down the narrow brick lane, with the right-side wheels on the sidewalk at times in order to pass a parked car. It stopped in front of the driveway at 12 Church Street. The driver stepped out. He was a portly gentleman with white hair and a beard, who looked remarkably like Santa Claus in a black suit and chauffer's cap. He opened the left passenger door, and Olivia the party girl emerged holding a champagne bottle in one hand and a bouquet of champagne flutes in the other, her keys dangling from a finger.

"Thank you, Santa Baby," she cooed at the driver. "I'll be right back with my friends."

"Yes ma'am." He nodded and took in the rearview as Olivia sashayed down the sidewalk in a red dress and heels.

Just before she reached the door, Nate, who was walking in the opposite direction, bumped into her.

Olivia stumbled and squealed.

The driver's nose lifted, like a hound sniffing the breeze. He took a step in Olivia's direction.

Nate grabbed her shoulders and steadied her. "Pardon me, ma'am."

In her outside voice, she said, "That's quite all right, handsome. Why don't you come along with us? I'm just going inside to get my friends. We're going to have a Christmas party. We have the limo for the whole day."

The driver returned to an at-ease position by the car door.

Nate let go of Olivia's left shoulder, then her right. Only because I knew what was happening and had the benefit of binoculars, I saw him slip her keys out of her fingers. "Thank you, ma'am. I'd better not. My wife's expecting me."

"That's too bad." Olivia pouted, playing it up.

Nate nodded goodbye and continued down the street.

Olivia stepped in front of the door. "Aunt Dean? *Aaaa-unt Deeeean.* My hands are full. Can you open the door?"

In the background, I heard steps on the porch. Moments later, the front door opened and Miss Dean appeared. "Lord a mercy, Olivia. What's all this noise?"

Though the whole scene was being videoed, I snapped a few stills of Miss Dean.

"My hands are full. Are you ready?" Olivia turned and called to the driver. "Hey, Santa Baby, can you pop this cork?"

He rushed over. "Yes, ma'am."

She handed him the bottle. "Is everyone ready?"

"I suppose we are," said Miss Dean. "I declare, Olivia, this is mighty generous of you, but a little more notice would've worked out much better."

"Now, Aunt Dean. That would've spoiled the surprise." Olivia held her left hand out towards the driver. He took a flute and filled it.

"Well, I suppose." Miss Dean stepped onto the sidewalk.

Sounds of heels on wood and women chattering drifted across the street.

The driver passed the glass to Miss Dean, then took another flute and filled it for Olivia.

A stunning redhead, who might've approached six feet tall even without the five-inch gladiator heels, appeared in the doorway. I snapped a few photos with the Canon. Her black slim-fit slacks, lace camisole, and black jacket suggested Forever 21.

Miss Dean said, "Olivia, I'm not sure you've met Lori. She's only moved in recently. Lori Russell, this is my niece, Olivia."

I opened the Voice Memos app. "Tall redhead. Lori Russell."

"It's lovely to meet you," Olivia said.

"Likewise." Lori's small voice didn't match her bold appearance.

The driver, who had the routine down now, handed Lori a champagne glass.

Miss Dean turned towards the door just as a black-haired girl with pale skin stepped out. "Olivia, you remember Amber."

"Of course. Hey, Amber!" Olivia hugged her like they were long-lost sorority sisters.

I snapped a photo of the odd look on Amber's face and recorded her name and description.

A brunette and a blonde joined the group. Miss Dean announced Dana and Heather as if they were being presented at their debutante ball. None of the women were inappropriately dressed. Though their hair colors represented most of the usual hues, the styles were similar—long and smooth. They looked like typical early-twenties college students and they all seemed vaguely uncomfortable. Santa gave them each a glass of champagne. I documented their names and basic descriptions.

"Aunt Dean," said Olivia, "aren't we missing someone?"

"Wendi and her beau have gone to Innsbruck for the holidays," said Aunt Dean. "She wanted to see snow. Nathaniel spoils that girl rotten, I declare."

"Well, then." Olivia raised her glass. "I'm so happy y'all could come out with me today. This is going to be so much fun. Merry Christmas. Cheers!"

Everyone clinked glasses and drank. The blonde, Heather, smiled.

"Is everyone ready?" Olivia asked.

"What the hell is going on here?" Seth filled the doorway, his eyes beaming anger at Olivia. In a flannel shirt, jeans, and work boots, he looked the part of handyman.

Lori cringed. Heather and Dana exchanged glances.

"Now, Seth," said Aunt Dean. "I told you we were going out for some girl time."

"I know what you told me," he said.

"Don't be rude." Miss Dean lifted her chin and gave him an imperious look. "We'll be back this evening. I'll call if we're delayed past dinner."

Seth glared at Olivia. "You're up to something."

Olivia waved at him dismissively. "Oh, for heaven's sake, Seth. We're going to get our nails done. Have a massage. Maybe do some shopping."

"Well then, you'll need someone to help with the packages. I'll come along just in case," said Seth.

Olivia did an amazing performance of a startled look. "No need for that. Our driver can handle it. I'm sure you could use some down time."

"I don't need you to tell me what I could use." He headed towards the car.

"Seth Quinlan," said Olivia. "You absolutely will not ruin our day out. I simply will not have it."

"You don't have a choice." He stepped closer to her, got into her face.

She stared him down. "What is your problem?"

"You," he said.

Miss Dean moved in and stood between them, forming a triangle. "Listen here. The two of you are family, this is Christmas, and we are making quite a scene. Everyone, get in the car this instant." She turned and walked towards the limo.

Seth gave Olivia a triumphant smirk and sauntered towards the car. Olivia glared at his retreating back. Her left eyebrow arched, her eyes killing him a thousand times over with poison darts. Then she snapped back into party girl mode.

"Whatever. Seth, I declare you will not spoil our fun. Y'all drink up. We have plenty more champagne."

The driver helped the ladies in the car. After he closed the door, he shook his head, squared his shoulders, and got into the drivers' seat. The limo rolled down the street. I heard Nate on the stairs. Then the sound of trumpets, like the ones used to announce royalty, rang out from my phone.

"Hey, Mamma."

"*E-liz-a-beth Su-zanne Tal-bot.*"

Those eight syllables, enunciated with precision, spelled Big Trouble. "What's wrong?"

Nate walked through the door.

"Not a single solitary thing, except that your sister and I have been waiting here for thirty minutes at Maddison Row with Nicolette for your final dress fitting. Nicolette has reminded Merry and me five times that this final fitting should've been two weeks ago, as if she or I either one had a say in the matter."

I squeezed my eyes closed. "Oh, Mamma, I'm so, so sorry." I'd completely forgotten about the fitting.

"Where on the Good Lord's earth are you?"

"I'm only a few blocks away."

Miles maybe. Maddison Row, the bridal boutique, was on Spring Street. I looked at Nate.

He must've recognized the desperation in my eyes. He stood at the ready, the question in his eyes, *What can I do?*

"I suppose if you're driving that explains why you didn't respond to Merry's messages. But really, you could've called." She tsked. "You were bound to get overwhelmed. We didn't have nearly enough time to plan this wedding. I don't know why you children couldn't wait until spring. We'll see you in a few minutes. Drive safe." Mamma ended the call.

Merry had texted me? I looked at my phone. *Sonavabitch.* I'd missed five texts with escalating urgency. I'd been so wrapped up in the show Olivia was putting on, I hadn't seen the messages.

I looked at what I'd left the house in that morning. Ann Taylor skinny jeans, a blue twinset, and black ballet flats. This would not fly with Mamma for a final fitting at such a nice salon.

"I need a dress."

"Why?" Nate's look telegraphed his incomprehension.

"The fitting. I forgot all about the fitting."

I could swing by Anne's on King Street on the way. It would take an extra few minutes. What in the name of sweet reason was I thinking? I'd never picked out a dress in less than an hour in my entire life.

I'd just have to go as I was. That was all there was to it. Mamma wouldn't be happy, and that snooty wedding coordinator, Nicolette, would turn up her nose, but it wouldn't be the first time for either circumstance.

Nate walked over and stood in front of me. He put his hands on my arms and rubbed.

"You look gorgeous. You always look gorgeous."

"You are a prince. But you don't understand—"

"But I do. You, Slugger, are the bride. This is *your* day y'all are planning. You can go in your pajamas if you like. It's that wedding Nazi your mamma hired who doesn't understand."

"But Mamma—"

"Your mamma loves you. She wants to share this with you. Go drink champagne with your mamma and your sister. Ignore that Nicolette. Fire her ass, better yet."

I giggled and shook off the anxiety. Nate was right. Nicolette was hired help. I ran into the bathroom to freshen up. A little powder, mascara, a fresh coat of lipstick. I ran a comb through my hair and looked at myself with a critical eye. It would have to do. *I* would have to do.

"I would drop you off," Nate said, as I stepped back into the bedroom. "But one of us needs to get these cameras installed and the phone tapped. Everything I'll need is in the back of the Explorer, so you can't drive off in it. I called Scoop. Your car should be downstairs any moment."

Scoop was a free electric car service in the city. You watch the advertising on the back of the headrests and tip the driver. "I was just wishing we had both our cars here—thanks. Can I borrow your phone? I want to text Olivia from it so she can just reply if she runs into trouble."

"Good idea." He handed me his phone.

I texted Olivia: *Forgot dress fitting. This is alternate contact in case of change in plans.* Olivia would understand.

I grabbed a few items I'd need when I got back from a utility bag we traveled with and transferred them to a zippered compartment in my large Kate Spade tote.

Nate stepped to the window. "Scoop's here. Run along now. Have fun. Say hi to your mamma and Merry for me."

He kissed me on the forehead, swatted my bottom, and pushed me towards the door. I gave him a look over my shoulder that promised a great many things.

EIGHT

Maddison Row sat on the corner of Spring and President. It was a darling boutique in a large, three-story, white building that was likely once someone's home. It had been modernized, and the street level windows and doors redone in warm, natural woods. The black-and-white-striped awnings made me smile.

I rushed through the door and immediately began apologizing. Lindsey, the store manager who'd been working with us, talked me down.

"You're here now. Everything's fine. Your mother and sister are right back here." She led me to the viewing room.

Mamma and Merry folded me into a group hug and a cloud of happy chatter. No one mentioned my attire. Nicolette hung back, a tight smile on her face. A table against the wall held a bottle of champagne and four glasses.

Merry rushed to pour the bubbly. "We have to toast." She filled our glasses and handed me mine.

Mamma smiled, tears in her eyes. She and Nicolette picked up their flutes.

Merry said, "To my sister. The most beautiful bride ever."

"*Aww.* You're so sweet." I drank, then hugged her tight.

"Your shoes are in the bag by the dressing room," she said.

Shoes. Panic with a chaser of sweet relief flooded through me. Lindsey couldn't check the length without the shoes I'd wear down the aisle. I held Merry at arm's length and beamed gratitude at her.

"*Thank you*. You win Maid of Honor of the Year and World's Best Sister Ever."

"Here we go." Lindsey carried in the dress and hung it in the dressing room.

"I can't wait to see you in it again," said Mamma.

I handed Merry my champagne glass and stepped behind the black and white print curtain.

Moments later, I emerged.

"Oh." Mamma covered her mouth with both hands.

"You. Look. Fabulous." Merry grinned.

Nicolette nodded. "It's lovely."

"Oh, I love that dress on you," said Lindsey.

Lindsey led me to a black square box between antique floor-to-ceiling mirrors with silver and pearl frames. "Do you have your shoes on?"

"Yes." I'd successfully resisted both Nicolette and Mamma and was wearing Kate Spade satin flats with pearl-accented bows on the toes. And I would totally be wearing the blue Kate Spade Happily Ever After flip-flops at some point during the reception.

Was that me in the mirror? The dress was perfection—the Ellie from Amsale Aberra's Christos Bridal Line, it was a fit and flare gown with a champagne satin ribbon at the waist. Illusion netting with oh-so-delicate floral appliqué at the neckline and cap sleeves. The skirt had a tulle overlay that gave it an ethereal feel without making me look like a Disney princess or a meringue. I looked into the mirror behind me. The deep V in the back made the dress nearly backless.

"You look so beautiful," Mamma said.

I smiled at her. Who wouldn't feel beautiful in this dress?

Lindsey checked me over thoroughly, examined the length. "The fit looks perfect to me. What do you think?"

"I love it," I said.

Something in my peripheral vision caught my eye. I turned my head. Colleen. She wore a wide smile. Tears slid down her face. What I wouldn't give to have her alive and one of my bridesmaids.

"When do you want to pick it up?" Lindsey asked.

"Friday?"

"We'll have it steamed and ready to go."

"Sugar, are you sure you don't want to wear a veil?" Mamma asked. "It's not too late. They have some lovely ones here in the store."

I stepped down, walked over, and put my hand on her arm. "Mamma, I wore a veil the first time. I'm going into this marriage eyes wide open. And I'm not hiding any part of my true self. It's symbolic for me."

"I understand." She smiled and nodded.

Lindsey said, "I love the floral antique brooch. It's going to be perfect with your hair up in a side sweep."

"Run and change now," Mamma said. "I want to have lunch with my girls." The look she gave Nicolette issued no invitation to join.

I floated back into the dressing room.

Mamma said, "Honey, after you change, put on some lipstick. You look a little pale."

Merry laughed.

"You need some, too, Esmerelda," said Mamma.

An hour and a half later, after a decadent lunch at Charleston Grill and more champagne, I texted Nate from the backseat of the Prius I'd been Scooped up in: *Sit rep?*

Half done.

I replied: *On my way 2 help.*

Doors locked. Fence post by door.

Then I texted Olivia: *Hey, r u free 4 dinner this evening?*

A few minutes later she replied: *Would love 2, but am having a girl's day with friends. Having early dinner together. Won't be back til after 6. Raincheck?*

Sounds good, I responded.

If Seth happened to steal a look at her phone, this exchange wouldn't raise his suspicions. But it told me things were going well, and we had until at least six to finish up. It was nearly three o'clock.

My phone made the Law and Order noise. *Boink-boink.* Damnation. Sonny. I could not talk to him yet. I sent the call to voicemail.

The driver dropped me off in front of the bed and breakfast. I scanned Church Street. No one in sight. I jogged over to number 12. The keys dangled against the inside of the wide post. Nate had hung them from a long piece of fishing line looped around the ball-shaped finial. I pulled on the string, retrieved the keys, and slipped them into my pocket. I pulled a pair of latex gloves out of the zippered compartment in my tote and pulled them on. Then I opened the door and slipped through, closing it right behind me and locking it.

I climbed the steps to the porch, walked past the front parlor windows, and stopped by the front door. There, from the supplies I'd stashed in my tote earlier, I pulled a vacuum-sealed bag. I tore open the plastic and shook out a disposable hooded coverall. I stepped into the built-in shoe covers, pulled the jumpsuit on, and tightened the hoodie around my face. The last thing we wanted to do was contaminate a possible crime scene.

We also wanted to be sure to leave no trace we'd been there. Who knew how far the investigation into this house would lead, or where it might eventually take the Charleston PD? While I had been inside the foyer and the parlor, I would have a hard time explaining if forensics were to find something I'd stepped in on Stella Maris or one of my hairs in another part of the house.

I let myself in the front door. The house was still. I texted Nate: *Foyer. Where r u?*

Upstairs. Front bedroom.

The staircase was a switchback, with a Palladium window at the turn. The raised panel wainscoting and woodwork detailing was the work of a craftsman. I made my way up the steps. A few of them creaked, but for a house built in 1810, it was remarkably well-maintained.

I turned towards the front of the house and stepped into the bedroom directly over the front parlor. The engraved silver doorplate announced I was entering the Calhoun Room. Dressed just like me, Nate stood on a chair near the center of the room. He was affixing a device with Velcro to the ceiling that looked exactly like any other smoke detector, but in fact held a motion and voice activated camera that would stream audio and video directly to our laptops across the street via Wi-Fi, courtesy of the mobile hotspot he'd installed in our room.

"I thought we were going to use the air purifiers," I said. We had several versions of these devices.

"We had twelve of those. But this house is a huge monstrosity. I used six downstairs—front parlor, foyer, second parlor, dining room, kitchen, and keeping room. The ceilings are too tall to put the smoke detectors down there without a ladder. The bedrooms...most of them don't have much clutter. Not many things on shelves and surfaces. I was afraid the air purifiers would be noticed anyway, so when I ran short, I started using these. Even though the rooms already have smoke detectors, these are much less likely to be spotted." He shrugged. "If they are, most people would assume one is a smoke detector and the other carbon monoxide."

"Where do you need me to start?"

"I can handle the equipment. Phone tap is in. Because the house is likely to be searched soon, I used the butt sett and put a recorder with a Wi-Fi transmitter on the junction box. If we can't get all our equipment out before the search warrant is executed...Well, there's no way they wouldn't recognize a recorder found inside the house for exactly what it is. Thought maybe you'd want to search the rooms. I haven't had a chance to get to that."

"I'll start with Miss Dean's. A ledger would come in handy."

"Master's on the back end of the house. Three other bedrooms on this floor, and one on the third floor. Two more above the garage."

"So eight bedrooms total, plus Seth's in the guesthouse?"

"Right. None of Olivia's keys fit the guesthouse lock. I had to get out the pick set for that. I did search the guesthouse while I was out there. Nothing helpful whatsoever. He drinks Budweiser and plays video games. I put a camera in the main room—small kitchen and a living room—but not his bedroom. We're short on cameras, and I don't know about you, but I'm not thrilled about all these bedroom cameras to begin with."

I shuddered.

"Me either. But this is the quickest way to find out what we need to know. If any of these folks know anything, they're more likely to talk about it behind closed doors. And, if any of the residents are in danger because of something *they* know, we're close enough to intervene if necessary. These cameras serve two purposes: surveillance and protection."

"I'm aware. Just unenthusiastic."

"I don't intend to watch the...action scenes. And neither will you."

"I hope you're not suggestin' you think such a thing would hold appeal for me."

"Of course not. I'll be down the hall. It's three fifteen. We need to be out clean by six."

"Roger that."

I followed the Oriental runner from the front bedroom to the back. A four-poster bed with cream-colored spread and taupe, brown, and robin's egg blue accent pillows sat in the center of the right wall. To the left was a sitting nook anchored by a fireplace, with a chaise and a club chair and ottoman.

As with the rest of the house, the heart pine floors gave the space warmth. The furniture appeared to be heirloom quality antiques. This had to be the most tastefully decorated whorehouse in the history of whorehouses.

Methodically, I searched the room, beginning with the nightstand drawers. Thirty minutes later, I verified there were no hidden safes behind the paintings. I scanned the room. There was simply no place else to look. The closet and bathroom, while modern, well-appointed, and organized, were equally unrewarding. If Miss Dean had written records of her rents, she kept them somewhere other than her bedroom.

Was there a desk in the house? I went back downstairs. The front parlor held floor-to-ceiling bookcases, but no drawers. I didn't have enough time to fan through every volume in the library.

The second parlor, to the right of the foyer as you came in the front door, was decorated similarly to the one in the front of the house. But there was a lovely desk in front of one of the windows. The room appeared to have more furniture than the others I'd seen. Had the desk been moved from the library to make room for the Christmas tree?

I sat in the wooden chair. The single drawer in the top center was locked. Damnation. I ran back upstairs and retrieved the pick set. It took me seconds to open the old lock. Inside the drawer, along with assorted office supplies, I found a leather-bound journal. I pulled it out and laid it on the desk. I held my breath as I opened the cover. Pay dirt.

The first page was dated June 14, 1995. Under the date, the first name listed was Bounetheau. I sucked in air. I was well acquainted with that family, and not in a good way. But that was a whole nother story. Underneath the name were months, beginning with June and ending with December. Each month had $1,000 beside it.

The next name was Huger, but the list of months began with July. The line for each month had $2,000 beside it. So a second room in the boardinghouse, as it was at that time according to Olivia, was occupied in July, at twice the rent as the first room.

In August, it appeared another tenant had moved in, and the last name listed was Middleton. The Middleton room had cost $1,000 per month. September brought the additions of Rutledge, and Simmons, both with the figure of $1,000 for each month. By December of 1995, the sisters had been bringing in $6,000 per month in rent for five rooms. One of the bedrooms would've been Mary Leona's at that time, but that still left one room empty.

The next two pages covered 1996. The five names remained the same, and the rooms were filled for all twelve months. I flipped through the book. There was a lot of data here. I turned to the last pages with entries. The entire year of 2015 had the names Calhoun, Huger, Gibbes, Prioleau, and Russell listed. Still five rooms rented. That meant there must be two empty bedrooms in the house. Had Miss Dean not been able to bring herself to add Mary Leona's former room to the rent roll?

Sweet reason. In 2015, all the rooms were going for $10,000 per month, with the exception of the Huger room at $20,000. Miss Dean had brought in $60,000 every month that year. And the girls were given an allowance on top of that, Olivia had said. Clearly there were men in Charleston with way more money than sense.

I pulled my iPad out of my tote, opened the scanner app, and started scanning with the most recent pages. If something interrupted me, I wanted the most relevant data secured. It was tedious work, with nearly forty pages of information covering twenty years.

No first names were recorded and no name for the "niece." It was a rent ledger for each room, with the room names changing periodically. When I'd scanned all the pages, I put the journal back where I'd found it and re-locked the drawer.

The next piece of information I wanted was first names for the gentlemen who paid the rent and real names for the residents. We needed to know who we were dealing with before I could start investigating them.

I returned to the front bedroom upstairs, the Calhoun room. Nate had finished and moved on. I studied the room. Like the master bedroom, it was tastefully decorated in shades of cream and taupe. Here the accents were green. On the dresser, a silver tray held a crystal decanter of amber liquor, a single matching rocks glass, an ice bucket, a bottle of Schug pinot noir, and a single wineglass.

A picture frame on the left bedside table held a photo of the raven-haired girl, Amber, and a brown-headed, clean-shaven man with intelligent eyes and a nice smile. I pegged him at forty-ish. Though clearly much older than Amber, he wasn't what I'd been expecting. He didn't look like a dirty old man. Something about him shouted his pedigree. It appeared they were at an outdoor party, a pool in the background. I snapped a photo of the smiling couple.

In the bottom drawer of the left bedside table, I found a zippered portfolio. I laid it on the bed, opened the zipper, and eased it open. The document on top was a grade report from the College of Charleston for the second summer session. Amber McDonald had taken FINC 402 – Derivatives Securities. She'd made a 4.0.

I leafed through the portfolio. Additional grade reports, school correspondence, a passport, various other personal documents—all in the name of Amber McDonald. I photographed her passport.

I glanced at the time on my phone. Four twenty. From what I'd seen, this room could've belonged to any college student, except it was far neater than any I'd seen when I was in college myself. I would've liked to've searched her room further, but I had six more bedrooms to go through. With meticulous care, I put the portfolio back in order, zipped it, and returned it to the drawer. I did a quick search of the medicine cabinet in the adjoining bath, but found nothing more unusual than Tylenol.

The next room down the hall on the right was the Russell Room. It was smaller than the room on the front of the house, but similarly decorated. The silver tray on the dresser held the same refreshments. The only variation was the pinot noir here was an Estancia. Again, a single framed photo of the redhead named Lori with an early forties gentleman who reminded me of Kevin Spacey with a mustache. The picture could've been taken at the same event—a summer party.

Lori's portfolio was similar to Amber's, but harder to locate. I worked my way methodically through all the furniture, then moved to her closet, which was a revelation in so many ways. Clearly "Kevin Spacey" Russell had a thing for role-playing. An assortment of costumes hung in Lori's closet, everything from a Catholic schoolgirl uniform, to sexy nurse, to cheerleader, to french maid, to a business suit with a skirt far too short to wear to any office.

The information identifying Lori as Lori Stowe, a twenty-two-year-old Information Systems Specialist student at Trident Tech, was hidden between sweaters folded on her closet shelf. I snapped photos of her passport and the framed photo.

The next room on the right was the Huger room. It was the same size and layout as Lori's room and had the basics the other rooms had—antiques and a neutral décor. Why was this smaller room worth twice as much as all the others? The silver tray on the dresser held a decanter of dark liquor, ice bucket, and two rocks glasses—no wine. The bedside photo was of the brunette, Dana. The gentleman she was with also looked to be in his early forties, and boy, was he a looker. Salt-and-pepper hair, happy brown eyes, a chiseled face.

In the closet, in an otherwise empty makeup travel case, I found a portfolio like the ones the first two girls had. These cases to hide your real identity must be a custom of the house. Dana's legal name was Dana Clark, age twenty-seven. She was a graduate nursing student at MUSC, working on her MSN. She was studying to be a nurse practitioner. Her passport had stamps from all over the world. I snapped a photo of the identification page, put everything back, and left the closet.

I continued down the hall to the last room on the left, the Prioleau Room. The neutral color palette in here was accented with soft rose. Two crystal decanters were on the silver tray in this room. One held an amber liquor, the other clear. As with the last room, there was an ice bucket and two rocks glasses. Smiling back at me from the bedside picture frame—another pool party shot—was one of the blondes, Heather. But the gentleman in the photo appeared to be close to her age. He had brown hair, round, wire-rimmed glasses, and a confident grin.

Heather's secrets were in the large bottom drawer of her dresser. Some of her secrets reminded me of Victoria's—bras, panties, bustiers, stockings, garters, teddies, baby doll nighties, et cetera. As squeamish as digging through someone else's underwear drawer made me, nevertheless, all kinds of ideas popped into my head regarding last minute trousseau shopping.

The zippered portfolio identifying Heather as Heather Wilder, a graduate student in environmental studies at the College of Charleston, was in the bottom of the drawer. Heather was twenty-seven. I took my photos, slid the portfolio back under neatly folded silk and lace, and moved on.

On the third floor, I found the Gibbes Room—the one that belonged to the couple who'd gone to Innsbruck. This room was large, with views of both Church Street and the harbor beyond a line of rooftops and treetops. Like all the others, it had a modern, private bath. The picture from the pool party showed Wendi, another blonde with large green eyes, and the man who must be Nathaniel Gibbes. He appeared to be in his mid-thirties. I stared at the photo. Did this sandy-haired man have a wife? Children? He should be coaching soccer. As in Heather's room, Wendi's hostess tray indicated both parties preferred the liquor in the decanter. I sniffed. Smelled like bourbon to me. Wendi's bureau sported nice lingerie, sexy, but nothing more adventurous than what I had in my own drawer. I moved to the closet.

A long alligator case in the corner caught my eye. I pulled it out onto the bed and opened it. Oh, sweet reason. It was a portable stripper pole that appeared to work something like a tension drapery rod when assembled. Interesting. Could be fun for consenting adults in the privacy of their own home. I put it back where I found it.

Boink-boink. Sonny's ringtone. I stared at his photo on the screen for a few seconds feeling guilty, then sent the call to voicemail. He hadn't left a message the first time he'd called, but I could guess what he wanted.

A backpack on the floor of Wendi's closet held a few textbooks and her portfolio. Her real name was Wendi Hill, age twenty-five. She'd graduated from Charleston Southern University, a Christian affiliated institution supported by the Baptist denomination, with a double major in psychology and sociology. No doubt her alma mater would take a dim view of her current situation. I snapped my photos and went to find the entrance to the wing over the garage.

I went back to the main floor and walked towards the back of the house. From the foyer, I passed through the parlor where I'd found the desk, the dining room, and into a modernized kitchen a realtor would no doubt describe as "gourmet." Restaurant-quality appliances, vanilla-glazed modern cabinetry, and granite countertops somehow managed to look as if they belonged in the historic house.

Beyond the kitchen, a cozy keeping room with a fireplace, more bookcases, and deep furniture invited one to sit a spell. From both the kitchen and the keeping room, there were views of a pool and spa hidden from the world by garden walls and greenery.

A nook recessed in the back kitchen wall hid the back staircase on the left. To the right was a walk-in pantry. Straight ahead, a door led to steps that went down into the garage. I flipped a light switch. The gold Cadillac likely belonged to Miss Dean, and the large black Dodge truck must've been Seth's. I took pictures of the license plates for documentation.

I checked the shelves on the back wall, and every corner of the neat garage. No bloody tarps, no hand truck with or without blood smears. No stairs led from this level to the living area above. I turned off the light, closed the door, and headed up the back staircase.

At the top of the steps, to my right, just before the master bedroom, a slim door I'd mistaken for a closet led to a landing over the garage. Charleston single houses typically had straightforward floorplans. This home felt a bit like a maze.

On the landing there were three doors. To my left was an exterior door leading to steps to the parking area. The doorplate on the right hand door identified it as the Rutledge Room. No Rutledge was on the current rent roll. I opened the door. It was decorated in keeping with the remainder of the house with one exception. Unlike the other rooms, this one had no rug on the pine floor. There was no photo, no clothes, no personal items.

I exited the Rutledge room, stepped towards the last bedroom in the main house, and stopped short. The nameplate read Huger. The ledger had only one line for Huger, so I had assumed there was one Huger renter. Did he require two rooms? Were there two Huger men involved? I opened the door. Just inside was an entry hall, leading into a large room with a sitting area. It was roughly the same size as the master bedroom in the main house, and it had a spacious modern bath with a deep, jetted tub and separate oversized shower.

There was no photograph on the bedside table in this room. The hostess tray held only bourbon, but a small wine cooler filled with champagne was hidden inside an antique console that had been retrofitted. The other side held a small refrigerator filled with fruit, cheeses, olives, et cetera.

The furniture yielded no portfolio, but in addition to a drawer full of lingerie similar to what I'd found in Heather's room, an entire drawer full of gadgets greeted me. I had to look through them—the portfolio could be on the bottom. I reached in my tote and pulled on a second pair of gloves.

There were clearly labeled bottles of massage oil in a variety of flavors, tubes of lubricants, and a wide variety of things that, while I had no personal experience of, I recognized. But there were also items that genuinely perplexed me, left me feeling curious, and unsophisticated.

Was this adventurous play what drove married men to mistresses? Were there some games they couldn't bring themselves to ask their wives to play? I picked up a yellow and purple tear-drop-shaped object that could've been a child's toy or a dog's chew toy. I tilted my head and scrutinized it.

The damn thing started to vibrate. How did you turn it off?

"You almost finished?"

I jumped three feet. "Oh!"

"Slugger? What've you got there?"

I felt myself turn fire-engine red. "I swear I don't have the first idea. I'm just trying to turn it off."

Nate didn't even try to hide his grin. "Let me see if I can help." He took it from me, did something to it, and it stopped vibrating. He set it on the dresser.

"What is that?" I asked.

"A massager." He smothered a chuckle.

"How do you know that?"

He shrugged. "They're fairly common." He looked into the drawer and whistled.

"Each of the girls had a hidden portfolio with ID. This is the last room. One of the other girls hid her private papers in the bottom of her lingerie drawer."

"You gettin' yourself an education?"

"I wasn't aware I needed one."

"Now don't go puttin' words in my mouth. Do you want me to finish looking in there?"

"No, I'll do it."

He looked at me for a long minute, continuing to grin. "All right then. Where do you want me to start?"

"I haven't checked the bed or the closet."

"I'll start with the bed. That's quick work."

I turned my attention back to the drawer. I wasn't going to pick up anything I didn't have to. I moved a few larger items to the top of the dresser, then slid the smaller things from one side of the drawer to another to check the bottom. What was the glass egg-shaped thing for? *Oh sweet baby Moses in a basket.* Handcuffs. Tassels. Clamps. I made quick work of clearing that drawer bottom. Once I was sure there was no portfolio, I put everything back and closed it firmly.

"You wouldn't believe some of this stuff," I said as I turned towards Nate.

He was examining something at the top corner of the bed. "I believe I would."

"What did you find?"

"Restraints."

I turned and made haste for the closet, which was a walk-in. I flipped on the light. An eclectic wardrobe greeted me. Everything from business suits to summer frocks to racy cocktail dresses. And leather pants, silk blouses, and all manner of lingerie. An entire wall was shelved for shoes, most sporting high heels with a message. While the variety of clothing was perplexing, the closet was nowhere close to full. Unlike the other rooms, there didn't appear to be clothes a college student would wear to class or out with friends.

A built-in unit in the back right was partially lined with pegboard and had shelves below it. This section held all manner of paddles, straps, and whips, et cetera, many hanging from hooks on the pegboard. I'd known this was coming as soon as I'd heard the word "restraints." I'd heard about the *Fifty Shades of Grey*. No wonder this couple had the room over the garage. And no wonder the girl next door had moved out. I'd bet these were not quiet neighbors.

I ignored the implements and searched the shelves and hatboxes for the portfolio.

Finally, I emerged from the closet. "There's no portfolio here," I said. I gave Nate the Cliff's Notes version of what I'd found so far, and the Huger puzzle.

"It's five past six," he said.

"Hell's bells." I glanced at my phone. "No further texts from Olivia."

"We've got to move."

I gave the room a final glance to make sure everything was as we'd found it.

"Which one of them do you suppose is the dominant?" Nate's tone was casual.

"I couldn't possibly care less."

"You sounded a little like your mamma just then." He grinned.

I arched my left eyebrow at him, turned, and strode out of the room.

Nate followed. "Do you have everything you came in with?"

"Yeah. Just my tote." I did a quick double check. Everything was there. "You?"

"Yeah. I took all the equipment out of the boxes and left those in the car. Brought everything over in this trash bag, which now has Velcro backing in it and not much else."

We crossed into the main house and moved quickly down the steps and out the front door. Once we were on the front porch, I locked the door behind us. Then we moved to the end of the piazza closest to the door leading to the street. Here we had more cover from the view of anyone strolling down the sidewalk who happened to glance over the fence. The front part of the side yard wasn't nearly as private as that on the other side of the garden wall, where the pool was located. We both stripped out of our coveralls and put them in the trash bag.

"Ready?" Nate asked.

My phone dinged a text. I glanced at the screen. Olivia: *Turning onto Atlantic.*

"Hurry," I said.

Nate opened the door, and as nonchalantly as if we did this every day, we walked onto the sidewalk, him carrying a large black trash bag. We crossed the street on a diagonal, and passed directly through the gate at the bed and breakfast. Nate went to stash the bag in the Explorer. I did a quick scan of the street. A couple walked from the direction of South Battery up Church. They seemed lost in conversation. On the other side of the street, a jogger kept a steady pace towards South Battery.

The nose of the limousine appeared at the corner. Nate grabbed my hand and we dashed up the steps.

Showtime.

NINE

Gloves or no gloves, pawing through a whorehouse filled with other people's pleasure gadgets deserved a thorough soap scrub with a generous hand-sani chaser. I craved a hot shower, but there was no time.

At six twenty, I called. "Miss Dean, this is Liz Talbot, Olivia's friend? We met last night."

There was a pause where I imagined she was recalling my odd attire. "Yes, my dear. What can I do for you?"

"I apologize for the short notice, but I need to speak with you privately as soon as possible, regarding a matter of great urgency—Olivia's troubles?"

"Oh, dear. I've been out all day, and I'm completely exhausted. Could we talk in the morning, perhaps?"

"I'm so sorry to press you. It's a terrible breach of manners, really. But I truly need to speak with you this evening."

"Well, I suppose I'll have to rally, then, won't I? How soon can you be here?"

"I'm in Charleston, nearby, in fact. I could be there in five minutes."

"Give me ten if you don't mind. The door to the piazza is unlocked."

"Thank you so much, Miss Dean. I'll see you shortly." I ended the call.

Nate slipped the headphones from his ears to under his chin. He'd listened over the wiretap he'd installed earlier. "Well done."

"Nothing to it. I won't be long."

"Take your time. Get what we need. I've got this."

"We've got a lot of work to do." I wanted to get back to my research on Thurston Middleton and pull all the pieces together about the women who lived across the street and the men in their lives as quickly as possible.

"Agreed."

We'd positioned a small chest to Nate's right and put both laptops there so he could monitor the screens and watch the house at the same time. I pointed to the corner of the display on Nate's laptop. "I managed to get feeds from all fifteen cameras up, but the images are small. Some of them are dark because no one's in the room—no sound or motion. You've got eight on your laptop and seven on mine. Why did you put a camera in the vacant room?"

"Can't hurt anything. You never know. Someone could duck in there for a private phone call."

I shrugged. "Also, on this tab," I clicked to another window, "my photo stream. All the photos I've taken so far on this case have uploaded."

"That will come in handy, thanks."

"Okay, normally, I'd tape my conversation with Miss Dean, but since we'll have a record of it from the feed, I won't bother with that. She'll be more forthcoming if I don't pull out my iPhone and ask."

Nate's brow creased. "I like conversations that are admissible in court best, but in this case, I agree."

I verified the contents of my tote—Sig, Taser, pepper spray, hand sanitizer—along with my cosmetics bag, et cetera. Then I popped in my earwig and tucked a thin transmitter coil under my sweater. "I'll do a communications check from the street." I leaned in for a bye kiss.

He put his hands around my face, brushed back my hair. "Be cautious."

"Always."

"That is not even a third cousin to the truth."

"Back soon." I was out the door.

From the sidewalk in front of the bed and breakfast, in a quiet voice, I said, "Everyone in their rooms?"

"Sound quality is fine." Nate's voice was in my right ear. "And no. Miss Dean is in the right hand parlor. Amber and Lori are in the front parlor by the Christmas tree. Dana is in her room reading. Heather is in the kitchen."

"Roger that." I crossed the street, opened the door, and climbed the steps to the porch. I glanced in the second window to the front parlor.

Amber and Lori must've heard me on the porch. Both of them stared towards the windows.

I knocked on the front door.

Miss Dean opened the door immediately. "Come in, child. Let's talk in the keeping room." She gestured to my right.

I headed into the parlor.

Behind me, Miss Dean said, "Girls, let's all freshen up before dinner."

I didn't hear a response, but shoes on hardwood told me Amber and Lori were heading upstairs. I passed from parlor to dining room, and waited for Miss Dean to catch up.

When we entered the kitchen, she also told Heather to freshen up before dinner. Must have been code for "go to your room," especially considering I knew they'd all already had dinner. Heather responded without comment as well. Miss Dean did not introduce us.

When we reached the keeping room, she said, "Please, have a seat. Can I get you anything?"

"No thank you, ma'am. I appreciate you seeing me on such short notice." I sat on the end of the sofa closest to a chair that looked well-used.

Miss Dean settled into it, then looked at me expectantly. "Please, tell me what I can do for you. You mentioned Olivia's troubles. Is she all right?"

"Yes, Olivia is fine—for the moment. But I'm afraid things are about to take a turn for the worse unless we act quickly."

Her blue eyes locked onto mine.

"Tell me everything."

"I will. But first I need your word that you will not mention any of this to Seth."

She sat back a little.

"Very well. You have my word."

"Olivia is afraid of him."

"That's absurd. Seth is family. Yes, he's upset with the terms of Mary's will—and mine. This is his home. Has been for most of his life. But he would never harm Olivia—or anyone, for that matter."

I studied her carefully. Miss Dean was likely good at poker. "That may very well be. But we can't take any chances."

"I've given you my word. I'll say nothing to Seth."

"All right. You've heard, no doubt, about Thurston Middleton's death."

She covered her mouth with her hand, closed her eyes, and shook her head. "Ghastly business, that."

"Did you know Thurston Middleton?"

"Why, of course I did. He was my neighbor. Lived just a block down on Meeting Street."

"Can you think of any reason why he would've been inside your house last night?"

"What? Goodness no. Why would you ask me such a thing?"

"Because the reason Olivia called me last night—the reason I left home in my pajamas to rush over here—is because she found a dead body in your front parlor."

She stilled, sized me up with her eyes, deciding how much to trust me. I let my statement lie there. The longer she was quiet, the longer she failed to protest such an assertion, the more likely she either knew it was true, or knew it wasn't beyond the realm of possibilities.

Finally, she said, "The poor girl has been under so much strain. It's no wonder she's hallucinating. I would've dealt with the issue between her and Seth and saved her so much anxiety. I only wish she'd come to me sooner."

"Have you? Dealt with Seth? Can Olivia now stop paying him blackmail money?"

She looked away. "I've taken steps. Spoken to a few family friends I trust."

"Why not speak directly to Seth? Are you afraid of him as well?"

"Goodness gracious, no. Why would I be afraid of Seth?"

"I can't think of a reason, unless he's a bit unstable to begin with, and the prospect of losing his home has unhinged him."

"He won't ever lose his home. That provision is in both Mary's will and mine. He is to live in the guesthouse for the rest of his life or until he chooses to leave. Olivia is to continue to employ him as handyman unless he quits."

"Why not just leave the house to him? You must know the problems this creates for Olivia."

She shook her head slowly.

"Seth has no head for business. He couldn't manage the boardinghouse on his own. He would end up losing it. It's our family home. Olivia must take care of our family legacy. It's a matter of duty. She's the last remaining Beauthorpe woman."

"So again, why not speak to Seth yourself about how family doesn't blackmail family? If you're not afraid of him, that is."

"Seth is mercurial. I didn't want an incident with him. I'm an old woman. I don't like drama. I thought it would be better for all of us to let friends handle the matter. Maintain peace in the household."

"Who did you ask for help?"

"I'd rather not say. This is a family affair."

"Getting back to Olivia, and her 'vision,' don't you find it odd that she had this experience the evening before Thurston Middleton turned up dead in White Point Gardens, not a block away?" I said.

"Well of course it's odd. Odd things happen every day. But his death has nothing whatever to do with us."

"So you are certain Thurston Middleton could not possibly have been in your home Monday evening?"

She hesitated, looked away.

"I wouldn't go quite that far. I can't think of a reason why he would be. That doesn't mean he didn't have one." Miss Dean was practiced in the art of ambiguity.

"Can you tell me who all *was* in the house Monday night, to the best of your knowledge?"

"And how will that help Olivia, pray tell?"

I shrugged. "It's possible someone played a practical joke on her."

Miss Dean raised an eyebrow at me.

I returned the gesture. "It's also possible someone murdered Thurston Middleton, who was in your parlor for reasons unknown. Then the killer, or someone else accustomed to cleaning up messes around here, moved the body to a bench in White Point Gardens."

"You're suggesting Seth killed Thurston and moved the body?"

"That's one possibility among many."

"That's preposterous. In the unlikely event that Thurston was in my house, why on earth would Seth kill him? He'd be more likely to offer him a drink."

"So they knew each other."

"Yes, of course. As I said, we were neighbors."

"But if someone else killed Thurston, and Seth found the body. He would remove it from the house to avoid exposing the house to police scrutiny during an investigation, would he not?"

"What are you implying?"

"Just that Seth would know you wouldn't want the police marking the parlor off with crime scene tape, interviewing your residents, making their family members uncomfortable coming to visit and all."

"Miss Talbot, I fail to see how this discussion will help my Olivia in any way. As I mentioned on the phone, I'm exhausted. I don't think I can help you."

"Liz," Nate said into my ear, "get out of there. Seth is leaving the guesthouse. Could be heading your way. Nothing to be gained by tangling with him."

I stood and handed Miss Dean my card.

"If you think of anything, please don't hesitate to call."

She stared at my card for a moment. "You failed to mention you were a private investigator."

I passed through the kitchen. "Did I? My goodness gracious. I'm so sorry. You know, I've been under a great deal of stress myself. Forgive me. Yes. I am a private investigator. Robert and Olivia are my clients."

Nate said, "I've lost him. Should've put a camera outside."

"And what have you been hired to do, exactly?" Miss Dean followed me, moving quicker now than she had earlier.

"I'm afraid that's confidential. You have my card. Good night, Miss Dean."

She followed me to the front door. "I'll see to it Seth leaves Olivia alone. I've already told her I would do that. There was no need for you to get involved in our private family business."

I winced, my hand on the doorknob. "Yeah...if it weren't for the body in the parlor, I'd almost agree with you. But you see, it became my business when Olivia called me and asked me to come over. After that point, if a crime was committed, I could be an accessory after the fact, or perhaps be charged with obstruction, if I don't give the information to the authorities."

"*Liz*. He's coming in the back door to the keeping room."

I continued, "Oh, and one of your family members hired me. There's that. Good night, Miss Dean."

I closed the door behind me, then listened to the sounds of her locking up.

"I'm out. Heading back."

"That was too damn close."

"Listen to them. I'll be right there."

TEN

Nate was staring at the screen when I rushed into the room.

"What'd I miss?" I asked.

He held a finger to his lips, then unplugged his headphones so the sound played over the laptop speaker.

Aunt Dean was speaking. "Why didn't you tell me?"

I hurried over to watch the feed.

Seth sprawled on the sofa where I'd sat moments before. "I didn't want to upset you." His tone with her was solicitous. His expression one of genuine concern.

"Seth, we can't keep things from one another. Promise me you won't ever do that again."

"I promise, Aunt Dean."

"Are you certain you removed all traces of this unpleasant incident?"

"Yes ma'am. I swapped out the rug for the new one you had me order for the Rutledge room—it looked the same to me. I ordered another one just like it already."

"What did you do with the soiled rug?"

"I put it in a dumpster in North Charleston. Someone's probably already swiped it out of there, taken it home, and put some bleach on it. That or it's in the landfill."

"And you give me your word you didn't harm Thurston?"

"Yes ma'am. Had no call whatsoever. Hel—heck, I liked Thurston. I'da voted for 'im."

"Why on earth did you leave him in such a public place—make such a spectacle? I've always admired your discretion in such matters."

"I figured if he disappeared, him being a politician and all, folks would be digging up his past like it was money in the backyard, trying to figure out what happened to him. Now they have a murder to solve. The focus will be on who wanted him dead right now. Who he's piss—made mad lately."

"I hope you're right, but I suspect his background will be explored exhaustively regardless. Have you any idea what he would've been doing here?"

"No ma'am. That right there is a mystery to me."

"I can't imagine, either. Nor how he got in, for that matter. He hasn't had a key in years. Not since he married Julia."

Seth changed position on the sofa. He studied the ceiling, shook his head.

Miss Dean didn't take her eyes off of him. "Who all was here Monday night?"

"Aside from the girls, just you and me. And Raylan. He dropped by to see me."

"Raylan?"

"Yes ma'am."

"I wasn't aware the two of you socialized."

Seth shrugged. "We don't much."

Miss Dean looked at her watch. "I'm very tired. I'm going upstairs now. This entire affair has me quite rattled."

"Aunt Dean, you don't need to worry. I took care of things."

She leaned forward, eased to the edge of the chair.

He jumped up, held out a hand to help her.

"Thank you, dahlin'. You get your snack now. I know you didn't care much for your dinner."

"Girl food," he snorted.

"I'll see you tomorrow. Good night." She offered him her cheek.

He obliged, leaned down and kissed her on the cheek.

"Good night, Aunt Dean."

She patted his shoulder. "You're a good boy. Thank you for lookin' after me."

"You know I'll always take care of you."

She smiled.

"I know you will."

Nate let out a long whistle.

"My thoughts exactly," I said. "Now what did I miss?"

"Just her explaining to him how Olivia had forgotten her purse on the foyer table and had come back for it. He heard her talking to you. She didn't tell him anything about you period. And she didn't mention Olivia saw the body in the parlor last night. She told him she'd heard noises, and was concerned when Thurston's body turned up close by. Made it sound like a fishing expedition. He told her the truth right off—about him moving the body anyway. There could be quite a lot he didn't tell her. There's plenty she didn't tell him, in spite of her insistence that they tell each other everything."

"Interesting. So Seth has no idea Olivia was even there."

"If he saw her, he didn't mention it."

Our eyes were still glued to the screen. Seth made himself a sandwich.

"I'm starved," I said. "We need to order a pizza or something."

"Already taken care of. I ordered sandwiches from Bull Street Market over on King. They should be here momentarily."

"Oh, thank heavens."

Miss Dean passed by the foyer camera and started up the stairs. The young ladies were in their rooms.

I glanced back to the kitchen feed. "He sure doesn't look worried, does he?"

"Not in the least."

"I've got to tell Sonny about that rug. There's a chance it's still wherever Seth dumped it."

"How are you going to do that without spilling everything?"

"I'm thinking."

After a moment, Miss Dean appeared in her room. She closed

the door behind her and leaned against it for a moment. Then she moved over to the sitting area and set her purse on the chaise. She rummaged through it and came out with a notebook of some sort. She moved her purse to the floor and stretched out on the chaise. Then she reached for the cordless phone on the table beside her. She consulted the phonebook, then punched a number into the phone.

Nate switched the audio feed to the wiretap.

After three rings, a man answered. "Hello, Miss Dean. How are you this evening?"

"I'm well, John. I hope you are."

"I am, thank you. What can I do for you?"

"Do you recall the matter we discussed on Monday? The one I mentioned to two of our friends as well?"

"Yes. I'm terribly sorry we haven't had time to see to it yet. I promise we'll take care of it tomorrow."

"Oh, that would be a weight off of me. Thank you, John. I know I can depend on you to look after me."

"Yes, you most assuredly can. Do promise you'll let me know if there's anything you need. Call me anytime, for any reason."

"I will, thank you."

"And I do hope to meet with Olivia soon. It's important we all get to know her—important she understand she can depend on us as well."

"I will speak to her straightaway. It may be after the holidays, will that suit?"

"Certainly. Just let us know."

"I will. Good night, John. And Merry Christmas."

"Merry Christmas to you."

She ended the call.

"Which one of these men is John?" I asked.

There was a knock on the door.

"Food," said Nate. "It's paid for, and the delivery guy has been tipped."

I opened the door only as far as I had to and exchanged my

thanks for the bag of food. I opened the bag, unwrapped a sandwich, and grabbed two Cheerwines from the cooler. By the time I got back to the screen, Miss Dean was back on the phone. I handed Nate half a turkey sandwich.

"Thanks," he said.

On the screen, we could see Miss Dean with the phone to her ear. It was ringing. From the kitchen, Seth walked through the keeping room, then out the back door.

A woman answered the phone. "Hello?" Her voice had the thick sound of someone who had been crying.

"Julia, dahlin', it's Aunt Dean. I'm so sorry to hear about Thurston. I wanted to see how you were gettin' on. Is there anything I can do?"

"Oh, Aunt Dean," Julia said. "I just can't believe it. My heart's broken. If it weren't for the boys, I'd probably fall completely to pieces."

"I can imagine how difficult this must be. The two of you have always been so very close. Made for each other. I've always said it."

"Who on earth would do such a thing—to Thurston, of all people?"

"It must've been some gang initiation ritual, is all I can think of. You hear about that sort of thing more and more often it seems. This stunt they pulled with poor Thurston smacks of random violence, I'd say."

"Perhaps you're right. Thurston never had a single enemy. Everyone who knew him loved him."

"Well, of course they did. I loved him very much. Have you made plans for the service, dear?"

"No, I have to do that tomorrow. Aunt Dean, I just don't know if I can do this."

"Nonsense. You're very strong—always have been. And your boys need you. You can be strong for them, can't you?"

"Yes." It was a whisper.

"Of course you can. And please do let me know if there's anything I can do."

"I will."

"You know I'll always be here for you, Julia."

"I know—thank you, Aunt Dean."

"Get some rest now, dear." She ended the call.

"Is it just me?" I asked. "Or is Miss Dean awfully friendly with the widow Middleton?"

"They are neighbors. Folks in Charleston are friendly as a rule."

I felt my face squinch and forced myself to smooth the lines. "I think there was something more there."

"Could be, I guess." He sounded skeptical.

"And there was something in Mrs. Middleton's voice that rang a bit off."

"What do you mean?"

I winced, shook my head. "Something wasn't right about that conversation."

For a long time Miss Dean sat there while we munched on turkey sandwiches and waited to see if she had more business to tend to. Eventually, she put the phone back in its cradle, maneuvered herself to a standing position, and went into the bathroom.

Nate tapped a few buttons and closed the video on her room. "She's getting ready for bed most likely. If we hear anything we think we need to see, we can turn it back on."

"Agreed." I fetched another sandwich and divided it, giving Nate half. "As soon as I finish eating, I'm going to go through Miss Dean's ledger pages. I think I remember seeing a Middleton in there the first couple years. It must've been Thurston. That's the only reason he'd have had a key before he married Julia."

"True. And that gives him a solid reason for being in that house. He's getting ready to run for office. To quote our buddy, Seth, the media and the opposition will be digging up his past like it's money in the backyard. Thurston had to know that. If he knew about that ledger, or even suspected such a thing existed, he very likely went looking for it."

"And if the desk is normally in the front parlor, but was moved to make room for the Christmas tree, then it makes sense that's where he'd look first." I chewed for a few moments. "So we have answers to the two biggest questions we started out with. There was a body in the house. It was Thurston. *And*, we know he must have been the intended victim, and we most likely know why he was there. And Olivia isn't crazy."

"I wouldn't carry our budding narrative of the crime quite that far."

I punched him in the arm.

"Hey, look at this." He pointed to the feed for the keeping room. Heather, the blonde, stepped out the door to the pool deck and closed it carefully behind her. "What is she up to?"

"She's sneaking out. I'm going to follow her, see where she goes," I said.

"Keep your earwig in. Hand me your iPad so I can follow you on GPS. Times like this, we need more screens."

I passed him the tablet, kissed him, and was out the door.

ELEVEN

I waited in the shadows behind the gate at the bed and breakfast. Moments later, I caught movement to the left of Miss Dean's garage. My eyes adjusted to the darkness. A low brick wall ran along the side yard between 12 Church Street and its nearest neighbor to the north. Heather scrambled over it and jogged to the end of the neighboring driveway. "Got her," I said. She'd circled behind the garage.

I waited a few beats, then opened the gate and followed her, staying on the left side of the street. When she turned left on Atlantic, I hung back, peeking around the corner. She turned right on Meeting. I jogged to catch up with her. There would be more traffic on Meeting. I would be less conspicuous.

I unzipped a compartment in the side of my tote and pulled out a burner phone. I'd taken to keeping a fresh one on me for emergencies. I dialed Sonny.

"Ravenel." He answered on the first ring. An edge in his voice testified to his stress level.

"I have an anonymous tip for the detectives working the Thurston Middleton case."

"Dammit to hell, Liz. Why have you been avoiding me? Why are you calling me from a burner? Why were you asking me about missing persons and what Middleton was wearing? Fill me in."

"There's an expensive rug in a dumpster somewhere in North Charleston. It has Thurston Middleton's blood on it. Someone should find it before the dumpsters are emptied." I ended the call before he could excoriate me. He didn't know it, but I'd just given him a lead on evidence he almost certainly never would've found otherwise. He'd thank me later. That's what I was telling myself, anyway.

Through my earwig, Nate said, "Of course I could only hear your end of the conversation, but I'm guessing he's not happy."

"That would be an understatement," I said.

Heather made a left on Broad, then a right on King. We passed Berlins, then Bull Street Market. She was on the phone. I could hear her talking, but couldn't make out what she was saying. I swapped my earwig to my left ear, then reached into my tote, pulled out an amplifier, and slipped it into my right ear.

"I've just been so busy with school...Yes, classes are out now...I'll see you soon...Love you, too, Mamma."

To Nate I said, "Seems like she just wanted some fresh air and to talk to her mamma. I wouldn't call mine from the bawdy house, either. I'm going to follow her a little further just to be sure."

"Roger that."

Heather picked up her pace. We crossed Queen Street, and foot traffic picked up. The farther up King we traveled, the thicker the stream of people. Even on a chilly, damp, December night, King Street was busy. Though it seemed later, it was only a little after eight.

I stepped off the sidewalk and went around a palm tree to avoid colliding with an oncoming couple. After we crossed Market, it got harder to keep Heather in sight. Taxis and limos dropped parties off for dinner. Groups of people congregated on the sidewalk. At Wentworth, I crossed the street and moved in closer behind her. She turned left on Vanderhorst. Oh, thank heaven. "She's going into Kudu. I'm heading inside."

I inhaled deeply the rich, warm aroma of coffee. Kudu was quiet that evening. Not surprising—the College of Charleston students had gone home for Christmas. It was getting on towards closing time. Heather ordered a latte, waited at the counter while it was prepared, then headed for the nook in the back left corner. I followed suit.

I ambled towards the back, blowing on my mocha latte and scanning the room with my peripheral vision. Heather was at a table near the back wall. Was she waiting for someone? I needed to talk to the residents of Miss Dean's establishment. We were in a public place. What the hell? I slipped the amplifier out of my ear and dropped it into my tote. Then I put on my sunniest smile and slid into a chair across from Heather.

For a moment, she stared at me, like maybe I was some poor soul who wasn't quite right.

"Hey, I'm Liz Talbot. Please forgive the intrusion. I know it's an appalling breach of manners, but I have a time-sensitive matter I need to discuss with you." Heather's blue-green eyes were huge, guarded. "You must be Heather." I extended my hand.

She followed suit. She couldn't help herself, I'm sure. Southern women are steeped in manners from birth.

I said, "I need to ask you some questions. And I promise to keep everything you say confidential. Well, unless you've committed a crime, or are planning one."

"What the—?"

"I'm a private investigator." I pulled out a business card and laid it in front of her. "I think we have some common interests. I'd like to help you if I can."

She looked at my card, then at me.

"Exactly what common interests are you referring to?"

"I'm afraid that's confidential," I said. "But here's what I know. You currently live in—let's call it a boardinghouse, shall we?—over on Church Street. Several other young women live there, and y'all have gentlemen callers from some of Charleston's oldest families. How am I doing so far?"

"How is this any of your concern?" Her tone wasn't rude. But she was spunky, not easily intimidated.

"I'm glad you asked that," I said. "It turns out, there's some unsavory business going on in that house. I don't want to get into details, but I have reason to believe that one or more of you ladies may be in danger."

Heather inhaled sharply.

I continued, "My goal is to be a quiet catalyst for change by first encouraging all of y'all guests to check out, then persuading Miss Dean to relocate to a nice retirement home. I'd prefer to do this without causing anyone undue embarrassment." I was ad-libbing, trying to get her to talk to me. But as soon as those words were out of my mouth, an idea popped into my head.

Then Colleen joined us. She occupied a chair at the next table, but sat on the back, defying gravity because she could. "Why didn't you get one of those pastries in the case up front?"

I tuned her out.

I continued, "The less you know about my case, the better off you'll be. I need you to trust me on that. But to keep you safe, we need to be working towards the same goal."

Colleen said, "That's a stretch."

I thought hard at her. *Ultimately, my client wants the place closed and sold. You said yourself that would be the best way to protect Robert and Olivia.*

"Assuming we can keep Olivia out of jail," Colleen said.

Heather said, "Let me get this straight. You, who I don't know from Adam's house cat, want me to move out of my home just because you say someone there may be in danger?"

Are you getting anything from her? I thought hard at Colleen. She could reliably read my mind. Sometimes she could read other folks as well, but her ability depended on several factors. Some folks were easier to read than others. Sometimes it depended on whether or not what the person was thinking was relevant to her mission. Often it seemed to me the phase of the moon was a factor.

Let me focus a little harder...no...sorry. Wait. She thinks Henry's parents sent you.

Henry. Her 'beau's' first name must be Henry. Heather looked at me expectantly. I gave my head a little shake, tried to get Colleen out of it. "I know this sounds crazy. But I truly think you're in danger."

"And I think you're nuttier than Granny's fruitcake."

She stood.

I put my hand on her arm. "Please. I promise I'm trying to help you. Talk to me for just a minute. Why would someone as smart as you live with Miss Dean?" According to her portfolio, she was a grad student in environmental studies.

"Excuse me?" She pulled her chin back. Her expression said, *Lady, you've got a lot of nerve.* "You don't know anything about me."

Damnation. The filter on my mouth fell off. Wedding brain. "I mean, if you tell me a little about what living there is like, perhaps you can convince me there's nothing to worry about."

"Why exactly would I care what the hell you think?"

"Because I know the woman who owns half that house very well—Olivia. She's a dear friend of mine. And she's worried."

"You know Olivia?" Heather said. "I just spent the day drinking champagne with her. She didn't look the slightest bit worried to me."

"She wanted to spend time with y'all, to see if everything is okay."

Heather sat back down, took a sip of her latte. "Prove to me you know Olivia Pearson."

I pulled out my iPhone and scrolled through photographs until I came to one of us shopping for bridesmaid's dresses. There was a shot of me with Olivia in her dress. I showed it to Heather. "I'm getting married Saturday. Olivia is in the wedding."

She scrutinized the photo. "All right. What do you want to know?"

"How did you first come to live there?"

"My boyfriend, Henry, set it up. I was sharing a condo with two other grad students—shared a room with one of them. No privacy. Henry wanted a place where we could be alone."

"And you can't be alone together at his place?" I asked.

"It's complicated. His parents are proud of their family name. They want Henry to marry someone from the upper crust, if you know what I mean. I grew up in a trailer park on a red dirt road in

Georgia. I'm not what they have in mind. His family is very close. They're always dropping by his condo."

I waited for her to continue.

"Henry loves me. No man has ever spoiled me like this. He just needs time to win his family over."

"Do you love him?"

She set down her cup and stared at the surface of her coffee. "Maybe. I don't know. I'm not sure I know what love feels like. I've dated men I thought I was in love with at the time. Every one of them was using me in one way or another."

"And Henry isn't?"

She shook her head firmly. "No. If anything, sometimes I worry—" She looked away, sipped her latte.

Had she been about to say she worried she was using Henry?

I spread my hands. "What's the attraction of living at the...boardinghouse? Didn't you just have to sneak out to have a cup of coffee?"

"Yeah, okay. Aunt Dean has some crazy rules. I'll give you that much. She wouldn't like me being out. Henry's coming over tonight. Aunt Dean would say I should be making myself pretty for him. I'd get a lecture on keeping my man happy if she knew I was here."

"What other rules does she have?"

Heather gave me a facial shrug. "There's a weird vibe. Like Aunt Dean sends us all to our rooms if she's having company. And that Seth...he's always sneaking around, spying on everyone. He gives me the creeps to tell you the truth.

"But then again, Aunt Dean's is perfect in a lot of ways...It's a gorgeous home, South of Broad. It's romantic. The other girls are all really nice. I don't have to have a roommate, but I'm not alone, either. I have a large room with a private bath. On good days, Aunt Dean is like a housemother. And she has people to cook and clean, which is a godsend with my schedule."

"How long have you lived there?" I asked.

"Three years."

"And the other girls?" I asked. "I heard one of them hasn't been there long."

"Lori," said Heather. "She moved in during September."

"Is there a lot of turnover?" I asked.

"Dana, Amber, and I have lived there for years. Lori is new, but her boyfriend, or whatever, has that room on reserve. It was empty for a while before Lori moved in, but someone else lived there a while back. Mr. Russell is a long-term client.

"Wendi's been there about a year, maybe eighteen months. The room she's in, the Gibbes room, used to be Aunt Dean's sister's room."

I asked, "Have you met any of the other men?"

"Not really. I've passed a few of them coming and going. Most of them are older than Henry. I know the family names, but not the men. Occasionally Aunt Dean throws a party. Everyone comes, but no one interacts with the other couples. It sounds odd, I know, but I guess I'm used to it."

"Have the other girls mentioned their 'boyfriends" first names," I asked.

"Dana's boyfriend's name is James." Heather blushed. "The rest of them, I don't know. We're encouraged to be discreet. Dana talks about her business more than most. They're...into some rough stuff. She has a bedroom her boyfriend never goes into. They have a playroom over the garage." She avoided my gaze.

Huger. Two rooms.

"Boy howdy," said Colleen.

"Heather," I said, "do you know the names of any of the household help?"

"No. That's one of Aunt Dean's rules. We aren't allowed to talk to them at all. Ever. A cleaning crew comes in once a day at nine. They're thorough, but in and out pretty quick, and they never open closets or drawers. There's food in the kitchen for breakfast and lunch. A cook delivers dinner and Seth puts it on the table."

"Have you ever heard anyone mention the name Thurston Middleton?" I asked.

Heather stilled. "I don't think so."

Colleen said, "Liar, liar, pants on fire."

"Are you certain," I asked. "This is important."

"Well, I mean, of course. Everyone knows the name. Thurston Middleton. His family has lived in Charleston for generations, I hear. He's involved with several local charities—an advocate for the homeless, environmental issues. He and his wife host a Thanksgiving dinner at a soup kitchen. His wife—Julia is her name, I think—and her pugs are all over the media. She's an animal rights activist. They're public figures—even the dogs. "

I recalled seeing photos of the socialite and her two pugs in an online magazine article while researching Thurston Middleton. "Can you recall his name coming up with any of the other women who live in that house?"

She had a shell-shocked expression. "Never."

Colleen said, "She's getting ready to bolt."

I moved to safer ground. "Where do the girls who live there park their cars?"

This topic didn't calm her. She spoke faster.

"Everyone has monthly parking in a lot or garage downtown— different places. Aunt Dean isn't involved with that at all." She stood. "I have to go. Henry will be at the house to see me soon."

"You have my number," I said. "Call me if anything develops, or if you think of anything I should know about the house and the folks who live there. I need a way to get in touch with you in case of an emergency."

"I don't think that's a good idea. Olivia can reach me through Aunt Dean." Heather walked away fast.

I finished my mocha, then walked outside.

Colleen followed me out to the street.

To Nate I said, "On my way back. Did you listen?" The conversation would've transmitted though the wire I still wore underneath my clothing.

"No. Too much going on back here. I can only listen to one thing at a time."

"I'll let you focus on what you're doing. See you soon."

"Roger that."

I pressed the button on my earwig twice to temporarily disconnect communications with Nate. Then I popped in both my earbuds—the ones that came with my iPhone. The long strings hanging from my ears convinced random strangers I wasn't talking to myself. I made the right off Vanderhorst and was back on King Street.

"Have you learned anything?" I asked Colleen.

"You mean aside from Heather knows more than she's telling about Thurston Middleton?"

"Yes."

"I spent some time in the brothel today."

"Your mamma would be so proud."

Colleen laughed her signature bray-snort laugh. Then she sobered. "There are lingering spirits in that house."

"Really? From what era?" Colleen had run across a debutante from the 1860s in another recent case.

"This one. They haven't been dead that long. One of them, her name is Roxanne Trexler. She lived in the Rutledge room for five years."

"What else did she tell you?"

"William Rutledge killed her by accident. They were cutting up. She fell and hit her head on the corner of a heavy table."

"You're not serious."

"Yes, I am. If he'd hurt her on purpose she would tell me. She'd have no reason not to—she'd want justice. Except..."

"Except what?"

"When Seth found out, he killed William Rutledge, and not by accident."

"*Damnation.*"

"Well, I guess that could be in his future. That's not for me to say."

"Hell's bells, Colleen. Try to stay on topic. I'm trying to get our friend who's still alive out of this mess and it just keeps getting messier. And I'm getting married in four days. And it's Christmas."

My phone rang. Sonny. Shit. Shit. *Shit.* I sent him to voicemail. I did not want to talk to him just yet. Not on my phone, anyway.

"Does Roxanne know where the bodies are buried?"

"Seth dropped William Rutledge off in a dumpster in North Charleston."

I remembered that case, from a year or so back. A homeless person had found the body. It was quite the scandal. "Seems to be a recurring theme with him. What about Roxanne?"

"Seth was in love with her—for years. He couldn't bear to let her go."

"I don't like where this is headed."

"She's buried behind the house—near the guesthouse. Seth put in a new flowerbed and there's a little bench. He likes to sit out there."

"Sweet reason. We've got to talk to Olivia. If she'd signed that house over to Seth years ago, she'd be in the clear. But it's too late now. All of this will come out too fast, and there's no way to keep her out of it."

"There are far worse things than scandal," said Colleen. "Olivia will survive this, and then no one will have anything to hold over her. She and Robert will be fine. If we do this right."

"I have a plan."

"I picked up on that," she said.

"I figured, when you showed up. What do you think? Can you scare the girls into moving out real quick? Before anyone has a chance to hurt one of them to keep them quiet?"

Colleen grinned.

"I can. Roxanne will help. And I bet the three men buried under the pool will, too."

"*God's nightgown.* What happened to them?"

"They became problems. Seth handled them."

"Does Miss Dean know?"

"I have no idea. I can read her mind, but she thinks mostly on how much she misses her sister. She worries about what will become of her family home once she's gone. Will Olivia sell it? And she worries about Olivia and Raylan. Seth, too. She cares deeply for all of them. Family is very important to her. "

King Street was a blur. This case had spiraled so far out of hand. I took several deep breaths. Then I pulled out the burner phone and called Sonny.

"I would hate like hell to have to arrest you," he said when he answered. It was the second call from the same burner, so he knew it was me. But he and I both knew he'd never prove it, even if he wanted to.

"This is an anonymous tip from a concerned citizen. The rug you're looking for—check the dumpsters in the area where William Rutledge's body was found first."

TWELVE

"Hard Candy Christmas" was playing again downstairs at the Bed and Breakfast. I hurried up to our room. "What've I missed?"

Nate slid the headphones to his shoulders. "Rush hour at the house of ill repute. The first car pulled through the gate right after you left. Lexus sedan. Driver either had an electronic opener or someone was expecting him. The gate opened as he pulled up. I snapped the plate and ran it. James Huger. But here's the more interesting part. I got a photo of him when he walked around the front of the car and opened the door for a woman with a scarf over her head and shoulders."

"Dana?"

"No," said Nate. "Dana was in her room at the time."

"Oh no. Don't they have enough going on in that room over the garage? Please tell me there aren't three of them in there."

Nate pointed to the screen. "Dana never left her room."

She was propped on her bed doing her nails.

"I don't understand," I said.

"I'll come back to them," Nate said. "This gentleman arrived next..." He picked up the Canon and showed me the screen. "...from the direction of South Battery. By process of elimination, he must be Mr. Russell, Lori's beau."

"I wonder why he walked over?"

"Like all the rest of them, he doesn't live but a few blocks away. Probably one of the things that makes this place so attractive. A gentleman can go out for a walk after dinner, pop in to see his mistress, and walk home. Much less suspicious than leaving in the car."

"Dear heaven. Who else?"

"William Calhoun pulled in a half hour ago. At least his BMW did.

"Finally, young Henry Prioleau arrived mere moments ago. I got his license plate and a photo of him. He turned around after he got out of the car and opened the backdoor to get a package."

"Likely more lingerie," I said.

"Twenty-seven years old, driving a Mercedes, and keeping a mistress." Nate shook his head.

"Did you see Heather go back in?"

"The same way she left. She beat Henry by five minutes."

"So we have a full house?"

"Indeed," said Nate. "It would appear if our killer is one of the patrons, he's bold. Not shy of returning to the scene of the crime so soon."

"So much for the process of elimination."

"On that note...One item of interest came up in conversation. It seems Seth's statement to the contrary notwithstanding, at minimum, three of these gentlemen were in the house last night: Huger, Calhoun, and Russell. Amber and Lori expressed surprise to see Calhoun and Russell, respectively, again so soon. The conversation between James Huger and whoever he's with included something along the lines of how they rarely get to sneak out two nights in a row."

"Let's go back to James Huger now," I said.

Nate ran a hand through his hair. "I think we have to assume he's a hound dog with two women on the side. But it seems he's neglecting Dana. Pays a lot of money to keep her there, though."

"Did you get a look at the woman in the scarf once she was in the bedroom?"

He shook his head. "They started going at each other as soon as they closed the door. But there was something strange...they were subdued. So far I've turned off the feed on three of the four occupied bedrooms because we can surmise the activities they are pursuing, and it is not relevant to our investigation."

"Interesting. The men who were there last night, I mean. And James Huger's second mistress. She didn't have a portfolio like all the others. And no street clothes. She can't possibly live there. She must come and go with him. Do you need a break?"

"I'm good."

"I'll get to work on organizing what we have and finish the profiles," I said, "as soon as I get back."

Nate raised his eyebrows. "Where're you off to now?"

"I'm going to take a walk over to Meeting Street."

"Didn't you just come that way?"

"Yes, but I thought you might need a break. I'll be right back."

"What are you—"

"I'm just going to see who all's out and about this evening."

I kissed him and was out the door. Truthfully, I felt a little guilty about where I was headed, and I didn't want him to talk me out of it. The clock was ticking. Desperate measures were in order.

I headed towards White Point Gardens on Church, made a right, and a block later hung another right onto lower Meeting Street. The Middleton home was only a few houses up, on the left. I walked slowly.

My phone rang. Nicolette, the wedding Nazi. What in heaven's name did she want at this hour?

"Hey, Nicolette."

"Hey, Liz, sorry to bother you. Are you getting excited?"

"Very. What can I do for you?"

"Well, I've been working on the centerpieces. I know you want a variety, and I have flower arrangements ordered as we discussed for half the tables. The others I've ordered candlescapes for. But the florist only has sixteen of the candle-centric pieces. We have thirty-eight tables total, unless you want to go back to ten tops as I recommended."

"No. I really don't want folks crowded together. Eight at a table is plenty."

"But ten really is standard, and you can see how it would make things work out with the centerpieces."

"Nicolette, when I said half, I didn't mean precisely half of the tables had to have candles. Tell her to use what she has and do flowers for the remainder. Or buy some more candles, for heaven's sake. For what we're paying her, she can make this work, I'm sure."

"Yes, but I really think you'll be happier and things will be simpler if we go to ten tops."

"No, I really won't be." She was testing my sunny disposition.

"Fewer tables will allow more floor space inside the tents—more room for everyone to mingle."

"You know what really appeals to me most right now? Eloping. Vegas looks better and better by the second. I've already had one big church wed—"

"Very well, Liz. I'll speak with the florist."

"Thank you, Nicolette. Bye now." I ended the call.

Across the street, the Middleton home, a two-story butterscotch-colored house, was trimmed for the holidays with greenery and red bows. Two sets of steps, one on each side, led to a semi-circle front porch. Double piazzas ran along the left side of the house, facing the side yard. Every light in the house seemed to be on. My heart hurt for the family inside. It was beyond sad that such a festive-looking home was in mourning.

Thankfully, the media wasn't camped out in front of the house. I paused by a palm tree, my phone still in my hand as if I were checking my GPS, or perhaps a message. A runner passed behind me.

Thirty minutes later, the front door opened. A feminine figure dressed in exercise togs emerged with two pugs on leashes. No matter what tragedy befalls us, others depend on us to carry on. Often those that need us most give us great comfort. Julia Middleton's sons and her dogs would see her through this. She wouldn't have someone else walk the dogs this evening. I would walk Rhett myself—would want him close.

She came down the steps and headed towards White Point

Gardens. I waited a moment, then walked in the same direction, but stayed on my side of the street. At the corner, she turned right on South Battery and I followed.

I took a deep breath, steeled myself. "Mrs. Middleton?"

She stopped and turned. "Yes?"

I caught up to her. Even with no makeup and red eyes, she was lovely. Porcelain skin, high cheekbones, her blond hair short, chic. "I'm sorry to bother you, ma'am."

"Are you with the press?" Bold, like a warrior princess, this widow was not to be trifled with. I sensed great strength in her.

"No, no. My name is Liz Talbot. I'm a private investigator."

"I'm sorry?"

"I'm a private investigator. I know this will sound odd, and I'm keenly aware that it's a deplorable intrusion on your grief. But I think we can help each other. Will you talk with me for a few moments?"

She stared at me. A car drove past, then another.

"You know something about Thurston's death?"

"I do. But I want to be discreet in how and when I share what I know with the police. I don't want anyone to be unnecessarily subjected to embarrassment."

"If you intend to blackmail me, it won't work."

"Blackmail you? Mrs. Middleton, I assure you, nothing could be further from my mind."

I looked her straight in the eyes.

"Very well," she said. "Walk with me. Bentley and Bess need their exercise." She moved to the right side of the sidewalk.

Bentley and Bess led the way and we followed.

"Was someone blackmailing Mr. Middleton?" I asked.

We walked for a few steps before she answered. "That Neanderthal bastard, Seth. All of this is sure to come out. I haven't told the police any of it yet. But I've thought about it, and I plan to tell them tomorrow. That's the only way they'll be able to get justice for Thurston."

This was what I'd heard in her voice on the phone with Miss

Dean—what Julia didn't say, the familiarity. "Seth knew that Thurston was once a client at 12 Church Street?"

She turned and looked at me. "Client isn't the right word, exactly. I lived there before we married. I was a student. It was a simple boardinghouse back then. Two sweet little old ladies trying to hold on to their family home by renting rooms. Nothing more."

"But the room was named for Thurston?"

She sighed. "He knew Aunt Dean and Aunt Mary Leona. He made the arrangements for me to live there to help them out. They were just getting started. He was afraid they'd lose their home. I couldn't have afforded it at the time. So yes, he paid the rent. No good deed goes unpunished, as they say."

"When did Seth approach Mr. Middleton with his blackmail demands?"

"A few weeks ago. He'd heard Thurston planned to run for office. Thurston had no idea what that place had turned into. When Seth told him, he didn't believe it."

"But then he came to believe it?" I asked.

"He started asking around. Normally, Thurston is above that sort of gossip. It's not something anyone would tell him because everyone who knows him knows he wouldn't be interested in hearing it. But he didn't have to ask many questions before some of his friends were happy to tell him. Don't misunderstand me. What that house is...that's a tightly held secret. But within a certain group, the information isn't hard to come by if you know who to ask."

"What did Thurston plan to do?" I asked.

"He wanted to talk to Aunt Dean. Try to get the business back on the right track. She really is a sweet lady. She's always been very good to me."

"What about Seth? Was Mr. Middleton going to pay him?"

"Not a chance." She shook her head.

"So he was prepared for this to come out?"

"I wouldn't say prepared. He was very concerned about my reputation. Would he have preferred it not come out? Of course.

But he wasn't going to pay a blackmailer. He thought about turning Seth in to the police, but that would've left Aunt Dean alone. She's in her eighties."

"He sounds like a very nice man—an upright man."

"He was. His death is a great loss not just to me personally, but to the community. He would've made a wonderful congressman."

"I'm certain he would have." My phone vibrated. I pressed the button to send the call to voicemail.

We crossed the street and turned south on King.

After a few moments she asked, "What's your involvement in all of this?"

"I have a client who asked me to get involved."

"Someone else Seth is blackmailing?"

"I'm not at liberty to say."

"It wouldn't surprise me. Seth is a menace. Thurston was concerned he might be a danger to the women who live there, but some of his friends convinced him that three of the men who have done business with Aunt Dean for a long time keep him in check."

"That's my impression," I said. "Though I think Miss Dean does a fair job on her own."

We crossed to the far side of Murray to walk along the waterfront. The breeze was bracing. Before long we could see the yellow crime scene tape, still wrapped around trees in the park.

"None of this seems real," she said.

"I can appreciate that." We walked on in silence. "Mrs. Middleton—"

"Please. Call me Julia. I think we're past formalities."

I nodded. "Julia, do you think Seth killed your husband?"

"I would bet a great deal on it. He was livid that Thurston made it clear he wasn't going to pay him. His threats were more frequent, the tone uglier. I think in the end, Thurston would've turned him in to the police after he made sure Aunt Dean was taken care of. Seth likely guessed as much."

"Do you know if your husband still had a key to Miss Dean's house?" I asked.

She glanced at me. "He kept one after I moved out in case the sisters had some sort of emergency. I imagine he still had it somewhere. Why do you ask?"

"It's a loose end," I said. "Can you think of anyone else who would've had a motive to kill your husband?"

"No. Everyone loved Thurston. He shined, you know, with this light from within. He was a good man."

"After he looked into the house on Church Street, did he find that he knew any of the men who are currently clients there?"

"He knew most of them. He was astonished to learn that James Huger is among them. Like Thurston, James helped out Aunt Dean and Aunt Mary Leona in the beginning. Honestly, he rented empty rooms—two of them, just to help them get by. But things were very different then."

"So they went way back, Thurston and James Huger?"

"All the way back to the cradle. Their mothers are friends. And James and his wife, Beatrice, are dear friends of ours. James positively dotes on her. They have five children—all adopted from foreign countries—about the same ages as our boys. They're very philanthropic. James was a campaign contributor—he was organizing a fundraiser." She shook her head. "You think you know people."

"Who else did Thurston know? Current patrons at Miss Dean's, I mean."

"Arthur Russell. That didn't come as quite the surprise. Arthur is notoriously unfaithful to his wife. And William Calhoun—that was a shocker. He's a neurosurgeon—married to a beauty queen—she was Miss Something-or-other. If she finds out, that will be a messy divorce."

Arthur Russell. We had our final first name. "And the others?"

"We know Nathaniel Gibbes and his wife socially. The other man is quite a bit younger, unmarried. We've met him—Henry Prioleau. We know the family. They own Rut's New South Cuisine. Not our sort of place, really, but the restaurants are quite popular. The Prioleaus—that branch of the Prioleaus—are very concerned with branding the restaurants with Southern Friendly. One might say they overdo." We rounded the point of the peninsula and headed north on East Battery.

"Do you think it's possible any of those men would've killed Thurston to silence him—to keep him from disturbing their extracurricular arrangements?"

She was quiet for a long moment. "I would hate to think someone would commit murder over such a thing, but I suppose it's possible. But I still think it was Seth."

I nodded, drew in a deep breath. "I'll walk you home. And maybe you shouldn't go out by yourself for a while."

"Why on earth not?"

"If it was Seth, he knows that you know everything Thurston knew. He has to know you'll suspect him and will likely talk to the police about the blackmail. You're as much a threat to him as Thurston was."

THIRTEEN

This time, the tune of "Blue Christmas" welcomed me to the bed and breakfast. It was almost ten, and the downstairs appeared deserted. A tray of Christmas cookies was on the foyer table. I grabbed a couple Santas and climbed the steps.

When I opened the door, Nate said, "Well, that was audacious."

"You listened?" I handed him a cookie.

"Of course I did. You ran out of here without telling me what you were up to."

"We're hard-pressed."

"I know. And, hey..." He shook his head. "It paid off. Well done, Slugger."

"I'm not proud of myself. Bothering a widow on the very day her husband's body is discovered. Mamma would skin me alive."

"Mrs. Middleton seems to be holding up, from what I could tell. I think she'll be grateful in the long run," Nate said. "During the...lull...while everyone was socializing, I called in a favor and verified Nathaniel Gibbes and Wendi Hill flew to Vienna on Saturday the thirteenth. After a phone canvas of the nicer hotels, I found them at the Grand Hotel Europa in Innsbruck. The concierge has helped them with entertainment virtually every day, and they've ordered a great deal of room service. I think we can safely rule them out."

"Thank heavens we can rule someone out." I sighed, bit Santa's head off. "What's going on across the street?"

"Things have mostly quieted down. All the clients have gone home except Arthur Russell. Huger just left with the same woman who arrived with him. I couldn't get a shot of her face, even her hair color, for the scarf and sunglasses. Seth is watching TV."

"Prioleau's already gone?"

"Yeah. Just a few minutes ago."

"He sure didn't stay long," I said. "We have all their names, and not one of them is John. Miss Dean called John for help. Who the devil is John? I need to get to work on pulling background on all these people."

I settled in with my laptop. Then my phone vibrated. Mamma. And the call I'd sent to voicemail earlier was from her. "Hey, Mamma." I reached for my happy voice.

"*E-liz-a-beth.*" She must've been tired. She didn't trot out the rest of my names.

"Mamma, what's wrong?"

"Where are you? Merry says she's staying with Rhett."

"I'm in Charleston. Nate and I have a case. We're staying over here tonight."

"You do recall you're getting married on Saturday?"

"I don't have anywhere else to wear that gorgeous dress."

"Why on God's green earth can't you take the week off like normal people?"

"We'd planned to. But something came up."

"You need to learn to say 'no' to people. You have a life aside from your job."

"I know, Mamma."

"Don't patronize me, Elizabeth. I called to see when Nate's parents are arriving. You never told me. I've asked a dozen times."

"Hold on a sec." I held my phone against my leg. "When are your parents getting here?"

Nate's eyes widened. He swallowed, rolled his lips in. "Tomorrow afternoon."

"Did they decide where they want to stay?" I asked. We'd invited them to stay with us. Mamma had likewise extended an invitation. Between the two houses, we had eight guest bedrooms.

"In a hotel. In Charleston."

"Why? They won't even be able to get back here after the reception's over. The ferry will've stopped running."

"My guess is they're not planning to stay for the bouquet toss."

That hurt my heart. Not because I cared one whit about those cold fish jerks, but for Nate. "Oh no. Sweetheart, I'm so sorry."

His face closed. "It's fine. I'm fine. Whatever they do or don't do is not going to have one iota of impact on our wedding and our party."

I'd kept Mamma waiting too long. I raised the phone. "They're staying in Charleston."

"What? Why on this earth would they do that?"

"Well, Mamma, I suppose they have mixed emotions about me marrying their other son." Nate's older brother, Scott the Scoundrel, was my ex-husband, whereabouts unknown, but likely in a country with no extradition. That was a whole nother story.

Mamma huffed. "Poor Nate. Is he all right?"

"I think so."

"Bless his heart. I'm still mad as fire at those people over the rehearsal dinner. They should be ashamed of themselves."

Nate's parents maintained they couldn't manage to coordinate a rehearsal dinner on Stella Maris from Florida, which everyone knew was ridiculous. Nate had quietly taken care of it himself. "I know, Mamma. They've made their own hotel arrangements, anyway, so we don't need to worry about where they're sleeping."

"I assure you I won't waste another millisecond of my time worrying about them. Have you spoken to Nicolette?"

"Yes. I told her again. Eight to a table. If some of them don't have centerpieces, I seriously doubt the world will stop turning."

"If she calls you again, tell her to call me if she needs anything else between now and Saturday."

"Thank you, Mamma. I will."

"We'll see y'all Thursday evening."

"Thursday?" Hell's bells. What else had I forgotten?

"Thursday night. We're having family Christmas because you and Nate will be in St. John over Christmas, remember? Which I still object to, by the way. It's not like you and Nate haven't been honeymooning for years now. You could've waited until the day after Christmas to leave. It might not be too late to change your tickets."

I was not going down that road with her.

"Oh, right. For a moment it slipped my mind. We'll see you Thursday at six."

"Fine. Give Nate my love."

"Will do. Bye now."

"Bye-bye."

I heaved a deep sigh. "I still have to find Daddy's Christmas present. He's always the hardest to buy for. At least this year he didn't ask for something ridiculous." For a number of years, he'd sent us all on a scavenger hunt by asking for things he thought would be hard to find. A digeridoo. A toucan bird—I'd gotten a ceramic one. A hippopotamus—Merry found one made of concrete for the yard. The list went on.

"I'd get him a gift card," said Nate.

"I can't get Daddy a gift card. It has to be something personal."

"Just don't get him another gun."

I gave Nate my best *Oh please* look. Then I set to working on profiles and organizing the information we'd gathered so far. I liked to know everything I could about everyone involved. You never knew what might be important. After digging a while, among other things, I established that none of the parties involved had criminal or civil action records. All of the bordello patrons came from old Charleston money.

The number of people involved made it difficult to see all the pieces to my puzzle. I needed a whiteboard and photos. I'd taken plenty of snapshots, but had no quick way to print them. I improvised with a quilt on the floor and some index cards from my tote. After laying it all out, I stood back to view my handiwork.

The bordello clients were down the left side of the quilt, with their "nieces" across from them on the far right. At the bottom, I added the former residents, boyfriends, and other assorted characters:

William Calhoun
Brown hair, nice smile
39 years old
Beauty Queen wife
Highly respected neurosurgeon
Friend of Thurston Middleton
Negative patient ratings/bedside manner

Amber McDonald
Black hair
23 years old
College of Charleston
Financial Management

Nathaniel Gibbes
Sandy hair
35 years old
Out of the Country

Wendi Hill
Blond
25 years old
Stripper pole
Out of the Country

James Huger
Salt-and-pepper hair, handsome
42 years old
CEO, Huger International
Friend and campaign contributor
Two rooms, mystery woman
Devoted husband, father
Philanthropist

Dana Clark
Brunette
27 years old
Nursing student, MUSC
Lots of passport stamps
Fifty Shades
Not as discreet as others

Henry Prioleau
Brown hair, round glasses
27 years old
VP, family restaurant business
Rut's New South Cuisine
Hiding something
Negative comments/TripAdvisor/
Short fuse

Heather Wilder
Blond, blue-green eyes
27 years old
Grad Student
Environmental studies
Interesting lingerie
Spunky

Arthur Russell
Kevin Spacey with a mustache
40 years old
Owns antique store on King Street
Serial adulterer
Knew Thurston Middleton

Lori Stowe
Redhead, tall
22 years old
Trident Tech
Information Systems
Costumes

Seth Quinlan
Longish brown hair
Burly
46 years old
Blackmailer
Murderer
Loved Roxanne
Protective of Aunt Dean

Robert Pearson

Raylan Beauthorpe

Julia Middleton

William Rutledge
(Deceased)

Roxanne Trexler
(Deceased)

Next, I made a card for Thurston Middleton and placed it in the middle of the quilt.

Thurston Middleton
Devoted husband, father
Philanthropist
Entering political arena
Once paid for Julia's room at Miss Dean's boardinghouse
Would not cave to blackmail
Tried to help Miss Dean, protective

"I need some yarn."

Nate looked over his shoulder. "Maybe Annelise has some."

"She wasn't downstairs the last time I came in. I don't want to disturb her. I bet she has spaghetti in the kitchen."

I headed downstairs. The music was off, the house quiet. In Annelise's well-organized pantry, I quickly scored a box of Mueller thin. On my way back, the four remaining Christmas cookies on the tray in the foyer called to me. It would've been a shame to let them dry out overnight. I scooped them up and slipped quietly back upstairs.

"Arthur Russell just left," said Nate when I'd closed the door. "He does favor Kevin Spacey a bit, in a *House of Cards* sleazy politician kind of way."

"Everyone looks sleazy sneaking out of a whorehouse."

"Fair point."

"I'm just trying to keep some sort of visual. Without photos to put on my board, the descriptions help."

"Whatever works."

I opened the box of spaghetti and took out a few noodles. Using three pieces end-to-end, I made a line connecting Julia Middleton to Thurston Middleton. My instincts said there was no way she killed her husband. But experience had taught me that people can fool you, and family members are very often liable in the deaths of their loved ones.

Next I connected James Huger to Thurston Middleton. They'd been close friends, and Huger was a campaign contributor. He had the strongest connection I knew of aside from Julia. Then I made connecting lines to Thurston's card from Arthur Russell and William Calhoun, the other two men Julia had mentioned Thurston knew well. Seth had the best motive I knew of. Spaghetti line for him. Raylan Beauthorpe and Robert Pearson both had opportunity.

Nate stared at the screen.

"Are you connecting people who knew him?"

"People who knew him and people who had motive, means, or opportunity."

"I see," said Nate. "Well, I suppose that thins the herd by a few."

"The three men we know were in the house last night are Calhoun, Huger, and Russell. They're already connected."

"So are we eliminating Henry Prioleau?" Nate asked. "I'd say he has as much motive as the rest of them."

"Agreed. And just because we haven't found a connection yet doesn't mean there isn't one. His family's chain of restaurants is very popular. The one here in Charleston is highly rated. Most of the reviews on TripAdvisor and so forth are very positive. But the few that aren't make the whole family sound a little nutty. Henry in particular reportedly has a very short fuse. Apparently, he doesn't handle criticism well. I have a lot of work to do, and precious little time."

"Me, too." Colleen faded in. "We need to get the girls out of the house tonight."

I nodded.

"Nate, I think we need to move the girls to a safe place."

"Okay, that came out of left field. What makes you think they aren't safe where they are?"

"It's a gut feeling." My gut's name was Colleen. I stared at my quilt. "It all comes down to motive. Whoever killed Thurston Middleton very likely did it for one of two reasons. Scenario one: to maintain the status quo at the bordello. The underlying motive would be lust, maybe even love, or money, depending on who the killer was—which side of the transaction they were on. If this was the motive, then Julia is also in danger if the killer knew her history with Aunt Dean."

"Julia, yes. The women in the house across the street, no."

Colleen said, "I don't need his help. Or permission, for that matter. I can have that house cleared out in five minutes flat."

I tamped down my irritation.

"Exactly, Nate, but scenario two is anger and/or revenge. If it was Seth, he was royally pissed off that Thurston wasn't paying him blackmail money, and was afraid Thurston was going to the police.

And he probably thought killing Thurston would solve most of his problems, keep the bordello open. As long as he takes care of Julia quickly."

"And if it was someone else?"

"Then the killer was angry that Thurston planned to put a stop to all the sex and/or money. The killer was smarter, perhaps knew Thurston better. He maybe knew that killing Thurston wouldn't keep the bordello open. Things had gone too far. Julia knew that Thurston was investigating Aunt Dean's boardinghouse, as did anyone else Thurston had confided in—possibly someone connected to his campaign. Killing Thurston served no real purpose except to make the killer feel better. This killer saw the bordello as irretrievably lost already. Leaving Thurston on the floor in the bordello probably gratified the killer's sick sense of poetic justice."

Nate looked thoughtful. I continued, "This scenario scares me most because the killer will almost certainly want to cover his tracks, eliminate anyone or anything that could tie him to the bordello as soon as possible."

"You're assuming our culprit is one of the men?"

"I'd say that's far more likely. Could one of the women have struck a six-foot-tall man in the head from behind with enough force to kill him? She would've had to've held the pineapple over her head with both hands and attacked while he was walking towards the door."

"It would be easier if we knew their fitness level. Height and upper body strength are huge factors here. The tall redhead maybe could've done it if she works out," Nate said. "Still…I agree. It was more likely one of the men. And we don't know if the motive was lust, money, revenge, or something else we haven't uncovered yet."

"Exactly. I think we should err on the side of keeping everyone who might possibly be in danger safe."

Colleen said, "And we need to step on it."

"Hold on a minute," said Nate. "You've just made a compelling case that we have a perfect trap already set. If you honestly believe the killer is coming back to permanently silence his mistress, why don't we wait until he shows up and grab him?"

Colleen started glowing.

"That won't work."

"Because we turn off the cameras when they start touching each other," I said. "We can't assume every man who shows up is here to kill someone. We can't possibly know who's in danger until it's too late to intervene."

"All right," Nate said. "Fine. How are we going to convince the ladies to leave, and what safe place did you have in mind?"

"Hmmm..." I grasped for a glimmer of a notion.

My phone rang. I glanced at the screen. Olivia. I tapped the button to accept the call.

"Hey, Olivia, you okay?"

"*Ohmygod. Ohmygod.*" It sounded like she was hyperventilating. I pressed the speaker button and laid the phone on the dresser so Nate could hear. "Seth just called Raylan. Raylan called me. Then Seth called me. *Ohmygod.*"

I said, "Olivia, slow down. What did Seth want with Raylan?"

"Aunt Dean somehow figured out Thurston was killed in the house. She *said* she heard noises. She *said* when Thurston's body turned up at White Point Gardens, she wondered if there was a connection. But Seth didn't believe her. He knew Raylan was there last night."

"Oh no." This was on the fast track to torment. It was one thing for Aunt Dean to know Seth had removed a body from the house. She was no threat to him. Anyone else Seth believed had witnessed that body in the house was in danger.

Olivia babbled on.

"Raylan. *Ohmygod.* I had no idea he was there. Seth thought Raylan must've seen the body and told Aunt Dean. Raylan...he didn't know that Seth didn't know I was there. He told Seth neither he nor I had seen any dead bodies."

"Oh no." Seth hadn't known Olivia was there until Raylan told him.

"Oh yes. Well, of course now Seth knows *I* saw the body and he has it in his head that I told Aunt Dean. Which of course I did no such thing. But he is livid. Liz, *he threatened my children* if either Raylan or I tell anyone there was a body in the house last night." She broke down into sobs.

"Olivia. I need you to calm down. Let me think." Based on what Colleen had told me, even if Seth hadn't killed Thurston, he was a stone-cold killer several times over. I glanced at my watch. Nine forty-five. I looked at Nate and murmured, "We've got to neutralize him now. Olivia and Julia are both at risk."

"What do you have in mind?" he asked.

"Olivia, where is Robert?"

"Right here, Liz." Olivia had her phone on speaker as well.

"Good. Robert, I need you to call Seth. Tell him that you and Olivia have discussed it, and you want him to have the house. She's going to sign it over to him tonight. You're drawing up papers and you want him to meet you at your office at eleven o'clock. This is important. Tell him you want this done tonight, as a gesture of good will. And throw in some things about how he is to stay away from your wife and children."

"But—"

"I'm not asking you to actually *do* this—draw up papers or give him the house. It's too late for that now. But I need you to get him to Stella Maris ASAP. He needs to be on the ten-thirty ferry. Tell him you'll get him a hotel room if he baulks about having enough time to catch the last ferry back tonight. Likely his greed will outweigh any minor concerns such as that. Just get him over there."

"And then what?"

"As soon as you're off the phone with him, take Olivia down to the police station and have her file a complaint. Blackmail, communication of threats, general jackassery...whatever else you, she, and Blake can think of. Get Raylan in on it—he was threatened, too."

Olivia commenced wailing.

"*Noooo.* Dammit, no. I've gone through way the hell too much trying to keep all of this quiet to let it come out now."

"Lookit," I said. "You are going to have to be strong here. There is so much going on in that house and it is all coming out, sooner rather than later. I can't stop it. There's just no way any of us can. People will talk, but so what? You haven't done anything illegal. You're just going to have to hold your head up and get through this. We'll all be there for you."

Robert said, "But even if Blake arrests Seth, he won't be able to hold him long. He'll get an attorney. Be out on bail in a few hours."

"Robert, you know how small towns work. Everything moves at a slower pace. It will take a while for his attorney to get over there. He's surely not going to hire you, and we're lawyer poor just now. The judge may go fishing tomorrow if the weather clears. Or he could be off for the holidays."

"I hear you," Robert said.

"We just need Blake to hold onto Seth for a day or so until Sonny comes to get him. And trust me, Sonny will be coming to get him."

"Are you going to call Blake?"

"As soon as we hang up. Bye now."

I selected Blake's name from my favorites list. He answered on the second ring.

"What's up, sis?"

"Robert and Olivia are on their way in to file a complaint." I brought him up to speed.

"I'll meet them at the station. There's a lot you're not telling me, right?"

I sighed. "Yes, but I promise to tell you as soon as I can—as soon as I have time. Please call me the second you have Seth behind bars."

"Will do. You still in Charleston?"

"Yes."

"Nate still there?"

"Right here, Blake," said Nate.

"Watch each other's backs."

"Always." We both spoke at once.

"Liz, you need to finish up whatever you're doing and come home. Mom's driving the rest of us bat-shit crazy because you're in Charleston and not here playing wedding with her."

"I know. I'll be home soon."

"See to it."

"I will, I promise."

FOURTEEN

At three minutes 'til ten, the garage door at 12 Church opened, and the black Dodge truck backed out.

"Thank God—Seth's on his way to Stella Maris." I called Robert to verify Seth had agreed to come. He'd been eager—no surprise there. Olivia, Julia, and the residents of 12 Church Street would be safe from him soon. But he wasn't the only danger. Time to commence Operation Clear Out the Bordello. The trickiest part of this was going to be explaining it to Nate without explaining Colleen to Nate.

Colleen sprawled across the bed, her head propped on one hand, impatiently drumming the fingers of the other.

"We've got to get those women out of that house while we can," I said.

"What exactly are you proposing?" asked Nate.

"I'll take the Explorer, load them up, and catch the last ferry over to Stella Maris. We'll stash them at our house with Merry. That way, they don't scatter, and Sonny can find them when he needs to. But they'll be safe."

"I'm not at all enthusiastic about having four houseguests who we know very little about, and what we do know doesn't reflect well on their character. But that's beside the point, really, because you'll never get them to agree to that plan, certainly not in less than an hour."

"First of all, these are students. The most significant thing about them is not that they're letting older men pay their rent and give them spending money." My back may have been up just a bit.

"Liz—"

"And secondly, I have to try. You stay here and keep an eye on everything. If I can't get them to leave, you can say 'I told you so.'"

He sighed. "As you wish. Proceed."

"If this works, I'll see you in the morning." I kissed him bye.

"I'll be with you every step of the way."

This was what scared the hell out of me. What exactly would he see? How much explaining was I going to have to do? "See, I'll be perfectly safe—you'll be watching."

"Like a hawk. Nevertheless. Be careful."

"Always."

Colleen appeared beside me on the sidewalk. "Let's start with Dana. She and Roxanne were friends. She'll be the easiest."

Or the most freaked out.

"Same thing."

Nate and I installed cameras with audio and video feed in every room. Can you interrupt the connection?

"Yes, but I'll wait until we're inside. Otherwise, he'll try to get you to abort."

I crossed the street and headed towards the street side door to the porch. *Okay. But here's the thing. I'm also wired. He can hear everything I say and anything I can hear. And he can talk to me on my earwig. I can't disable it. He has to be able to hear me. He'll worry, and may well come running across the street. But we can't let him hear you or Roxanne.*

"Sheesh. This would be easier if you just stayed outside."

And then how would I explain the girls showing up on the sidewalk?

"I'll handle it."

I unlocked the door to the porch, opened it, and closed it behind me. *How?*

"I'm going to screw with your transmitter."

Nate needs to be able to hear me, or—

"Prince Charming will come rushing to the rescue. Got it. I'll handle it."

Hey...leave the men from under the pool out of this. We don't need anyone going into cardiac arrest tonight.

"Fine. But it would've been more fun with them. Meet you in Dana's room." She faded out.

I let myself into the house. It was pitch dark. Didn't Miss Dean believe in nightlights? I turned on the flashlight on my phone, climbed the stairs, and made my way to the main-house Huger room.

The door to Dana's room—the one where she slept—was locked. Voices, low and urgent, drifted to me from inside. I knocked twice and the door unlocked.

"Wait," said Nate in my ear. "There's something odd going on in that room. The lights aren't on, but I can see flashes of glowing colored lights. I hear women talking, but I can't make out what they're saying."

I moved quickly into the room. Dana, Colleen, and Roxanne, the lingering spirit who appeared with flowing blond hair, were in a game of keep-away around the bed.

Colleen. Cameras. Audio. Transmitter.

In my ear, Nate said, "What the hell? Liz? Are you all right? All the audio and video feeds went to static. Can you hear me? What the hell is going on in there?"

"I'm fine. I can hear you."

Dana's head swiveled towards me. "How did you get in here? Who are you?"

Roxanne said, "Trust her. She will help you."

Colleen floated towards the ceiling and glowed in golden light. "Leave tonight, or by tomorrow you'll be one of us." She'd materialized, which meant Dana could see her.

I said, "I'm Liz Talbot, I'm a private investigator. You're in mortal danger here. Come with me. Please."

Dana looked from me to Roxanne, to Colleen, then back to Roxanne. "I thought you'd gone home. That's what they told us."

"What's she talking about?" Nate said into my earpiece.

"I don't know," I said.

Roxanne shook her head sadly. "Too many people have died here. Leave now."

Dana nodded rapidly. She fumbled for her purse and bolted for the door, passing me on the way.

I caught up with Dana. We slipped back into the main house. "I've got to get the others," I said. "Wait for me on the porch."

"I can help," Dana said. "I can talk to them."

The instincts of a nurse, to save others.

"Well I'll be damned," Nate said.

Colleen faded in beside me. "No. It's better if they're scared to come back here. The men will pressure them if they can get them on the phone."

"No," I said. "Go on outside and wait for the others. Keep them with you and keep them quiet. Hurry now."

Dana hesitated, then darted towards the stairs.

Heather's room was the next closest. It was also the closest room to Miss Dean's. "We've got to keep her quiet," I said.

"What?" said Nate.

"I need to be quiet. I don't want to wake Miss Dean."

"Roger that. I don't know what the hell happened to these cameras. I won't be able to warn you if she wakes up."

Colleen passed through the door, no doubt because she could, then opened it for me.

"I'll be fine," I said to Nate. *Showoff*, I thought hard at Colleen.

Colleen approached Heather's bed. She went to floating and glowing.

Roxanne appeared on the other side of the bed. She was transparent, but added no theatrics to her ghostly appearance.

I clamped my hand over Heather's mouth.

Her eyes flew open and she started slapping at me. Then she must've seen Colleen. She tried to scream.

I put my knee on the bed and pressed my hand tighter to her face. "Shhh. Hush now."

Heather scrambled to a sitting position.

Colleen said, "You are in grave danger. You must leave here tonight and never come back."

"Heather—Heather—it's me, Roxanne."

Heather tried to scream again. She went to shaking and rocking.

"You have got to be quiet," I said. "If Miss Dean hears you, we're all in trouble." I wasn't sure what I thought Miss Dean would do to stop us, or try, but I had a strong suspicion it was better for her to sleep through the exodus.

Roxanne said, "I died here. If you don't leave, you will too. Leave now. No matter what anyone says, don't come back."

I thought Heather's eyes were going to pop out of her head. I was afraid she might be having trouble breathing. "If I take my hand off your mouth, will you be quiet?"

Her head bobbed up and down.

Slowly, I released my grip and eased off the bed. "I told you before. You're in danger. Come on, let's get out of here."

Roxanne said, "You can trust her. She'll help you. Go on now."

Heather said, "What are you, the ghost of Christmas freakin' present?" She slid out of the bed and into a pair of flats near the bed. She grabbed her handbag, darted an expectant look towards me, then stared at the apparitions.

"Let's go," I said. "Wait for me on the front porch. Dana is already there."

Amber and Lori came along in much the same manner. Shortly, we were all on the front porch. Some of the women had on shoes, others were barefoot. They all had their handbags.

"Okay," I said, "we're going across the street to number fifteen. Through the gate, then back to the Explorer parked behind the house. Stay with me."

Once everyone was on the sidewalk, I said to Nate, "We're clear."

"Roger that. Keep me posted." His voice was tense. I suspected there would be much to talk about later.

"I'm getting static on this earwig now," I said. "I think all our communications have been compromised. I'll call you from the car." I pushed the button twice to disconnect.

I led the group to the Explorer. They stayed close and quiet. I opened the doors, put up the third row bench seat. Heather was the first one in. She moved to the back, buckled her seat belt, and hunkered down. Lori and Amber settled into the second row. Dana rode shotgun. Colleen had vanished in the commotion.

I turned around and headed out the gate. Once we were a few blocks away, I popped in my earbuds and called Nate on my iPhone to reassure him again. "I'll call you when we get to the house."

No one said a word until we were on the Cooper River Bridge. I said, "As I mentioned to each of you, I'm Liz Talbot. Olivia Pearson and her husband retained me. Y'all know Olivia, right?"

They replied in a chorus of "of course," "well, yeah," and "naturally."

"Where are you taking us?" asked Dana.

"To my house, on Stella Maris. I have a top-notch security system. You'll be safe there for a couple of days—until we can sort things out."

"What the hell was that back there?" asked Lori.

"Roxanne," said Dana. "She used to live in the empty room above the garage. They told us she moved home to Nebraska about a year back. Seth was heartbroken. He was always sweet on her. He must've known she was really dead."

Lori said, "So her...ghost...came to warn us to leave? Who else was with her?"

"I don't know who that was," said Dana. "Maybe someone else who died in that house. I'm just glad we got out."

"Me, too," I said. "And I'll do everything I can to keep you safe. But I'm going to need your cooperation on a few things."

No one said a word.

"First, I need you all to promise me you won't leave my house until we know it's safe. And I'll let you know when that is. Promise me? No one leaves—even for an hour?"

"I promise," said Heather.

"Me, too," said Dana.

Lori and Amber confirmed.

"And because your gentlemen friends will try to harass you and possibly even have you tracked, I need your cellphones."

No one piped right up and agreed to that.

"What if we just agree to not accept any calls from the men?" asked Amber.

"That will work up until the point one of you feels bad because they might be worried. Then you're all at risk. And if any of them has enough pull with someone inside the police department, he can maybe talk them into tracking your location. Again, you'd all be at risk."

"Who are we at risk from?" asked Dana.

"Seth, for one." I didn't fill them in on his impending incarceration. "And there's also a decent chance at least one of your...benefactors...has a violent streak."

Dana said, "There may be a misunderstanding about that."

I glanced over at her.

She smiled a sly little smile.

"I'm not talking about what any of you do for entertainment. One of these gentlemen may be under the impression that one or more of you know something that could get them arrested. For murder."

"Murder?"

"Who was murdered?"

"I don't know anything about a murder."

"Are you talking about the guy in the park?"

The car erupted in chatter. Disbelief, indignation, fear, and rebellion ran loose. I pulled to a stop at a light on Highway 17 in Mt. Pleasant. It occurred to me any one of them could be texting right then.

When the light changed, I pulled through the intersection, and immediately started looking for the next opportunity to get off 17. At the next light, I made a right, then a left onto Johnnie Dodds, then pulled into a Sherwin Williams parking lot and brought the car to a stop. For a moment, I entertained the notion of putting them all out right there. But if one of them came to harm, I couldn't live with myself. Also, Sonny would be that much madder if I lost his potential witnesses.

"Ladies, please," I said.

The noise level in the car grew.

I opened the car and got out.

Lori opened the passenger door behind me.

Colleen swooped in and hovered in front of the car, her red mane in a starburst around her head, shimmering, sparks flying.

In a collective gasp, the women hushed.

Lori slammed the door closed.

"Give her your phones," said Colleen.

They all scrambled to pass them forward. Dana took them and laid them on my seat.

I leaned in. One by one, I turned them off and dropped them in my tote. "I promise to give you these back as soon as the danger has passed."

"Do as she asks and you might live through this," Colleen said. Then she did a pyrotechnic stunt worthy of the Fourth of July and disappeared.

Tomorrow, no doubt, there would be wild speculation in the news about the strange lights in Mt. Pleasant. But the women in the car were blessedly quiet. I climbed back in, glanced around. Four pale, wide-eyed faces stared towards the front of the car. Dana's lips moved in what I'd bet was silent prayer.

I closed the door and drove towards home, praying the quiet would last. Time to call Merry and let her know what was coming her way.

FIFTEEN

Blake texted me while we were on the ferry: *Seth is locked up.*

I sent up thanks and relayed the news to Nate via text. I couldn't speak freely in the car, and I didn't want to leave my charges unattended by getting out.

He texted me back: *Good news for all. Hope Blake can keep him there 4 a while.*

I replied: *He will. Miss Dean's house unlocked. Keys on porch. Grab cameras tonight?*

Nate texted: *Good idea. Feed is hosed anyway. Don't know what happened. Best to get them out before Charleston PD goes in. Going now.*

Be careful. Miss Dean keeps a gun close.

Good to know.

Every light in my house was on. Merry waited on the front porch, her arms full of quilts. Rhett came running out to escort us down the driveway.

"Oooh," Lori said. "What a pretty dog."

"His name is Rhett," I said.

As soon as I parked the car, they all hopped out to pet him. They were still subdued, but they all cooed and talked baby talk to Rhett, who ate it up.

Merry made her way down the steps. The stack of quilts was up to her eyeballs.

I ran to help her.

"Here. Let me take some of those."

"I have hot tea and hot chocolate made," she said.

"Thank you. I know all of this wasn't part of the bargain when I asked you to stay here."

"They need help," she said.

This was Merry. Giving and softhearted to a fault. I hadn't had a chance to tell her much on the phone, but it didn't matter.

"Hey, y'all, this is my sister, Merry."

They kept petting Rhett, but looked our way.

"Merry, this is Amber, Lori, Heather, and Dana." Black hair, redhead, blond, brunette. I double-checked the names in my brain. Everything had happened so fast, I hadn't had a chance to get to know any of them well.

"Hey," Merry said. "It's good to meet y'all."

They all murmured greetings.

"Y'all sure do look a lot alike," said Heather. "You could be twins."

"We get that a lot," I said. Except I was two years older, four inches taller, and several pounds heavier. I didn't like to talk numbers.

"Y'all must be freezing," Merry said. "Here, take these quilts."

Merry and I handed them out, then made a second round making sure everyone was wrapped up and tucked in.

"Let's go inside," I said. "Merry has hot tea and cocoa ready."

"Can Rhett come inside?" Dana asked.

"Of course," I said.

Merry and I herded them indoors, down the hall, and into the sunroom.

"Everyone, please make yourselves comfortable," I said.

Dana, the brunette nursing student, Amber, the raven-haired whiz in business and/or finance, and Heather, the blond grad student in environmental studies, huddled under their quilts on the sofa. These were the three who'd lived at 12 Church Street the longest. Lori, the redhead information systems student, who was both the newest resident and the youngest of the group at twenty-two, curled into one of the wingback chairs near the fire Merry had built in the fireplace.

Rhett finally noticed I was there and came over for attention. I ruffled his head and scratched behind his ears, then patted him on his side. "You're a good boy."

He wagged his tail and gave me a sloppy grin. I went into the kitchen, and Rhett followed me. Merry had a tray of mugs and was headed in the other direction. I grabbed the thermal carafes. Soon, everyone had a warm drink and Rhett had settled between my wingback and the end of the sofa. Merry pulled in a chair from the kitchen.

"If you stay, you may hear things you'll be called to testify about at some point," I said.

"If you think I'm leaving, you've lost your mind," she murmured under her breath, a huge smile on her face.

I shrugged. "Suit yourself."

"I usually do."

"Mule." I shook my head and sighed.

"Takes one to know one." Colleen, who was still seventeen, the age she was when she died, joined us in spirit mode. I was the only one who could see her sitting cross-legged on the floor, aside from Rhett, who belly-crawled over and laid his head down beside her. Colleen obliged and stroked his head.

"I know you're all exhausted," I said, "and in shock from everything you've seen this evening."

I caught a glimpse of Merry's scrunched-up face in my peripheral vision.

I continued, "But I need to ask you a few questions. It's very important that you tell me anything that might be connected, even if you think it's unimportant. Do any of you know Thurston Middleton?"

Lori, the redheaded new girl with all the dress-up outfits, gasped.

Dana said, "The man they found dead in White Point Gardens this morning?"

Dear heaven, had it been that same day? "Yes." I looked from face to face, scanning for reaction. A mixture of confusion and lingering shock stared back at me from every face save one. I recognized fear on Lori's face.

"Lori?" I held her gaze.

"He was waiting for me in the lot where I park over on Elliott Street when I came back from class one afternoon a couple weeks ago—right before winter break. He must've followed me there from Aunt Dean's before then. He gave me his card, asked me to come with him for a cup of coffee. He said it was urgent he talk to me."

"Did you go?" I asked.

She shook her head. "No. I told him he could talk to me right there, but I wasn't going anywhere with him. He seemed nice, but you never know."

Her mamma had given her the same Ted Bundy lecture mine had given me. "Did he tell you what he wanted?"

"He asked me about Aunt Dean's, who paid my rent there. He said he'd heard some ugly rumors. He wanted me to confirm them. I told him it was none of his business and walked home."

"Did he follow you?" I asked.

"No."

"Did he ever contact you again?"

"No."

"Did you tell Arthur about the incident?"

Tears filled her eyes. Her lips, tightly clamped together, trembled. She nodded.

"What was his reaction?" I asked.

She wiped a tear from her face.

"He was so angry."

"Did he hurt you?" I asked.

She looked startled.

"No. Arthur is very good to me. He'd never hurt me."

"Did he ever mention Thurston Middleton to you again?"

"Not after that night. He told me to be sure to tell him if I ever saw him or heard from him again. But I never did."

I said, "Did Thurston Middleton ever approach any of the rest of you?"

They all shook their heads slowly.

Dana said, "I never met the man or talked to him. But James asked me if he'd approached me."

"When?" I asked.

"Probably right after that. It's been a couple weeks."

"Anyone else been asked about him?" I asked.

Heather said, "Henry asked me the same thing."

Who had told Henry? According to Julia, he wasn't close to the other men.

Amber said, "William never mentioned Thurston's name. But he did ask me recently if anyone had bothered me or asked me questions."

"Are any of you afraid of Seth?"

They exchanged glances.

I waited.

Dana, the *Fifty Shades* brunette, spoke for the group. "Seth would never hurt any of us. The men who pay our rent would be unhappy. Happy men who pay the rent are very important to Aunt Dean. But Seth is creepy. We just avoid him as much as we can."

Lori said, "When you're new, he spies on you. I've caught him following me a few times. He always just smiles and waves, like him being there's a coincidence, but I don't buy it."

"How is your relationship with Aunt Dean?" I asked.

Amber said, "She's mostly like a grandmother. Some of her rules are odd. But you can't beat the perks of living there. Dinner on the table every night at seven. Someone else does all the laundry. Most of our time is our own to study, focus on school."

"So none of you are at all afraid of Aunt Dean?" I asked.

They all shook their heads.

"Was everyone home Monday evening?" I asked.

"Yes," said Dana.

They all nodded.

"And dinner was at seven?" I asked.

"No," said Dana. "Aunt Dean was tired. Dinner was at six Monday."

"And after dinner...did you all go to your rooms?"

There was a chorus of "Yes," and "I did."

"Who all had company last night?"

Dana, Lori, and Amber raised their hands. This confirmed what Nate had heard earlier when Lori and Amber had been surprised to see their gentlemen callers again so soon. But Dana had not seen James that evening. She'd been in her room when he snuck in the mystery woman. Had she really been with James and the mystery woman the night before?

"What time did the gentlemen arrive, and when did they leave?" I asked.

"James came earlier than usual, shortly after seven. He left around eight fifteen," said Dana.

I felt my face scrunch. I'd talk to her later, privately, about the mystery woman. There were too many people coming and going between seven and nine on Monday for some of them not to've bumped into each other. "How does James come and go from the house? Through which door?"

Dana said, "He drives through the gate—he has an automatic opener—then comes up the steps to the landing over the garage. He almost never goes into the main part of the house." Where her room was located. And where Thurston had been killed.

"Lori?" I asked.

"Arthur came and went around the same time," she said. "But he comes in through the street door to the porch, goes down the back porch steps to the pool deck, then comes in through the keeping room doors and up the back staircase from the kitchen."

"So James and Arthur wouldn't have crossed paths, and neither of them were ever in the foyer," I said.

"Right," said Dana and Lori.

Amber piped up. "William arrived about seven twenty. He was there a little more than an hour. He comes and goes through the front door and the porch entrance to the street."

So William did go through the foyer. What and who did he see?

"Once they arrived, did any of the three men leave your rooms for any length of time before they left for the evening?"

"No." All three heads shook.

I gave Dana a stern look.

She glanced away.

"Did any of you come back out of your rooms later in the evening?" I asked.

Heather had a queasy look about her. I let my gaze rest on her and waited. Finally, she said, "I came back down to the kitchen for a glass of milk. I'm on a diet, and I'm supposed to have a protein snack in the evening."

"What time was that?" I asked.

She shrugged. "Around seven thirty."

My skin tingled. "Did you come down the front staircase or the back?"

"I came down the front. But I went up the back," she said.

"Did you see anyone downstairs?" I asked.

She shrunk deeper into the chair and the quilt. "When I was coming down the stairs, I saw someone—a man—in the foyer. I saw him from behind. I didn't know who it was and I was in my pajamas. I waited on the stairs and he went out the front door."

"Were any of the lights on?" I asked.

"No."

"Did you turn on a light?" I asked.

"No," she said. "I'm always afraid I'll surprise someone—one of the men. If the lights are off, I just leave them off. I can see with the light in the refrigerator in the kitchen."

"Did you see anyone else?" I asked.

She said, "I was sitting at the kitchen counter drinking my milk. I heard a noise in the front of the house. I told myself, this house makes all kinds of noises. It was nothing. But it scared me. Then Seth came in. I told him about it. He made a joke about the house being haunted. I didn't want to be alone with Seth, so I went up the back staircase to the second floor and then up to my room."

"Where did Seth come in from?" I asked.

"He came through the back door in the keeping room," she said. "I guess he came from the guesthouse."

Just then I was thinking how Heather had likely seen Robert go out the front door, heard someone else kill Thurston, and solidified Seth's alibi.

"That's about the size of it," said Colleen.

I jolted. *Are any of them holding anything back?*

"Yes," she said. "Dana has a secret. But it's not relevant. Otherwise, they're telling you the truth, at least to the best of their knowledge."

So none of these women killed Thurston.

"No, but they are all in danger."

From who?

"I don't know. It's your job to figure that out."

Nothing we learned tonight helps Olivia.

"No," said Colleen. "And things are about to get hairy for Olivia. She's going to want you to hold her hand. But you can't. You need to focus. The best way to help Olivia is to figure out who killed Thurston. But even that won't protect these women."

Dana said, "I'm so exhausted. Can we talk more tomorrow?"

They all chimed in in agreement.

"Sure," I said. "Follow me." We all went upstairs, and Merry helped me get them settled in two of the remaining guest rooms. None of them wanted to sleep alone.

SIXTEEN

At seven thirty the next morning, I was showered, dressed, and headed downstairs, eager to get back to Nate. The aroma of coffee wafted up to greet me. Who was up? I hustled down the hall to the kitchen. A woman who looked like my sister, Merry, was washing strawberries at my old-fashioned farmhouse sink.

"Who are you and what have you done with my sister?" I asked.

"I figured you'd have to leave," she said. "Those poor girls are going to be hungry when they wake up."

I gave her a quick hug. "Thank you."

Then I headed for the coffee pot. I grabbed a to-go mug. "I'm going to arm the security system when I leave. Rhett can come and go through the doggy doors, but please keep our guests indoors. They may be in danger."

She gave me an inquiring look. "What exactly happened last night? Why were they in shock? What did they see?"

I knew this was coming. I narrowly escaped her questions the night before. "I basically snuck into their rooms and told them they would die if they didn't leave with me. I'm sure it was unsettling."

Merry rolled her eyes. "So you're not going to tell me."

"Listen," I said. "The men who employ them will be looking for them. I have their cellphones. If they ask to use a phone, tell them no. Keep your cellphone on you."

"Okay, but what if someone is worried about them?"

"If anyone wants to let family know they're okay, call me. I'll relay a message. I just want to keep them safe for a few days until we've neutralized the danger."

"You'd better tell Nicolette you're going to have four more guests at the wedding," Merry said in the tone one reserves for tormenting siblings.

I took a long drink of coffee. "I hope this is resolved before Saturday."

"I can handle things here," she said. "Go do what you need to do."

I opened a drawer near the refrigerator, reached far into the back, and brought out a Sig P290. "Just in case. It's loaded. Eight rounds. Granddaddy's shotgun is in the foyer closet if you need it." I put the handgun back in the drawer and closed it.

Merry's eyes went large and round, but she nodded. Daddy had made sure we all knew how to handle guns if the need arose.

"I'll let Blake know what we've got going on here. He may stop by—at least have someone drive by occasionally."

"We'll be fine," she said. "There's no way the men involved could know where you've stashed their women, right?"

"One of them could think to look here if they chased it hard enough," I said. "They know Olivia owns half that house and she lives on Stella Maris. Olivia's aunt could cave under pressure and tell them I'm involved. It's best to stay on guard. When does Joe get into town?" Merry's current boyfriend would be here for the wedding and for Christmas.

"This afternoon," she said.

"Good. Have him come straight here. There's strength in numbers."

"That was my plan." She went back to arranging fruit on a platter. "But don't be sending Daddy over here with a shotgun."

"No." I chuckled. "Mamma would not understand this situation, and she would definitely not countenance Daddy being any part of it. I'm out of here. You know the alarm codes if you need them. Call me if anything comes up."

I gave Merry another hug, holding onto her longer this time.

Then I patted Rhett and asked him to hold down the fort, and I was out the door.

I checked in with Nate once I was in the car. "Did you get some rest?" I asked.

"Not as much as I would've liked. We had drama here."

"What happened?"

"After I got the cameras out, I decided to keep an eye on things for a while, see if anyone came to call well past normal visiting hours."

"And?"

"Lo and behold, at ten after two, a gentleman approached from up towards Atlantic. He was dressed all in black athletic clothes. Had a ski mask over his head."

"*What*? Please tell me you didn't go down there," I said.

"He went in with a key. I called 911 from a burner and reported a burglary in progress."

"And then you went down there, didn't you?"

"Miss Dean was there by herself, Slugger. I wasn't sure how long it would take the police to arrive. So, yes, I went down there. Don't even pretend you would've done anything different."

I stayed quiet.

"When I went in, I heard someone walking around upstairs, so I went straight up. But I stepped down the back staircase towards the kitchen a few steps and watched to see what he would do. This guy went from room to room. He wasn't just looking for his woman, he was doing a bed check. Just as he headed for Miss Dean's room..." He sighed.

"What happened?"

"Well, I ran up the back stairs, which put me between him and her. He wasn't expecting me, of course. I had the element of surprise. I tackled him—"

"Wait. Why didn't you just pull out your weapon and hold him until the police got there?"

"I didn't think it was a good idea to carry my weapon into a situation where I could end up in a face-to-face with the police, explaining how I'd followed a burglar inside. Miss Dean doesn't know me. I could've ended up looking like an armed intruder."

"You went in there unarmed?"

"Yes, and I lived to tell. Stay with me. Like I was saying, I tackled him. Tried like hell to pull that mask off. But he was scrappy. And he was carrying a sizable knife strapped to his leg. He didn't pull it, though. He wriggled away and took off down the front stairs. Of course, he didn't know the police were on their way. I figured I'd best slip out the back before Charleston PD showed up and thought I was the burglar. Seemed prudent to avoid getting tangled up in a police report. I went over to the landing above the garage and down the steps to the parking pad. There was a police cruiser on the street, but the officers were on the front porch trying to raise Miss Dean. I hopped the picket fence to the sidewalk, headed towards Atlantic trying to get a bead on the guy in the ski mask, but there was no sign of him. I walked around the block and came back to the bed and breakfast."

"Thank God you're all right."

"Nothing to worry about."

"So the guy must've slipped past the police?"

"He may've gone out the keeping room door, or through the garage. But they didn't put anyone in the back of the patrol car."

"How long were the police there?" I asked.

"Not long. I suspect Miss Dean convinced them it was a prank. She didn't know at the time that she was alone in the house, and her default setting is to keep the law from coming inside."

"And then what happened?" I asked.

"I went to bed. I missed you."

"I missed you, too. That guy...he likely meant to kill everyone in that house."

"I imagine you're right," said Nate. "It's a good thing you got most of them out."

"It's a good thing he didn't pull that knife with you unarmed. I can't help but wonder why he didn't."

"My guess is me turning up dead in that house would've focused attention on it before he had a chance to find and tie up all his loose ends. That would've been contrary to his goals."

"I suppose that makes sense," I said. "Before the episode with the intruder, when you were getting the equipment, were you able to get the camera out of Miss Dean's room?"

"I cracked the door. She was snoring like a rusty chainsaw. I got the camera—she snored through the whole thing. I'm amazed the police got her awake."

"So we're out clean?" I asked.

"Roger that."

"That's a relief. I'm going to run by and talk to Blake, then I'll be on my way back."

"See you soon."

Colleen appeared in the passenger seat. "He would've killed them all. Miss Dean, too."

"But couldn't Roxanne have just scared him off?"

"Roxanne's a lingering spirit. She doesn't have the tools I have to work with, and she has a very narrow worldview. She only knew what to do and when because I told her. Ghosts can only manifest for so long. She couldn't have protected them. Besides, scaring him off once wouldn't solve the problem. Removing them from harm's way did."

"And you could lend a hand for a while last night, but couldn't stand guard because that's not part of your mission."

"Exactly," she said. "Humans have free will. I can only intervene on behalf of people directly relevant to my mission. We've been over this a time or three." She faded out.

I walked through the door of The Cracked Pot at eight.

Moon Unit Glendawn, who owned the place, pounced on me straightaway. "There's the bride! How are you, sweetie? I can't wait 'til Friday night. We are going to close The Pirates' Den down." My bachelorette party was scheduled for Friday night, after the rehearsal dinner.

"I can't wait," I said. I spotted Blake at the counter.

"Me either. We have all *kinds* of things planned for you. Merry hasn't let on, has she?"

"She hasn't told me a thing, I promise."

"She'd better not."

"Moon, I need to talk to Blake for a minute. Could I get some breakfast?"

"Sure thing, sweetie. You want the usual?"

"Cheese eggs, ham, grits with red eye gravy, and biscuits."

"I'm glad you're not starving yourself the week before the wedding like some brides do," said Moon. "It's just not healthy. Makes 'em mean as snakes, too."

Colleen must've heard the word biscuits. She popped in beside me. "And two ham biscuits to go."

"And two ham biscuits to go, please," I said to Moon Unit.

She'd become accustomed to my add-on takeout order and given up questioning it. "Coming right up."

I slid onto the stool beside Blake. "Any chance I can get you to move to a booth so we can talk?"

He looked at his breakfast, identical to the one I'd ordered, except his eggs were over medium. "Grab my coffee."

He picked up his plate and the biscuit basket and moved to the back booth.

Colleen took the opposite side and moved over next to the window.

I set his coffee down and slid in across from him, beside Colleen. "What's the sit rep on Seth?"

"He's still locked up. Asked for an attorney. Called one—I have no idea who. No one's shown up yet. Nell's supposed to let me know if someone does."

"Did he say anything?" I asked.

Moon Unit set a coffee cup in front of me and filled it. "You want juice this mornin'?"

"No thanks, Moon. Water would be great."

"All righty. I tried on my bridesmaid's dress again last night just for fun. It's the most gorgeous *thing*. I feel so pretty in it—all that lace. And such a pretty color. I love the name of the color: smoked pearl."

Blake said, "Moony, I need to talk to my sister in private. I'm giving her brotherly advice on being a good wife, seeing to the needs of a man. You know, things didn't work out for her the first time."

Colleen broke out into an uproar of bray-snorting.

I kicked my brother under the table.

Moon froze, speechless, which happens about as often as Venus and Jupiter align. She reddened, did an about face, and hurried away.

Blake cracked up.

"What is wrong with you?" I asked.

"You wanted to talk in private—talk." He dug into his breakfast, still grinning.

I shook my head, sighed. "Did Seth say anything when you arrested him?"

"He cursed me and all my ancestors real good. Robert and Olivia, too. That's about it."

"He'll be Sonny's problem soon enough. Do you mind if I talk to him?"

Blake's eyes narrowed. "Why?"

"Because I want to know what he knows."

"About the whorehouse, or about Thurston Middleton?"

"Thurston Middleton. I won't get a chance to talk to him after Sonny picks him up."

"If I let you talk to him, that could screw up Sonny's interrogation. You'll ask him questions. He'll have more time to make up answers. This is not a good idea."

"Damnation, Blake," I said, "I'm trying to help out Robert and Olivia."

Moon Unit set my breakfast and a glass of water in front of

me, but she didn't hang around.

I was starving. I picked up my fork and dug in.

This was fine with Blake. He wanted his turn at talking. "What else do you need to do to help out Robert and Olivia? I charged Seth with blackmail and communicating threats. The Pearson family is safe. The judge is out of town until tomorrow. Even when Seth's attorney shows up, he's not going anywhere until tomorrow morning soonest. If Sonny is waiting on him after he makes bail, so much the better. But I'm unclear on what else needs to be done to help out Robert and Olivia."

I sipped my coffee. Blake was a sworn officer of the law. I had to be careful I didn't tell him anything I wasn't ready to tell Sonny. And I needed to talk to Nate before we made that decision.

"Fine," I said, in the universal female tone signaling things were far from fine. I put together a perfect bite of eggs, grits, and gravy.

"I've got a bad feeling about all the stuff you're not telling me," he said.

The doorbells jangled. Blake looked up. "Raylan," he said to me. He threw a chin lift of acknowledgement in Raylan's direction. "Here he comes."

Raylan slid in beside me. I slid over towards Colleen.

"Hey," she said.

I threw her a look that said, *Oh please.*

She switched sides of the booth. "I'd rather sit by Blake anyway."

"I have no doubt."

I raised an eyebrow at her. She'd had a crush on Blake as a teenager.

Blake and Raylan looked at me.

"You have no doubt about what?" asked Blake.

Colleen commenced bray-snorting.

I purely hated it when that happened—when she baited me into speaking to her outloud when others were present.

I smiled sweetly at Blake. "I have no doubt that you have Seth all taken care of."

His look held a threat.

Raylan said, "I'm really glad to hear that. Can you keep him locked up?"

"As long as necessary," Blake said.

I turned to Raylan. "I wanted to ask you something."

"Shoot," he said.

"Monday night, at the house on Church Street, tell me exactly how you entered and left."

Blake's eyes narrowed.

Raylan said, "I went in the door to the porch, walked to the end of it and down the steps and around back to the guesthouse. Left the same way."

"And that was at seven twenty?"

"About that. I can't say exactly."

"Did you see anyone else, coming or going?" I asked.

Raylan cocked his head. After a moment, he said, "Now that you mention it, I thought I heard footsteps on the front porch after I turned the corner around back. I didn't think anything about it at the time. Honestly, I was glad not to run into anyone, knowing what all goes on there. Someone might've thought I was involved in that."

"What about when you left?" I asked.

Raylan looked over his shoulder, leaned in. "When I came out of the guesthouse, I saw someone walking across the yard, between the garage and the guesthouse. His back was to me. He went around the side of the garage and climbed over that little brick wall into the neighbor's driveway. I figured it was one of the...you know, the men who keep women there."

"Could you see what he looked like?"

Raylan pressed his lips together, shook his head. "It was too dark. It was a man, that's all I can say for sure. Probably about my height. He had on light colored pants, probably khakis, and a jacket."

"Like a sport coat, or a bomber jacket?" I asked.

"Looked more like a sport coat to me," said Raylan.

Blake said, "You need to let Sonny do his job. Don't you need to meet with Mom and that wedding planner about seating charts or something?"

"Are you and the guys still going to play a set when the band takes a break?"

Blake, Sonny, and a few of their friends had a band—The Back Porch Prophets. Blake played pedal steel guitar and keyboards. He also wrote some of their music. They played most Friday nights at The Pirates' Den, and the occasional other bar in the area. I'd asked them to play a set or two at the reception.

Blake scowled. "People don't want to hear original music at a wedding. They want stuff they can dance to. We don't do that many covers."

"Raylan, could I trouble you to let me out, please?"

He complied.

I stood. "Blake, folks'll have plenty of opportunities to dance. Haven't you heard? Mamma and Nicolette hired Big Ray and the Kool Kats. But I'm the bride. And I want my big brother to play." I leaned down to hug him bye.

He submitted, but muttered something under his breath that sounded like, "God, why couldn't you have given me brothers?"

SEVENTEEN

Arthur Russell, notorious philanderer, owned a King Street antiques shop. He came from money and had the luxury of spending his days as he chose. The store had only been open five minutes that Wednesday morning when I walked inside.

"Good morning." He smiled and walked towards me from a roll-top desk in the middle of the store. Nate was right. Something about him was sleazy, though he was handsome and well-groomed.

"Good morning," I said.

"Are in you in the market for a Christmas present, perhaps?" he asked.

I had no time for pleasantries, though I did still need a Christmas gift for Daddy. I wouldn't be buying it from Arthur. "Not today, thank you."

"Can I offer you a cup of coffee while you browse? I just made a fresh pot." His smile was more than a Charleston-friendly smile.

Was he flirting with me? Eeew.

"No thank you." I pulled out my PI license and photo id. "My name is Liz Talbot. I'm a private investigator."

His expression changed to one more guarded. "What can I do for you, Miss Talbot?"

"I have some questions regarding the house at 12 Church Street."

"Willowdean Beauthorpe lives there. Sweet lady. She's in her eighties, I believe. Her sister lived there with her until a few years back when she passed."

"And you had the occasion to visit someone in the house on Monday evening and again on Tuesday evening of this week."

"I drop by occasionally to check on Miss Dean. It's the neighborly thing to do."

"Did you see anyone else while you were there?"

He squinted at me for a moment. "Who, for example?"

"Did you run into Thurston Middleton?"

"Thurston? No, I most certainly did not. What would give you such a wild idea?" He either was practiced at looking bewildered or the expression was genuine.

"Who else, besides yourself, was aware that Thurston Middleton was investigating the house on Church Street?"

"Thurston. Such a shame—ugly mess, that. What have you to do with Thurston? Are the police not adequately investigating his unfortunate demise?"

"I've been retained on another matter. It's my understanding that before his death, Mr. Middleton was investigating the house on Church Street, and that you were made aware of his line of inquiry."

Arthur stared at me for a long moment.

I stared back.

Presently, he said, "I don't believe I'm obliged to speak with you, Miss Talbot."

I lifted a shoulder. "You're not. I can always turn what I have over to the Charleston police detectives investigating Mr. Middleton's murder. They can swing by." Of course I would give Sonny everything anyway. But Arthur didn't know that.

I meandered farther back into the store, letting my hand glide across the top of a mahogany chest. "How long have you kept a room at Miss Dean's house? Lori isn't your first girlfriend to live there, is she? The one before her—what was her name?"

"I don't mean to be rude, but what business is it of yours if I have a harem?"

"None whatsoever. And frankly, I couldn't care less. But I wonder...does your wife know? I'm guessing she does. But she likely prefers your infidelities not provide fodder for the local gossips. It would be a shame for all this nonsense to get tied up in with Thurston's murder investigation and come out in the newspaper."

Arthur's eyes glittered with controlled rage. "Very well, if you must know the details of my private affairs, I mentioned to James Huger and William Calhoun that it had come to my attention Thurston was poking his nose into our business. The three of us are old friends. We have common interests to protect."

"The three of you have tenure, so to speak, at the...establishment."

"I guess you could say that, if you like."

"So Miss Willowdean Beauthorpe would turn to one of you if she had trouble—needed help with something?"

"I believe that is Seth's job," he said.

I tilted my head, gave him my best try at a quizzical look. "Yes, but what if Seth were the problem?"

The top of Arthur's upper lip trembled, as if he were trying to quell a sneer.

"In that case, I suppose Miss Beauthorpe would call upon one of us."

"And has she called upon you recently?"

"She mentioned that Seth needed to be spoken to about discretion, family loyalty, that sort of thing. He's a grown man, but he never has quite matured. Sometimes we step in to assist her with matters related to Seth."

"And who exactly is John?" I asked.

Arthur threw back his head and laughed. "Miss Willowdean is the soul of discretion. John is whichever one of us she happens to be speaking to her on an untraceable phone."

How appropriate.

"When you were checking on Miss Beauthorpe Monday and Tuesday evening, did you notice anything unusual in the house—anyone there who didn't belong, anyone behaving in a suspicious manner?"

"Nothing like that at all. The only mildly remarkable thing was

Olivia Pearson's car parked out front. It was there when I came in and when I left. It's not unheard of for her to visit her aunt, but it doesn't happen every week."

I said, "One more question, Mr. Russell. Has Seth or anyone else ever attempted to blackmail you regarding your affiliation with Miss Beauthorpe's establishment?"

"Fortunately, no one has been that foolhardy."

EIGHTEEN

"Grandma Got Run Over by a Reindeer" was playing on the downstairs sound system at the bed and breakfast. At least it wasn't "Hard Candy Christmas." That song was a little too close to my heart just then.

"Hey, Slugger." Nate had a hug waiting for me just inside the bedroom door. "I was watching for you."

I hugged him tight. I needed a hug. "Arthur Russell is a creep of the highest order."

Nate pulled away just enough to look me in the eyes. "What have you been up to?"

"I drove right past his antique store on the way here. I figured why not stop. I had questions."

"Did he have answers?"

"Not very satisfying ones. I need to finish that timeline." I moved to my workstation in the corner, pulled my makeshift lap-desk onto my lap, and opened the spreadsheet I'd started earlier.

"We need to speak to Sonny," said Nate.

"Yes, we do. But I need to sort this out a bit more first."

Nate sighed. "We're pushing it now. We need to get Sonny on board before Blake has to release Seth."

"Seth is the least of our worries."

"Is that a fact? Correct me if I'm wrong, but he threatened Olivia and her children, and poses a threat to Julia Middleton. That was our working theory, last I checked."

And he'd killed at least four people who were buried across the street. "Okay, Seth is a problem, but he surely wasn't the burglar with the big knife, and he couldn't've killed Thurston Middleton, so he may not be a threat to Julia, at least."

"Walk me through that last part." Nate stretched out on the bed and leaned back on a stack of pillows.

"Hang on." I created a minute-by-minute timeline for Monday evening. "Everyone in the house had dinner together at six, after which they all went to their rooms. Olivia arrived at seven, and went through the foyer, up the front stairs to Miss Dean's bedroom."

"Okay."

"Almost immediately after Olivia, Robert arrived." I reached into my tote, pulled out my phone, and made a quick call to Robert to verify exactly where he'd parked and the time. I typed the info into my spreadsheet. "He drove around the block after he saw Olivia go inside, then he parked half a block back, at approximately seven-oh-three. He did not see anyone turn into the drive. So James must have arrived while Robert was circling the block. He drives in, using an automatic opener. So we'll say James arrived at seven-oh-two."

Nate shrugged. "Okay, James pulled in after Olivia, but before Robert arrived."

"Right. So Robert arrives and stays in the car for fifteen minutes—that's what he said, right?"

"That's how I remember it."

"Then how does he miss Arthur Russell coming in the street side door at around seven-oh-five?"

"It was dark. If Russell approached from South Battery like he did last night, and Robert was half a block away, he could've easily missed him."

"Maybe so. Arthur comes in and takes the front porch around to the keeping room doors and goes up the back staircase. He and James never cross paths, and neither of them are ever near the foyer. Neither of them leave their rooms until well after the murder—there's a caveat on James, but we'll come back to that—so if we believe Lori and Dana, neither of them could possibly have killed Thurston."

Colleen's voice echoed in my head. *Dana has a secret. But it's not relevant.*

"That is a damn shame. I wanted it to be Arthur."

"Me, too," I said. "The next thing we can document is that Robert went inside between seven fifteen and seven twenty, but mere moments before William Calhoun, who arrived just before seven twenty—he arrived upstairs around seven twenty, anyway."

"Robert is wandering around downstairs looking for Olivia, Calhoun comes in the front door and goes upstairs. That's who Robert heard." Nate said.

"Right. Then Raylan arrives shortly after William Calhoun, but Raylan never goes inside the main house. He walks down the porch, around back to the guesthouse to see Seth. I'll assign Raylan seven twenty-five. He parked on Murray and walked. And Raylan heard someone walking on the front porch right after he turned the corner."

"And we don't know who that was, but it could've been Thurston."

I said, "I think it must've been. The timeline is too tight for him to've already been in the house. Someone would've surely seen him. Robert claims he didn't. Neither James nor Arthur would have. We need to speak with William Calhoun. For now, I think we assume it was Thurston who Raylan heard on the way in."

"All right," said Nate.

"The next thing that happened is right around seven thirty. Robert gives up looking for Olivia, walks through the foyer and out the front door. Heather is coming downstairs and sees him leave— sees someone leave. Based on the timeline, I think it had to be Robert."

"Makes sense."

"Heather is in the kitchen drinking a glass of milk at the counter, and she hears a noise in the front of the house. She doesn't investigate. I'm thinking this was when someone conked Thurston on the head—likely someone who followed Thurston into the house. This happened sometime between seven thirty and seven forty."

"Proceed."

"At approximately seven forty, Raylan comes out of the guesthouse and sees a man walk around the back side of the garage and climb over the brick wall to the neighbor's driveway."

"When did he tell you that?" Nate asked.

"This morning at breakfast. I ran into him at The Cracked Pot."

"Description?"

"Just that he was about the same height as Raylan—and not for nothing, but virtually every man involved is within an inch of six-foot-tall—and had on what appeared to be khakis and a sport coat."

"So, not your average prowler or whatnot. And possibly our murderer."

"Exactly," I said. "Right after Raylan left, Seth walked through the keeping room door and joined Heather in the kitchen. Heather tells him she heard a noise. He makes a joke about the house being haunted, and Heather, who doesn't want to pass time with Seth, goes up the back staircase to her room."

"And since Seth cleaned up the mess so quickly, he must've gone straight to the front parlor to investigate, where he found the body."

Nate got up and moved to my quilt display. "Nathaniel Gibbes and Wendi Hill were in Austria. Still are." He picked up their index cards.

"Right."

"Julia Middleton was serving dinner to the homeless. I ran across a photo online this morning. Thurston's death is all over the news, of course. She is as well. I made some calls to the folks who run the soup kitchen. She was there from four-thirty until eight. Helped clean up." He added Julia's index card to the ones in his hand.

"And we know James, Arthur, William, and Seth couldn't have

done it." He picked up the index cards for those four men.

"Hold up on James," I said. "Dana claims she was with him and he never left the room. But remember, last night you heard James and the mystery woman mention sneaking out two nights in a row. If he always entertains them one at a time—and I seriously hope that's the case—Dana was in her room while James Huger was in the playroom with the mystery woman. We'd need to speak to her to confirm his alibi."

"That's true." Nate returned James's card to the quilt.

"Assuming all our other facts are solid, we know neither Lori nor Amber could have done it."

"Right." Nate picked up their cards. "That leaves us with James Huger, Dana Clark, Henry Prioleau, Heather Wilder—she could've done it on her way to the kitchen and made up the story to get Seth to investigate..." Nate's face creased. "Who are William Rutledge and Roxanne Trexler, both deceased, and how could they have killed Thurston Middleton?"

"I'll explain in a minute. Keep going." How in the hell was I going to explain that? What had I been thinking laying those cards out? I hadn't been thinking. I had wedding brain.

"All right...Robert Pearson, Raylan Beauthorpe—he also could've done it on his way out and made up the story about seeing someone hopping the brick wall to throw us off—and of course Olivia Beauthorpe, who you seem not to have a card for." Nate's gaze locked on mine.

"Right. I assume she's innocent. Robert and Raylan too. I don't know why I made cards for them or the dead folks. Those are people who used to live there. One of the, umm, girls told me their story. William Rutledge was found dead about a year ago in North Charleston. Roxanne Trexler was his mistress. She lived in the empty room over the garage, and Seth was crazy about her. The girls were told she went home. I'm thinking there's a possibility whoever killed William killed her too, but the body hasn't been found."

I kept my gaze neutral.

Nate said, "Occasionally, more and more often, in fact, I have a strong notion you're leaving things out that you don't want to tell me. It's an unsettling feeling for a man about to make a trip to the altar."

I closed my eyes and inhaled, then opened them and looked directly at Nate. "I give you my word I'm telling you the truth."

"I don't doubt that," he said. "I'm just not so sure it's the whole truth."

A little piece of me withered every time I had to lie to him. "What, about William Rutledge and Roxanne Trexler? Why would I withhold information about people who are dead and/or missing, who likely have no connection to our case?"

"There's a reason you put those cards out," he said.

I held out my palms.

"They *could* be connected."

Nate looked away, was quiet for a few moments. Then he said, "Let's finish our timeline. We left off at seven forty, which is approximately when Olivia found the body and ran back out to her car to call you."

"Right. That call came in at seven forty-five. That we have documented. And sometime soon after that, Seth discovered the body and commences cleanup."

"So Raylan—and the killer—must've left before seven forty, or Olivia would've crossed paths with at least one of them."

"He wasn't exact on the time—no one was, really. But I think we have the order right."

"What came next?" Nate asked.

"Around eight fifteen, James left through the garage entrance. Olivia was still parked outside. He, Arthur, and William—possibly the others, too—know Olivia owns half the house now."

"Who left next?"

"Arthur, through the keeping room door, also at about eight fifteen. He could've seen Seth carrying Thurston out wrapped in a rug, but claims he didn't see anything unusual. One would hope such a thing would be unusual. He did say he saw Olivia's car, both when he was going in and coming out. Then William left through the front door. He also could've witnessed Seth's cleanup, and would've seen Olivia's car out front. I arrived at eight forty-five. All traces of a crime were gone."

Nate said, "From what the 'young ladies' told you last night, we can infer all four of the men who pay for rooms in that house who were in the country when Thurston Middleton died knew he was asking questions and would likely make trouble for them. Three of them—Calhoun, Huger, and Russell—were in the house the night Middleton died. Two of them—Calhoun and Russell—have firm alibis for the time of death. Which leaves us with James Huger."

"From our remaining suspect pool on the quilt," I said, "our theoretical motives fit *four* people. James Huger, Dana Clark, Henry Prioleau, or Heather Wilder. I'm not sure Dana or Heather could've done it, given their height and Thurston's, and the weight of that pineapple."

"Which means," said Nate, "that either James Huger or Henry Prioleau is our culprit. Neither Robert nor Raylan would've had a motive to kill Thurston—nor would Olivia."

"We need forensics to tell us for sure if the women can be eliminated." I knew they could because Colleen had told me. But I couldn't tell Nate that.

"Which is why we're going to call Sonny right now."

NINETEEN

Sonny agreed to meet us at the bed and breakfast. We could talk much more freely in our room than in one of the local lunch spots. Because we were starving, Nate ordered more sandwiches from Bull Street Market.

Nate let Sonny in. He stared at me with this surly expression for way too long. Finally, he said, "We go way back. But our professional relationship is built on trust."

"You're mighty right it is," I said, staring him down. "And that means if I don't answer the phone, you should *trust* that I have a very good reason."

Sonny closed his eyes, rolled his lips in, put a hand to his head and shook it. "No. No. What that means is that I have to be able to trust that when I need you to pick up the damn phone and give me straight answers, you will *do* that."

I sat in one of the three chairs we'd arranged in a triangle. "Sonny, there are times you really don't want to know what you're asking. You just think you do."

"We're all a little stressed here." Nate sat in the chair to my right. "Sonny, I believe you'll find what we have for you very helpful."

Sonny huffed out a breath and sat in the remaining chair. "Let's hear it."

"Monday night, Olivia called me in a panic..." I started at the beginning and worked my way through Tuesday morning exactly as it had happened, leaving out nothing except Colleen.

"Well, that explains why you were asking about missing persons, and why you wanted to know what Thurston Middleton was wearing," Sonny said. "But what I don't get is why you couldn't've just picked up the phone when I called you back Monday afternoon and told me all that."

"Because at that point," I said, "we didn't know that Olivia hadn't had some sort of breakdown. I was in that house an hour after she called to tell me Robert was dead on the floor, and there was no sign of a crime. None."

Nate said, "It was reasonable to vet our information before we clouded your homicide investigation with something that could've well been a figment of Olivia's imagination."

Sonny sat back in his chair and crossed his ankles. "How did you do that, exactly? And how did you arrive at the conclusion that the body in the house across the street was in fact Thurston Middleton?"

"I spoke to Julia Middleton," I said. "I expect you've spoken to her by now about Thurston's investigation into the 'boardinghouse' and their association years ago."

"As a matter of fact, I have. And I have a search warrant for the premises which we'll execute immediately after we finish here. Julia didn't mention you."

I shrugged. "She's discreet. We have a lot more to tell you, but first, did you happen to get an anonymous tip regarding a rug that might be in a dumpster in North Charleston?"

Sonny heaved a massive sigh, crossed his arms. "Why yes I did. How did you know that?"

"I heard a rumor somewhere. Did you find the rug?"

"We found an expensive-looking light-colored rug with blood on it. The lab has it. We don't know there's a connection, but we will soon." His tone softened. "I don't want to know how you knew where to find that, do I?"

Nate said, "We're just happy you found it."

"I'm grateful to whoever called in that tip," said Sonny. "That rug would've been in the landfill before we even knew to look for one. And we would've never known where to look. But it would be nice to know that no laws were broken in getting that evidence."

I nodded. "It's important that evidence as critical as that rug hold up in court—not be the fruit of some poisonous tree or other."

Sonny looked away. He'd received my message. "What else do you have for me?"

"We have a great many anonymous tips," I said. "Do you want them or not?"

"*Dammit*, Liz." He looked from me to Nate and back.

"This is a complicated case," said Nate. "I predict you'll be glad for the information."

After a long pause, Sonny said, "Yes. Please. I'll take all the tips you have."

"You'll need to take notes," I said. "Trust me. I'd give you mine, but they're electronic, and that would ruin the whole anonymous thing." He pulled a pad and pen from his jacket pocket. "In a desk in the right parlor, you'll find a rent ledger. The most recent names are Calhoun, Gibbes, Huger, Prioleau, and Russell." I walked him through the first names that went with those surnames, and the associated women. I told him everything he needed to know, including the timeline we'd built, which should save him considerable time. I left out all mention of cameras, phone tapping, guardian spirits, ghosts, et cetera.

He made a few final notes, then asked, "Why again did you take these women to your house?"

I said, "Because we don't know who killed Thurston Middleton. And regardless of who did, when these men go to protecting their family fortunes from divorce attorneys, they may well try to cover their tracks. But we knew you'd need to talk to them, so we stashed them in a safe place."

"There's already been an attempt along those lines." Nate filled him in on the knife-carrying burglar. "Whoever it was had a key. Which means one of the patrons, or perhaps a former patron. He likely planned to get rid of anyone or anything tying them to that house—especially the women who could be called to testify."

Sonny said, "And Blake is holding Seth on blackmail and communicating threat charges."

"That's right," Nate said.

I said, "The judge will be back tomorrow morning."

Sonny nodded. "Good to know. We should have some hair and fiber evidence tying him to that rug. The warrant we have covers his truck. I'd better get someone over to Stella Maris. Is that everything?" He looked tired.

I winced. "When you serve the warrant, are you going to let cadaver dogs sniff around the yard?"

"What?" Nate gave me a look that said, *Here we go again.*

Sonny was quiet for a moment. "Given that we found that rug in the same dumpster where William Rutledge turned up a year ago, and the high profile nature of that particular cold case, I don't think that would be unreasonable."

Nate muttered, "William Rutledge." He looked at me for a long moment, then away.

I handed Sonny a sandwich. "You'd best eat. It's going to be a long afternoon."

"Thanks," he said. He unwrapped it and dug in.

I passed around drinks and Nate and I opened our sandwiches as well.

"Sonny?" I said, a few bites in. Maybe the food had taken the edge off his irritation.

He looked up at me, chewing slowly.

"When you know if Thurston could've been killed by a woman—if the angle is right, the upper body strength fits—will you let us know? We'll sleep better knowing none of the women staying at our house could possibly be murderers." And that my friend wasn't in danger of being arrested.

He closed his eyes and nodded.

TWENTY

We watched out the window as Sonny met two other Charleston PD detectives on the sidewalk. Moments later, a forensics unit arrived and parked on the street.

"I feel bad for Miss Dean," I said.

"Why? She's knowingly run a business that provides illicit services to married men for years. She's either remained silent when Seth committed and covered up heinous crimes, or she's been a party to them. Maybe even manipulated him into doing her dirty work."

"I just don't think she set out to do any of those things. She and her sister just wanted to save the family home."

"Regardless," said Nate. "At some point she crossed a line and she skipped right along and never looked back."

Across the street, the detectives and forensics team entered the door to the porch.

I heaved a deep sigh. "We haven't finished the job."

"This is Sonny's case now. Olivia's blackmailer is incarcerated."

"Still. I hate leaving a puzzle half-finished on the table."

Nate turned to look at me. "Well, I suppose an argument could be made that it's our duty to interview Miss Dean's current clientele in order to certify no one else was caught up in Seth's blackmail scheme."

"Exactly. Because we were hired to investigate the blackmail. Which has nothing to do with Thurston Middleton's murder, as far as we've been able to prove thus far."

"We wouldn't be doing our jobs if we didn't tie up the loose ends."

"Precisely." I offered him my sunniest smile. "And what kind of friends would we be to Sonny if we didn't check out those last few remaining alibi issues while we're at it? Save him a lot of time..."

Of the five current patrons at Miss Willowdean's cathouse, Dr. William Calhoun was our first priority. He was a potential witness. Before we questioned suspects, we needed to know if he'd seen anyone we hadn't accounted for or witnessed Seth's crime scene cleanup at 12 Church Street Monday night on his way out.

Dr. Calhoun was with a patient according to his receptionist, and no, he couldn't work me in. Appointments were booked four months in advance, she informed me, and his afternoon was booked solid and she highly doubted he would have a cancellation.

I'd already interviewed Arthur Russell. We knew he had an alibi and nothing to contribute to our investigation. And Nathaniel Gibbes was out of the country. That left our two top suspects.

Nate called and made an appointment with Henry Prioleau for one o'clock on the pretext we had emergency rehearsal dinner needs. Our original venue had canceled last minute. The receptionist enthusiastically confirmed he'd be happy to speak with us.

James Huger, CEO of Huger International, a holding company with offices on Broad Street, agreed to see us at two thirty. His secretary failed to hide the surprise in her voice when she came back on the line to confirm the appointment. We'd asked her to tell him our meeting request was in regards to Miss Willowdean Beauthorpe.

Henry Prioleau was vice president of the company that owned his family's chain of fine dining restaurants. Rut's New South Cuisine was named for Rutledge Prioleau, Henry's grandfather. The offices were on the top floor of the original restaurant on East Bay, just up from North Market. The building was red brick and was perhaps once a hardware store or some such thing.

His secretary told us to come in the side entrance and take the elevator to the third floor. We stepped from the elevator into a reception area.

"Hey, how are y'all?" A perky, petite woman with burnished brown hair stood.

"We're good. Hope you are. I'm Nate Andrews. This is my fiancé, Liz Talbot. We called about the last minute rehearsal dinner?"

"Of course," she said. "Now normally, someone in catering would help you with that, but you asked for Henry, right?"

Nate said, "We did. A friend of ours recommended him personally."

"I'm sure he'll be happy to help you. Right this way."

She led us towards the right front corner of the building. We approached a desk sitting outside of one of the offices. The receptionist said, "This is Gail, Henry's secretary. Y'all have a good day."

"You, too," I said.

"Hey, how are y'all?" Gail, an effervescent blonde, stood.

"We're good." Nate smiled.

Julia Middleton's comments on how the Prioleau family took their Southern friendly brand to extremes floated across my mind.

"Right this way." She escorted us the remaining twelve feet to a corner office overlooking East Bay. She knocked once and opened the door.

Henry was on his feet and moving towards us with a big smile. "Hey, how are y'all?"

"Good. And you?" Nate took the hand Henry offered.

"I'm great. Just great. I'm so glad you're here." He held onto Nate's hand for an abnormally long time, patted him on the back. I thought for a minute he was going to hug him. "Gail here tells me your big day is Saturday and you had some trouble come up with your rehearsal dinner venue for Friday night."

"That's right," said Nate. "We'd be grateful if you could help us out."

"Of course. We'd be happy to. Have a seat." Henry gestured to a pair of leather chairs in front of his desk.

I said, "Have we met before? You seem awfully familiar to me."

Henry took a seat behind his desk. "You've probably seen me in the restaurant. Our whole family works the floor here in our original location. We want to make sure everyone who comes in feels welcome—like family."

"I bet that's it," I said. "We were just here Monday night." We'd never dined at Rut's New South Cuisine.

He grinned. "I probably opened the door for you. I was at the door during the early evening, then working the floor chatting with folks. Did you sit downstairs or up?"

"Upstairs," said Nate.

Henry's face creased in confusion. "It's not like me to forget folks. I must be working too hard."

I said, "In fairness, we were deep into wedding discussions."

Nate said, "Likely we gave off an uninviting vibe."

Henry shook off his confusion. "In any case, we can offer you the private room upstairs. How many are you expecting for your rehearsal dinner?"

"Oh my," I said. "I was hoping to have it at my parents' house. We're going to have a hundred guests. The tents will already be up for the reception."

Henry winced. "A hundred people, you say? At your rehearsal dinner?"

"Yes," I said, "it's so close to Christmas and all. Our families are coming in early. We have big families."

"I see," said Henry. "Unfortunately, we don't do offsite events. And our private dining room will only accommodate thirty in any case. I'm surprised Gail didn't mention that."

"I'm so flustered these days," I said. "There's no telling. I'm sure it's my mistake. We have several meetings set up this afternoon."

Nate stood. "Sweetheart, with that in mind, we'd best get out of Mr. Prioleau's hair. We have several more stops to make."

Henry stood. "I'm terribly sorry we couldn't help you. Y'all come see us when you get back from your honeymoon."

"We'll do that," Nate said.

"Sweetheart," I said, "Don't forget, we promised to stop by Julia's as well."

"Of course," Nate said. "Such a tragedy."

"Do you know them?" I asked. "The Middletons?"

Henry's face went as solemn as an undertaker's. "Yes, of course. Such a shame. I don't know them well, but they were our customers. And naturally we're familiar with all they do for the community."

In a hushed tone, I said, "I just can't believe the rumors goin' 'round."

Henry stilled.

"Rumors? What rumors would those be?"

"You haven't heard?" I asked. "Apparently, Thurston was being blackmailed by some deplorable reprobate runnin' a bawdy house over on Church Street."

"That is scandalous," said Henry. "If you'll excuse me, I have another appointment."

I met his eyes squarely. "No one's been blackmailing you, have they, Mr. Prioleau?"

Something dark flickered in Henry's eyes. Then the jovial restauranteur was back. "Thank goodness I don't have to worry about that. Poor Thurston, my goodness. I hate to hear such things about such a good man." He showed us to the door.

We said our good-byes to Henry, then to the two girls up front.

Back out on the street, I said, "Those folks are almost pathologically friendly. Even for Southerners."

"Yeah," said Nate. "Something was a little too frenetic in their Southern friendly."

"Did you see the look on his face when I asked him about blackmail?"

"I did indeed. I think young Henry was badly rattled."

"He has an alibi for Monday night," I said.

"Nice sport coat."

I shook my head, "Sport coats are common attire. That doesn't prove anything."

"No, it doesn't. But it makes you think. Makes you wonder how hard it would be for the vice president to slip away from floor duty for a while. It's less than a ten minute walk from here to the cathouse."

I studied the cars in the parking lot. "You know what isn't here?"

Nate's gaze followed mine. "Young Henry's Mercedes."

I snapped a photo of the license plate on a brushed steel and red Ducati. "It would take a lot less than ten minutes on a motorcycle." For good measure, I got every plate in the off-street parking lot.

"Good afternoon. Can we get y'all anything to drink?" James Huger was the epitome of a Southern gentleman. If I wasn't mistaken, his was the voice on the phone with Miss Dean when she called "John."

"Thank you," Nate said. "We're fine."

"Did I understand correctly? You all are private investigators?"

"That's right," I said.

"Please, have a seat." James gestured to a leather sofa in a conversation area across the office from his desk. He took the wingback chair.

"You have a lovely family," I said. On walls and shelves in his well-appointed office, photos of James Huger with his elegant wife and their five children outnumbered the photos of him with dignitaries, but not by much. The family photos were candid shots from far-flung vacations. Everyone was smiling, laughing. I recalled how Julia Middleton had said James doted on his wife.

"Thank you," he said. "I'm very proud of them. Family is very important to me. To most of us, I suppose. Now. Please tell me, is everything all right with Miss Willowdean?"

I focused hard on not thinking about the contents of the playroom over the garage. "I'm afraid not."

"Is it her heart?" James asked. "I've tried to get her to see a cardiologist. Anyone fortunate enough to reach her age needs to see one regularly."

I said, "As far as I know, her heart is fine. Mr. Huger, can we speak confidentially?"

"Of course," he said.

"You were friends with Thurston Middleton, is that correct?" I asked.

He winced. Pain coated his words. "My whole life. He was like a brother to me. I was one of his chief supporters in his upcoming political campaign. Such a tragedy. My wife and I are grieving. And of course I'm heartbroken for Julia and the boys."

I nodded. "Did you know Seth Quinlan was blackmailing him?"

"I had no idea." He seemed genuinely surprised. "What possible grounds would he have had? Thurston was as straight an arrow as they come."

"Apparently," Nate said, "a long time ago, when Miss Willowdean and her sister first opened their boardinghouse—back when it *was* a simple boardinghouse—Julia lived there for a while. Thurston paid her rent to help Miss Willowdean get her business started. But in light of how the establishment has evolved over the years, and given Mr. Middleton's political aspirations, Seth believed he'd found a cash cow."

James was as cool as a cucumber.

"That's disturbing, to be sure. Do you believe there's a connection to Thurston's death?"

I said, "We're not sure what to believe. What do you think, Mr. Huger?"

"It's certainly possible, I suppose."

"Has Seth or anyone else ever attempted to blackmail you, Mr. Huger?" I asked.

His smile was genuine, though still tinged with grief. He seemed relaxed. "Me? No. There wouldn't be any point in that. People tell tall tales on folks with money all the time. One of the very few downsides to wealth. My solid record of public service speaks for itself, I'd like to think. People generally believe what they want to believe. To be honest, I've never much cared what strangers think of me."

My instincts said this wasn't our guy, partly because of what Colleen had said about Dana's secret not being relevant. But I also had the sense that his grief over Thurston's death was genuine— that he would help us if he could. "Did you happen to be driving through the neighborhood Monday evening?"

He flashed me a conspiratorial little smile. "Yes, as a matter of fact, I was. I had to run out right at dinnertime. Business." He shook his head as if to say, *It's always something.* "I would've driven by Miss Willowdean's house around seven, maybe a couple minutes after. Then again on my way back home about eight fifteen."

I didn't grill him about how that worked, what with him living on East Battery and lower Church being a one-way street a block out of his way to most places.

"Did you see anyone coming or going? Anything unusual going on?" I asked.

He pressed his lips together, shook his head. "I wish I could help. The only thing I noticed—and this isn't unusual at all—was that Miss Willowdean's niece was by to visit. Her car was parked on the street."

I changed channels quickly to gauge his response.

"I have racked my brain trying to figure out why a man would pay for two rooms at Miss Willowdean's."

"That is an intriguing question."

James looked directly at me.

"Especially a man who is so devoted to his wife and children."

Nate said, "Where on earth would one man get the time for three women?"

James laughed. "I can't imagine."

"Would you like to know my theory?" I asked.

"I'd be fascinated," said James.

"I think a man with five children, a live-in household staff, a wife off the cover of a magazine, and a historic home with interior walls that aren't well-insulated would have a unique problem."

Nate cheated a glance at me, then straightened in his chair.

James smiled. "I would agree with your assessment. Such a man would face challenges."

"How in the world would the couple ever enjoy privacy?" I mused. "Hotels certainly aren't the answer. Those walls would be even thinner."

"Indeed." James held my gaze, not quite smiling any longer.

"If the man were a true Southern gentleman such as yourself, his wife's privacy would be of the utmost concern."

He looked away, then back. "It would be his highest priority after his family's safety and well-being."

"And if money were not an issue, this hypothetical man could probably find a way to help out a neighbor in need and a college student while solving his own problems. He could even pay for some high-end upgrades to the neighbor's house so that it suited his needs."

James nodded. "I imagine he could."

"And if it all came out," I said, "well, it couldn't really *all* come out, could it? The gentleman's reputation might suffer. But no one would ever know his wife had ever visited his neighbor's home...except the college student who served as his cover story. And she'd be far too grateful that she didn't have student loans to ever breathe a word." James stared out the window.

"Of course," I said, "over time there would likely be more than one college student. But it would be helpful if they planned on grad school. All the better if they volunteered for medical relief programs and traveled extensively."

Nate said, "The two rooms over the garage have a virtually private entrance. Everyone who comes and goes at that house is concerned about keeping their own business quiet, not taking attendance on the young ladies who live there and checking it against patron visits."

James said, "In a hypothetical situation such as you describe, no doubt the neighbor originally ran a boardinghouse. She's likely been taken advantage of by men who aren't as devoted to their wives."

"The only remaining question I have," I said, "is would such a man resort to murder to protect his wife's privacy and reputation."

A startled look flashed across his face. "I would imagine these hypothetical people would both be horrified by the very idea. They would alibi each other, of course, which could be problematic. Except neither of them would have a motive." He met my gaze with sober, sincere eyes. "A reputation would never be worth a life."

I studied him for a moment, nodded. Then I stood and laid my card on the coffee table. "If you think of anything that might be helpful in solving Thurston's murder or protecting the other young women, please give us a call."

"Certainly. And if you could do me the great favor of being as discreet as possible with your inquiries, I would be very grateful. You never know when having someone in your debt could prove helpful. Especially someone with my resources and connections."

"Mr. Huger," I said, "we have no interest in, nor the stomach for, embarrassing you or your wife."

He nodded.

We walked out of the building and down Broad Street to our parking space. As we buckled in, Nate said, "Well, that was interesting."

"Indeed, it was. Mr. Huger is a complex man, to say the least. I wish he knew something we didn't. He seems to genuinely want to help."

"I'll say this," Nate said. "He goes to a great deal of trouble to be alone with his wife."

*   *   *

After our positive experience with James Huger, Nate and I decided to try the direct approach with our last subject. Perhaps he would likewise be filled with the spirit of cooperation. Dr. William Calhoun's office was in one of the Medical University of South Carolina buildings over on Jonathan Lucas Street. Nate camped out in the waiting room. I waited at the elevator in case there was a back entrance to his office. We both had earwigs in so we could easily communicate.

At four fifteen, Nate said, "He's on his way out."

"Roger that." I pretended to dig in my purse. A few minutes later, Dr. Calhoun walked towards me in khakis and a long-sleeved, blue button-down.

I looked up from my purse and smiled.

He smiled and pressed the down button.

"Oh, I feel so silly. I was distracted and forgot to push the button."

"It happens to me some days."

The elevator arrived and we both stepped on. In my ear, Nate said, "Taking the stairs."

The elevator doors closed. Two seconds later, I said, "Dr. Calhoun, I apologize in advance for this shameful breach in etiquette."

He gave me a quizzical look. "How do you know my name? Are you a patient?"

"No, I'm a private investigator."

He stiffened.

"I have no desire to hang your dirty laundry out on the line. If you'll answer two quick questions for me, I'll be on my way. Has anyone attempted to blackmail you regarding your patronage of the house at 12 Church Street?"

He stared straight ahead, not acknowledging my presence. The elevator doors opened on the first floor. Dr. Calhoun took off at a fast clip. I kept pace. Nate fell in behind.

"Dr. Calhoun? Did you see anyone doing anything unusual Monday night as you were leaving? This could be very important."

He kept walking and didn't say one word.

"Of course, I could stop by the house later and speak with you and your wife, if that's more convenient." A beauty queen, Julia had said—likely a vindictive one.

Dr. Calhoun said, "If you show up at my house, I'll call the police."

"That'd be great," I said. "It would save us all a lot of time."

He stopped on the sidewalk.

"Perhaps you should stop by the psychiatry department while you're here. Or maybe schedule an MRI. If it turns out your mental problems are caused by a brain tumor, give my office a call to schedule a consult."

He crossed the street to a parking garage.

I followed, with Nate a few steps behind. "Truly, if you answer my questions, you'll never see me again."

Dr. Calhoun stopped at the garage entrance. "I don't know what house on Church Street you're referring to. I haven't visited any house on Church Street this week, or in recent memory for that matter, so I could hardly have seen anyone as I was leaving."

I didn't care the teensiest bit for his tone. "I have photos," I said. "I can put you and your car at that house many, many nights." Okay, so I exaggerated.

His face took on a menacing look. "Are you trying to blackmail me?"

"Not at all. But I'd like to know if someone else has attempted to blackmail you."

He stared at me, didn't say a word.

"Did you see anyone inside the house Monday night as you came in at approximately seven-eighteen, or as you were leaving at approximately eight thirty-five?"

He got in my face. A bit of spittle was on his lip, giving him the look of a rabid dog.

Nate stepped between us. "Back off."

Dr. Calhoun gave himself a little shake, composed himself. "This young woman is in need of medical attention." He turned and walked away.

"He has a quick temper," I said.

"Indeed he does," said Nate. "And he's disinclined to be helpful. Slugger, I think we need to pack up our toys and go home. Sonny will get to Dr. Calhoun soon enough. You and I have a honeymoon to plan. We've given Robert more than the day we promised. Olivia is shed of her blackmailer. Our work here is done."

"All right," I said. "I just hate leaving puzzle pieces on the table."

"Come along and I'll see if I can distract you from worrying about your puzzle." His smile worked better on me than anyone.

We held hands and walked towards the Explorer, which was parked one level up in the garage.

Nate's phone rang. He glanced at the screen. "Here we go."

He pressed the button to accept the call. "Mother. Have y'all made it in?"

He looked at me, his expression one of a trapped animal. "That sounds nice. What time were y'all thinking?...You want us to pick you up?...All right then. See you soon. Bye now."

I said. "They're here?"

"Just checked into the Market Pavillion hotel over on East Bay. You'll never believe where Dad made dinner reservations."

"Seriously?"

"Oh yes. Rut's New South Cuisine is very convenient to their hotel and they're tired from the trip."

I felt a little jolt of joy. "That will give us another go at Henry. See, fate intervened on behalf of my puzzle. I'm going to have to freshen up. It's a good thing we went ahead and paid for another night at the bed and breakfast. But I really need a change of clothes. What time is our reservation?"

"Not 'til seven. We have plenty of time to go shopping."

"Why Mr. Andrews, you say the sweetest things."

"Now see, here is the part where I was looking forward—after the wedding—to being able to say something like, 'Mrs. Andrews, you look so beautiful in everything you put on, it's a pleasure to take you shopping.'"

"It bothers you, doesn't it? That I want to keep my name."

"Sometimes. You bring out the old-fashioned in me."

"But it doesn't—"

The sound of rubber on concrete, taking a corner too fast, interrupted me.

A familiar BMW hurled towards us.

Nate shoved me between two parked cars, then leaped after me. I scrambled for balance, grabbing ahold of the sedan in front of me with one hand and Nate with the other. We steadied each other. The car blew past us. The driver slammed on brakes, tires screeching.

The car rolled backwards at an angle, coming to a stop inches from the backs of the cars we'd taken refuge between. Through tinted windows, we could clearly see Dr. Calhoun. He revved the engine twice, then drove off.

"I'd say that was meant to convey a message," said Nate.

TWENTY-ONE

The Scoop car pulled to the curb on East Bay. Nate tipped the driver, hopped out, then circled around the back of the car. He opened my door and reached in to offer me his hand. I smiled my thanks, my eyes holding his smoky blues.

Nate murmured in my ear, "You look stunning. I can't wait to unwrap my Christmas present."

"So that's what this new dress is?" I grinned. "Wrapping?" I'd picked out a darling gold shimmery dress with a fitted waist and flared skirt at Anne's on King Street and still had time to stop by Bob Ellis for a pair of strappy heels of a suggestive height.

"Absolutely." He laced his fingers through mine and we waited for the Scoop car to drive away.

Across the street, the entrance to Rut's New South Cuisine was decked out in full holiday regalia. Garlands of fresh greenery with white lights and bows draped the large glass storefront windows and the double door. Ivy topiaries with more lights and bows in large gold pots stood on either side of the entrance. Our favorite restauranteur stood just outside the door chatting with a group of folks like they were old friends.

Traffic cleared and we crossed East Bay. Henry Prioleau caught sight of us. He patted the man he'd been speaking to on the back and stepped in our direction. "Well, look who's here. Y'all joining us for dinner again this evening? That's twice in one week. We must be doing something right." His smile didn't reach his eyes. He opened the door for us. The noise level inside hit me like a wall.

"We're meeting my parents," Nate said. "I believe they may already be here. Andrews, party of four?"

"Of course," said Henry. "Are y'all celebrating a special occasion with us this evening?"

Nate and I exchanged a glance. Henry didn't wait for a response. He escorted us three steps to the first in what appeared to be a line of hostesses. "The remainder of the Andrews party is here. Y'all enjoy your dinner." He hovered a moment, then stepped back towards the door.

The hostess looked at him as if she'd missed her cue. Finally she said, "Hey, how are y'all?"

"We're fine, thanks," said Nate.

"Are y'all celebrating a special occasion with us this evening?"

There wasn't a simple answer to that question. Nate said, "Just the season."

I could barely hear him over the cacophony of too many voices straining to be heard above the baby grand piano, at which someone was playing "Winter Wonderland" at three times the customary speed.

"Welcome!" The hostess's smile was wide and bright. She led us towards a sweeping staircase.

"Maybe it'll be quieter upstairs," Nate said in my ear.

"If not, I predict your mother is not going to be happy. And she already isn't happy." Glynneth Sloane McBee Andrews had not been happy when I married her older son. She quite possibly held me accountable for him turning out to be a scoundrel of the first order.

"Now, Slugger, that's not true."

I raised an eyebrow at him. He put his hand on the small of my back and we proceeded to the top of the steps. At the landing, the hostess paused at another hostess stand. An older woman standing there said, "Hey, how are y'all?"

"Great," said Nate.

"Are y'all celebrating a special occasion with us this evening?" Her smile was even wider and brighter than the hostess's.

"Just the season." Nate smiled.

"I just want to personally welcome you!" she said.

We nodded and smiled our thanks.

The hostess led us past her and into a room where it was thankfully, a few decibels quieter—at first. The farther we went towards the back wall, the louder the din. I spotted the Andrewses at a table near a front window. Nate and I waved at the same time.

Mr. and Mrs. Andrews stood as we approached. Mr. Andrews looked fit and distinguished, just a bit of grey at the temples. Blessed with timeless beauty, Mrs. Andrews's classic blond bob, high cheekbones, and flawless skin attested to her superb gene pool. One of the many things she held against me was, owing to a bad case of endometriosis that led to a complete hysterectomy, I would not be giving her grandchildren.

"Darling." Mrs. Andrews reached for Nate.

"Mother." He stepped in and gave her a hug.

"Liz, good to see you," said Mr. Andrews.

"Good to see you too, Mr. Andrews," I said.

"Oh, for Pete's sake. If you can't call me Zach, I don't know who should." He stepped around his wife to give me a quick hug.

"Elizabeth," she said. She didn't enunciate it quite as clearly as my own mamma when she was displeased, but somehow it came out sounding like I was in trouble.

"Hey, Mrs. Andrews," I said.

"You must call me Glyn." It came out sounding like a pronouncement.

Progress. In the entire time I'd been married to Scott, she'd never suggested such a thing. Glyn was what her friends called her.

I smiled. "Glyn. It's good to see you."

Nate and his dad exchanged a quick handshake-half-hug-shoulder slap.

"Hey, Dad," said Nate.

"Son."

The hostess hovered until we were all seated. "Tyler will be your head waiter. He'll be with you in just a moment."

"It's terribly loud in here," said Glyn.

"Yes, it surely is," I said. "I didn't realize it, but the wall behind us opens to the staircase. The piano music is funneled up to this end of the room."

"I'm sorry about that," said Zach. "The restaurant is highly rated on TripAdvisor."

"I'm sure we'll grow accustomed to it," I said. "And I've heard the food is divine." This was a stretch. But clearly, Zach had tried to pick a pleasant restaurant. We all had our happy faces on. I wanted to keep it that way.

"How are y'all this evening?" A young gentleman in dark slacks and shirt with a tie stepped up to the table.

"We're well, thank you," said Zach.

"I'm Tyler. I'll be serving you this evening." His smile was freakishly gay, his energy level positively zippy.

Was everyone who worked here on something?

Tyler handed us menus and left the wine list with Zach. "If you'd like, I can send over the sommelier to help with a wine selection."

Zach said, "I'm sure we can figure it out. Shall we start with cocktails?" He glanced around the table.

"Please," said Glyn.

"I'll have Woodford Reserve on the rocks," said Zach. "A Grey Goose cosmopolitan for my wife."

Nate said, "Wood Reserve, rocks, and the lady will have a Grey Goose pomegranate martini."

"Very well then." Tyler smiled, nodded, executed an about face, and disappeared.

"How many times have y'all been greeted and asked if you were celebrating a special occasion?" Nate grinned.

"I've lost count," said Zach.

"How was your flight?" I asked.

"Fine," said Zach. "We arrived safely, on time, and our luggage arrived with us. You can't ask for much more than that these days."

"I remember when flying was a treat," said Glyn. Her forehead creased. "I declare, it's amazing that piano player's fingers can move so fast. I've never heard 'Jingle Bells' at quite that pace."

Her right hand moved to her temple. I couldn't help but notice the two carat round diamond ring with sapphire side stones. I'd returned it to her when Scott and I divorced. It had been Zach's mother's ring and was meant for Scott's wife.

I played with my current engagement ring. It had been Gram's—my grandmother's—engagement ring. Nate would've bought me anything I wanted, but I wanted to wear Gram's ring. It was a lovely emerald cut stone, too pretty to leave in a box. For the first time, I missed having something he'd given me on my hand. Three more days.

"...to Florida to see us in the spring." Zach and Nate had been chatting.

Glyn said, "Yes, of course you must come. Before it gets too hot. We'll likely go back to Greenville for the summer. Or somewhere farther north. I can't stand the heat the way I once could."

"Highlands, North Carolina is nice," I said. "The summers there are milder, I understand."

Tyler brought our cocktails. As he set them in front of us, he said, "Sir, I'll be happy to send the sommelier over to help you select a wine."

Zach's smile was tight. "No, thank you."

Tyler did his about face again.

Zach raised an eyebrow, took a deep breath, and let it out. "Let's toast, shall we? Welcome back to the family, Liz." He lifted his glass.

I started to giggle, but smothered it.

Glyn said, "Zachary, really." She sipped her cosmopolitan.

"Thank you so much," I said.

Nate smiled. He was happy his parents were here. Things hadn't been easy for their family since Scott had fled the country.

The piano player raced through "The Christmas Song."

A gentleman in a suit approached the table. "Hey, y'all. I just wanted to stop by and make sure everything was all right here. How's your dinner?"

Zach said, "We haven't ordered yet. Our cocktails were just served."

"I hope they're all right," said the gentleman, who hadn't identified himself.

Glyn smiled, "They're fabulous."

"Wonderful," said the anonymous gentleman in the suit. "Enjoy your dinner."

He'd no sooner left, than another gentleman approached the table. "I'm Eduardo, the sommelier. May I help you select a wine for your dinner?"

Zach appeared to have trouble forming a response.

Nate said, "No, thank you."

"It's really no trouble at all," said Eduardo.

I sipped my drink.

Glyn took a long pull of hers.

In carefully parsed words, Zach said, "No. We would like to choose our own wine, thank you."

The sommelier left. We all drank. The piano raced through "Oh Christmas Tree."

Zach said, "Perhaps we should decide on food."

We all studied our menus. The dishes did sound delicious— lots of creative variations on Southern standards.

"Why don't we start with some oysters?" Nate said.

We all agreed that sounded good. The shrimp and blue cheese grits were calling to me. In short order we'd all decided on entrees. Zach chose a pinot noir that would work well with the steaks he and Nate had chosen, my shrimp, and Glyn's vegetable plate.

As soon as we'd placed our order and the menus had been cleared, I reached into my bag and pulled out the Purell. I smoothed on a generous coat. Who knew who all had handled those menus and what they might be carrying? I returned the hand sanitizer to my purse and glanced up.

Glyn stared at me. She executed a dramatic eye roll and

downed the last of her drink. She set down the glass and looked at Zach.

Zach flagged down a waitress. "Could you please send Tyler by, and let him know we'd like another round of cocktails."

"Certainly, sir." Her expression was something akin to fear. Happy fear. She scampered away.

"Excuse me," I said. "I'll just run and powder my nose." I had no intentions of going to the ladies room. I avoided public restrooms whenever possible. But they were likely near the back, where I'd have a good view of the room.

When I found the restrooms, I took in the scene before me. In addition to the waitstaff, several gentlemen in suits or sport coats, along with two women, one of them the older woman who'd been at the upstairs hostess stand, worked the room. They seemed to be performing an odd square dance, moving from table to table in time to the frenetic music. One of the dancers was Henry Prioleau.

I noticed a recessed area in the wall between the two restrooms. I stepped into the hallway. To my right was the elevator Nate and I had ridden to the third floor offices. It would be an easy matter to take it down and slip outside. I pondered our timeline for a moment. If Henry had slipped out, his intention had been to visit Heather. Since he didn't arrive, something had changed his plans.

"Did you get lost?" Henry stood in the doorway to the hall. His expression was openly hostile.

"I must have." I pushed past him and walked back into the dining room. It was in constant motion. If one of the folks moving from table to table were off the floor for a while, would anyone notice?

I navigated my way back to the table. Our second round of cocktails had arrived and Glyn had already downed half of hers.

Nate stood and held my chair for me.

Glyn said, "Ah. Such a gentleman. Someone raised you right."

"Yes, someone did," I smiled.

Nate said, "There's something I've been meaning to give you."

I tilted my head at him.

"We never did go shopping for engagement jewelry." He pulled out a large velvet box.

My heart went to fluttering.

"This was my grandmother's. She left it for me to give my wife." He opened the box.

The diamond and sapphire necklace was spectacular. The stones glittered in the candlelight.

"*Ohh*. Nate, it's gorgeous."

"Shall I help you put it on?" he asked.

"Please." I lifted my hair, trying hard not to think of the matching ring on Glyn's finger. Did she wear it all the time, or did she wear it for me special?

Nate closed the clasp and I let down my hair. "Thank you, sweetheart. I'm honored to have this lovely family piece."

Glyn finished her cosmopolitan. "Zach, would you order me another drink, please?"

Zach looked at her for a three count. She returned the stare. He flagged down the waiter. "Anyone else?"

"No, thank you," Nate and I said in unison.

Finally, Tyler brought our oysters. I needed a little food on top of a martini and a half. We passed them around. Everyone but Glyn took two.

"Darling," said Zach, "won't you try one of the oysters?"

"No thank you," she said. "Ah. There's my cosmopolitan."

One of the waitstaff set it in front of her.

A few sips in, she said, "Have you children considered adoption?"

Nate said, "We have plenty of time to think about that, Mother."

"Nonsense," she said. "You want to have children when you're young enough to run after them. Past a certain age it gets so much more difficult."

Whatever Nate might have said in response, I'll never know. Henry Prioleau appeared at our table. "Hey, how are y'all this evening?"

"Fine." Nate forced a smile.

"You know, it's the strangest thing," Henry said. "I checked our reservations for Monday night. It bothered me so bad to forget a customer. We didn't have a reservation in either of your names Monday night."

"That's odd," Nate said. "Computers so often lose things, don't they?"

"How're the oysters?" Henry's fake smile nearly reached his ears.

"They're excellent," said Nate.

"Wonderful, wonderful. Are y'all celebrating a special occasion with us this evening? Well, I guess you are. The big day's almost here. Did you work everything out for your rehearsal dinner?"

My insides clenched.

Glyn said, "Really? Are we never going to hear the end of this rehearsal dinner business?" She downed half her third drink.

Nate said, "Mother, everything is fine. We just had a last-minute glitch, but it's all been taken care of."

Henry said, "Y'all enjoy your dinner." He moved on to the next table.

"Honestly," said Glyn. "You'd think the steak Oscar for a hundred the first time you married one of my sons would've satisfied our rehearsal dinner obligation."

"Mother," Nate said, "the rehearsal dinner is a non-issue. Would you like some bread?"

"Bread? You know I don't eat bread. I work hard to maintain my figure." She gave me an appraising look. Glyn was likely a size four.

At five-eight, I was a size ten. I was comfortable with my size. I was fit. All during my three-year marriage to Scott—and even during our engagement—Glyn had sent me diet and self-help books. I glanced out the window.

Zach said, "Perhaps tonight you could make an exception."

A server arrived with our salads. He placed them in front of us and pulled out a peppermill.

Glyn said, "There's dressing on this salad. And croutons. I specifically asked for no dressing or croutons."

The server smiled and nodded.

"I'm terribly sorry. I'll replace it right away."

He took Glyn's salad and disappeared. He returned momentarily with a new one.

As he set it in front of her, Glyn said, "I'd like another cosmopolitan."

Zach said, "My dear, do you think that's wise?"

She tossed him a look that could've wilted all our salads.

The server ran away to find another drink. "Carol of the Bells" raced across the keyboard. I sipped my martini. Nate put his hand on my leg. I picked up my fork. "These salads look delicious."

Between the salads and the entrees, Zach excused himself. Nate squeezed my knee.

Glyn said, "Elizabeth, really—"

Henry appeared and interrupted her. "How are those salads?"

Glyn said, "Well, if you must know, I was first served one with dressing and croutons. I specifically asked for neither. This one seems satisfactory, though unremarkable."

Henry turned red in the face. He opened his mouth, but before he could speak, the woman I assumed was his mother grabbed his arm. "Henry, I need to speak with you for a moment."

He gave me a look of pure hatred, but walked away. Why me? I hadn't complained about the salad, though he'd likely poisoned mine. Did his mother keep him on a short leash after reading some of the negative TripAdvisor reviews? If so, perhaps he couldn't have slipped out.

Zach returned to the table.

Glyn said, "You missed the young man who stopped by earlier."

"No I didn't," said Zach. "Apparently, you have to shake his hand before you can go to the bathroom here."

By the time we'd finished our entrees, which were excellent, no fewer than eight people had stopped by to say hey and make sure our dinner was all right. The constant interruptions were almost a blessing in that they limited the need for conversation.

Glyn had picked at her food, but kept her thirst quenched. "Elizabeth, if you manage to drive Nate to a life of crime with your excessive demands for material things, I'm afraid I'm all out of sons."

I stared at her. Excessive demands? Material things? Scott was the materialistic one, not me.

Zach said, "Glyn, you've been overserved. That was uncalled for."

Nate looked at his dad as he rose, pulling me up along with him. "I'm going to take Liz home now. We'll see y'all on Friday." He tossed his napkin on the table, and with one hand at the small of my back, he escorted me downstairs.

The piano player dashed out "Hard Candy Christmas."

"Happy anniversary!" the bevy of hostesses shouted as we walked out the front door.

TWENTY-TWO

Thursday morning, I was so relieved to wake up in my own bed, I hated to get out of it. Nate and Rhett encouraged me into my running togs. We ran our usual route, with Rhett particularly happy for a return to our routine. Waves breaking, rushing to the sand, and sluicing back out made a perfect harmony. Pent-up stress left my body.

"If I apologized every day for the rest of my life, I don't think it could possibly cover last night. But I am so sorry," Nate said. We climbed the steps to the walkway across the dunes.

"You have nothing to apologize for. And yet you have, several times. Let's just forget it."

"When she drinks—"

"The filter comes off her mouth and she says what she really thinks."

Nate sighed. "We won't see them often."

It hurt my heart that he felt like he had to reassure me on this. I knew he loved his parents. Family meant so much to me, and I didn't want to stand between him and his. "In time, maybe she'll be okay with us. We'll go down in the spring like they asked. Just keep her away from the vodka."

Nate grabbed my hand. "Maybe we can get Dad to purge the house before we go."

"Maybe the first trip we can stay in a hotel." I grinned.

*   *   *

After breakfast, I settled into the office to pull all our case notes together and work on the report. Nate finalized our grocery order for St. John. Our villa would be stocked when we arrived. I was so looking forward to being alone with Nate for two weeks.

My phone *boink-boinked*.

"Hey, Sonny."

"Liz." His voice was tight.

"How did the search go?"

"Long. It went very long. We found a rent ledger in the desk drawer. Not much else of note indoors except an astounding variety of bedroom toys."

"I see." My chest tightened. Sonny was working up to why he'd called.

"Outdoors was much more interesting."

I'd seen the crime scene tape when we'd gone back to the bed and breakfast to get our things. "What did you find?"

"Two deceased white females, one who's been under a flowerbed for approximately a year. The other has been under an older flowerbed behind the garage for—we're not sure how long yet. ME's preliminary estimate is three years, give or take."

I breathed in and out. Two?

"Liz?"

"Yeah, I'm here. Any idea who they are?"

"We suspect the newer body is Roxanne Trexler. She's been missing for about a year. Trident Tech student. Her family's on their way in from Ohio. The older body, no idea."

"What did Miss Dean say? She doesn't know who it could be?"

"Miss Willowdean has a bad memory. She's very upset, naturally. Also seems disoriented. From her point of view, everyone in her home disappeared while she was asleep. I thought maybe you and Olivia could talk to her. She may recall more if she sees a familiar face. I don't know that it's a good idea for Olivia to speak with her alone. Too much up in the air."

"What do you mean?" I felt my face scrunch.

"I don't know yet how involved Olivia is in any of this. I'd prefer to have someone I trust be a party to the discussion."

"You don't trust Olivia?"

Sonny blew out a breath. "Someone more stable."

"Sure. Of course. I'll grab Olivia and we'll head on over."

"Thanks. I'm coming over there to get Seth. Fiber analysis connects the rug we found in North Charleston to the back of his truck. They're still working on some stray hairs, a few other tests. It seems William Rutledge was found wrapped in a similar rug. They're pulling that from evidence. I don't think we'll be letting go of Seth anytime soon."

"That's good to hear. Talk to you soon."

I filled Nate in. "I don't think it's a good idea for you to come with Olivia and me. Miss Dean will be more forthcoming if it's just the two of us."

Nate shrugged. "I'll finish the paperwork and get it to Robert. As far as we're officially concerned, that case is closed."

Olivia insisted on taking her own car to Charleston. "I have some shopping to do. I still haven't decided what I'm wearing to the rehearsal dinner. I want to wear something nice, but I don't want to have to change before the bachelorette party. I still wish we could've done that last week."

"Merry's fundraiser—" Merry was the executive director of a non-profit agency in Charleston that worked with at-risk teenagers.

"I know, I know." Olivia held up her hands. "I'm just sayin'...I need to go shopping."

We parked in the same spots we had Monday night. I got out of the car and waited. Olivia was still in her car. I walked up to the driver's side window. Her hands covered her face. "Olivia?"

She opened the door and climbed out none too quickly. "All that yellow tape. I just hate to see today's newspaper."

"Olivia. We'll get through this," I said. "Come on." I nudged her towards the door.

We found Aunt Dean in the keeping room. She was in the chair, which seemed to be her spot, facing the fireplace. Her back was to us as we entered the room.

"Aunt Dean?" Olivia spoke gently.

She didn't respond. Her silver head didn't move.

I moved to the sofa and sat on the corner closest to Miss Dean. Olivia pulled a chair closer to her aunt. Miss Dean's hands lay crossed in her lap. She stared at them.

Olivia reached for one of her hands. She took it between her own and rubbed. "Aunt Dean, are you all right?"

Miss Dean looked up at Olivia. "No," she said. "Everyone's gone. I don't understand."

I felt a pang of guilt. I should've made arrangements for someone to see about Miss Dean yesterday morning when she woke to an empty house. I'd simply not thought about it. What kind of a person was I?

Olivia said, "Aunt Dean, you know the guests are all students. They've gone home for the holidays. But I don't think they're coming back next semester. We'll work something out."

"But where is Seth?" Miss Dean's eyes never moved from Olivia. Her hands grasped Olivia's now.

Olivia's eyes held pain for her aunt. "Seth has done some very bad things. I'm very much afraid Seth is going to jail."

"What on earth?" said Miss Dean.

My highly suspicious nature reared its head. Miss Dean had been through a great deal, yes. But she'd been functional enough to discuss body removal with Seth just two nights ago. "Miss Dean," I said, "do you recall me coming over on Tuesday night?"

She turned to look at me.

"You're Olivia's friend."

"That's right," I said. "We discussed what Olivia saw on Monday night."

"You did this," she said, her voice rising in indignation. "You went to the police with your outrageous accusations about our Seth and now look what's happened. Every bit of this is your fault."

"Now, Aunt Dean—" Olivia said.

"Oh, no ma'am," I said. "I can't take all the credit. I didn't kill anyone, and I didn't remove any bodies. But everyone who did is going to jail. And those of us who know something, we'd best tell it so we don't go to jail too."

Miss Dean looked at Olivia. "Child, tell me you didn't kill that man. I couldn't bear it if you went to jail, too."

Olivia looked like she'd seen a snake. "Me? Why on earth would I kill Thurston Middleton? I barely knew him. When I saw the body, I thought it was Robert."

Miss Dean studied her carefully. "Maybe everything will be all right then."

I said, "Miss Dean, do you honestly not have any idea who killed Thurston?"

She shook her head. "It's been years since he paid for a room here. He must've been looking for my ledger. But why anyone would kill him—it's beyond me."

I said, "Let's talk for a moment about the young ladies in the flowerbeds." Apparently, cadaver dogs have trouble with bodies under concrete and chlorinated water.

Miss Dean stared at the fireplace. "Her name was Roxanne, but I don't recall her last name. I knew her as a Rutledge. William Rutledge's niece. William killed the poor girl. It was an accident. He adored her. Seth did, too. He couldn't bear to have her sent off to Ohio and buried. So he created a memorial for her out back. I thought it was a lovely gesture."

I took a deep breath. "Miss Dean, do you know who the other girl was?"

She met my gaze, clear-eyed, and shook her head. "I don't have the slightest idea."

Olivia patted her hand.

I said, "Can you recall any young ladies a few years back who left abruptly?"

"That does happen occasionally. I could check my ledger, but they took it."

Olivia said, "Think hard, Aunt Dean. Some poor girl's family doesn't know where she is."

Miss Dean stared at the fireplace some more. "Two come to mind that surprised me. I thought they were happy. One was one of Arthur's nieces. He has a gracious plenty." She looked at her hands.

"Do you know what her name was?" I asked.

Miss Dean shook her head. "I can't recall. But they all have red hair. I believe she was from around here."

If that was the case, there should be a missing person's report if she was the girl discovered in the flowerbed behind the garage. "Who was the other girl who surprised you when she left?"

"One of William Calhoun's nieces. He is such a dear man. Such a nice smile. He dotes on his girls. All of them have dark hair like our Amber. This girl's name was Victoria. She left in the middle of the night, just like Arthur's niece. It was right about the same time." She put a finger to her temple. "Victoria left first."

"Was she from around here too?" I asked.

"I don't recall. William could tell you."

I pondered the odds on that.

Olivia said, "Aunt Dean, I'm going to help you get some things together. I want you to come stay with Robert and me for a while. You can spend some time with Campbell and Shelby. Won't that be nice?"

"Oh, no dear. Thank you." Miss Dean patted Olivia's hand. "I'm an old woman. I like being in my own home. Bring the children over to see me, why don't you?"

Olivia's eyes got bigger. I highly doubted she'd be bringing her children over here. "Aunt Dean, it's not safe here. Until they catch Thurston's killer, you really can't stay here alone. I hear you had a prowler Tuesday night."

"That's what the police said. I have a gun, you know."

"Yes, I know," said Olivia. "All the same. Please come stay with us for a while, won't you?"

"You're a sweet child to ask me. But I want to stay here, in my home. This is where I belong."

I said, "Miss Dean, without Seth here to look after you, it really isn't a good idea."

"You girls run along now," said Aunt Dean. "I need a nap."

I looked at Olivia. She gave me a helpless look, shrugged.

I said, "Miss Dean, if anything unusual happens, call 911 first, then call Olivia or me, all right?"

"All right then," she said.

TWENTY-THREE

Of all the men associated with the best little whorehouse in Charleston, James Huger seemed the most normal. His taste in bedroom entertainment maybe should've given me pause, but I don't judge. As long as folks weren't asking me what I do in mine, I couldn't give a tinker's damn what consenting adults did behind closed doors. There were just some things I didn't want to know about.

I called and he agreed to see me right away, shocking his secretary yet again.

"Miss Talbot, what a pleasure," he said. He led me to the seating area where he, Nate, and I had spoken the day before. "What can I do for you?"

"You may have heard what all was found at the house on Church Street."

"Yes. I think they finished up too late to make the print newspapers, but we live in a twenty-four hour news cycle, don't we? I sometimes lament that circumstance."

"I spoke with Miss Dean this morning."

"How is she? I've been quite concerned."

"She seems in shock. Olivia is trying to get her to come stay with them for a while, but she's resistant. Perhaps you could speak to her? I think she respects your counsel a great deal."

"I'll do that very thing," he said. "Perhaps I can get her to see reason. She has no business being in that big old house by herself."

"Thank you," I said. "I wonder if I could ask you to search your memory a bit."

"Certainly."

"Do you recall a couple of young ladies—former residents—who moved out three years or so ago? One was a redhead, and the other a black-haired girl named Victoria."

"You're thinking these are the women found buried in the yard?"

"One of them. The other has been tentatively identified."

"Arthur's redheads tend to run together in one's mind. He has a type, I guess you could say. All local girls. He loves that Charleston accent. Can't abide anything else. I'm afraid I don't recall much about that particular girl except that she did leave rather abruptly."

"And the other girl?"

"Ah. Victoria. Yes, I do remember her. Striking young woman. William has discerning taste. His wife is a blonde. Former Miss Georgia. Finicky sort. He says she's frigid, but what do I know?"

James seemed awfully chatty today.

He gave me a rueful smile. "This is all coming out in the newspaper tomorrow. Most of it anyway. The gossips will feast on it for months. There'll very likely be a movie—you wait and see. I'm happy to tell you anything that proves helpful in identifying that unfortunate young woman."

"Thank you."

He nodded. "If memory serves, the lovely Victoria had a falling out with William. I don't recall the particulars. Only that she left in the middle of the night and no one heard from her again. Now, I'm not suggesting anything here. Make of it what you will."

"How long have you known William Calhoun?"

"All my life. We grew up together."

"Are you close friends?"

"I wouldn't say that, no. We've always run in the same social circles. We're friendly. But I wouldn't invite him over for a dinner party. My wife and his don't get on well."

"Have you ever known him to be violent?" I'd only known him since Tuesday, and I knew he was violent. I wanted to know how forthcoming James was actually being.

He paused for a long moment. "I have reason to suspect he has that tendency."

I nodded. "Do you know anything about Victoria? Where she went to school? If she was local? What her real name might've been?"

"William has a type as well. He likes very bright women, often in financial studies. Several of his alums are now successful investment bankers. She may or may not have been from Charleston, but she went to school here, likely at the College of Charleston."

"That's a start. Thank you."

"My pleasure." He didn't stand.

"Can you think of anything else I should know?"

He was quiet for a moment.

I waited.

Presently, he said, "Be careful, Liz. May I call you Liz?"

"Yes, of course. Be careful of what—of whom?"

"This whole thing began as a way to help two spinster sisters keep their family home. Everyone had the best of intentions. Property values here—I don't have to tell you. Folks moving in from all over pay top dollar for trophy houses they live in a month out of the year, if at all. Now that's not to say there aren't perfectly nice new folks buying here as well. But the nouveau riche, as it were, they'll pay anything for a historic Charleston home. It makes it difficult for the families who've lived here for generations to stay. Property values rise, and with them taxes. And it costs a fortune to maintain these historic mansions—not to mention heat and cool them. It's a shame, really. Parts of this city—South of Broad in particular—have very few children anymore because young families can't afford to live here. Everyone's moving to West Ashley, Johns Island, Daniel Island."

"I don't understand," I said. "I mean, of course I understand what you're saying, and I agree—it's a problem. But how does that connect to why I should be careful?"

He leaned towards me. "Because that house is worth a great deal of money. In many neighborhoods, all this scandal—bodies buried in the yard, for heaven's sake—why, that might make it difficult to sell a home. But this is Charleston. Spirits are a given. Ghost tours are big business. Don't encourage Olivia to sell that property. It's a goldmine, to be sure. But if she's of a mind, it would be lovely to have a family with children live there."

"Oh...I..."

"You thought I was about to caution you concerning your personal safety?"

"I did." I smiled.

He looked at me very seriously. "You're a professional investigator. Bodies and secrets are being dug up all around you. I figure you already know you're in grave danger, as are Olivia and Miss Willowdean. Here's my card. It has my cellphone number. Call me at any time for any reason."

TWENTY-FOUR

I made a stop by George C. Birlant Antiques & Gifts on King Street to look for something for Daddy. The silver antique hound dog statue that looked just like Chumley, Daddy's basset, would've been cute enough. The fact that it was also an open salt server with a spoon would appeal to his love of the unusual. Thank heavens that completed my Christmas shopping.

Sonny called and asked me to meet him for lunch at Closed for Business, a pub on King Street that he knew I particularly liked. He was there when I walked in, and motioned me over to a table by the wall. He'd already ordered my iced tea. I had a bad feeling. The kind you get when a guy takes you out to break up with you so you can't make a scene.

"Hey." I slid into a chair facing the wall.

"I don't have much time," said Sonny. "I took the liberty of ordering your usual."

"Thanks." I loved the Southern fried chicken sandwich with a side of fried green beans.

"I have bad news," he said.

"I figured. Just tell me."

"Seth is talking. Once he found out we were charging him with William Rutledge's murder, he started trying to make all kinds of deals."

"So the rug you found Rutledge in—"

"We don't have the tests back. But all we had to do was mention that rug and he tripped himself up. His attorney—high dollar, sharp lady from the Savage firm—like to've choked him to get him to shut up."

"The Savage firm?" I hated like hell to be on the opposite side of anything from them. Nate and I wanted to grow that relationship.

"Yeah. Anyway, she wants to negotiate a deal. Seth can give us Thurston Middleton's killer."

I felt sick on my stomach. "*No*. He'll say anything to save his sorry ass."

"Liz, he says he saw Olivia leaving the room right before he found the body. He believes Olivia killed Thurston. And the solicitor is considering making a deal."

"There's just no way Olivia did this."

The waitress put food in front of us. I didn't touch mine.

"I understand she's your friend. She's my friend, too. And Robert. This makes me sick."

I shook my head. "All you have is the word of a known killer. And not just William Rutledge. You wait. I'll bet you anything he killed those girls too."

"The solicitor will certainly take that into consideration. But understand. I can't refuse to arrest her. And right now, I have a witness. Olivia has motive. She—"

"Wait. What motive? What motive could she possibly have to kill Thurston Middleton?"

Sonny sighed. "You know that's a brothel, right?"

"We've covered that."

"Olivia owns half of it and stands to inherit the other half."

"Yes, but she didn't want it. Seth was blackmailing her. She wanted to sell the house, but her aunt wouldn't agree to it."

"And her attorney can bring all of that up in court. But the way Seth tells it, Thurston was likely looking for that ledger. He was getting ready to run for office. And he was going to make a big public deal out of closing that place down. Everyone with anything to do with it would've been in the newspapers. And Olivia owns half. She was trying to keep it quiet. Thurston was going to bring it all crashing down."

"That is all twisted around."

"Maybe so. But her fingerprints are on the murder weapon."

"Sonny, was there blood on the murder weapon?"

"No. Could've been wiped off."

"And fingerprints left behind? I saw her pick that pineapple up Monday night. She was showing me what had been on the floor beside a body she was convinced was Robert's. I thought she was hallucinating. But she picked it up to show me."

"That doesn't mean she hadn't picked it up earlier and smashed Thurston's head in."

"Could she even have done that?"

"Was she wearing heels?"

I thought back. *Damnation.* "Yes. But. She. Did. Not. Do. This."

"I don't want to believe it either. I hope she didn't. Maybe we'll find another piece of evidence. But as of right now, I have to pick her up for questioning, and unless she has some very good answers, I'm going to have to arrest her."

"Oh God. Sonny, no. Please don't do this."

"I don't have a choice. Where is she? I thought she was with you."

"You son of a bitch. You asked me to bring her over here knowing you were going to arrest her."

"That's not exactly true."

"Find her yourself. I've done enough of your work for one week. I will not do your dirty work too." I stood up so fast my chair fell over. I didn't stop on my way out to pick it up.

TWENTY-FIVE

It was hard to say what upset Mamma more: One of my bridesmaids being arrested for murder two days before my wedding, the fact that said bridesmaid was half owner of a bordello, or the presence of courtesans at the family Christmas party. But Mamma was definitely unhappy.

"Who did Robert hire to defend her?" Mamma handed me a casserole dish of chicken dressing.

"Charlie Condon." I added the dressing to the double-sided, u-shaped buffet Mamma was building in the kitchen.

"And Sonny actually arrested her?"

"Yes, Mamma, he did." I was so mad at Sonny I couldn't see straight. But a little part of me knew he'd had no choice. I wished mightily I hadn't gotten involved. I'd handed him information that had ultimately led to Olivia's arrest.

"Well, I have just never in my life...what is that boy thinking?" Mamma's loyalty ran deep, as did mine.

And Blake's. "He was probably thinking it would be better for him to arrest her and make sure she was taken care of than to let strangers go pick her up."

"Do *not* defend him," I said.

"Hell, Liz, there's a mountain of evidence against her. She's my friend too, but Sonny can't help that."

"It's all circumstantial," I said.

"Circumstantial evidence is still evidence," said Blake.

"*Enough*," said Mamma. "Blake, kindly do not leave your father unsupervised with our...guests."

"Nate's in there. So is Joe," said Blake.

Mamma gave him the look.

"Fine. When's dinner going to be ready? I'm starved," said Blake.

"I will notify you immediately," said Mamma. "Liz, check on Merry. See if she needs help."

I went upstairs to the room that had been Merry's before she bought her own cottage a few blocks away. "How's it going?"

"I've found something from the gift closet for everyone except Dana. Can you look while I wrap Amber's gift?"

"Sure." I walked back out to the hall and opened the shelved walk-in closet. Mamma was always prepared. Throughout the year, when she found sales, or unique things she liked, she stocked her gift closet. Then whenever four extra people showed up on Christmas, all we had to do was match a gift to the recipient. I picked out a set of lavender body butter, body wash, lotion, and bubble bath for Dana and took it back to Merry's room, where Mamma had set up the wrapping table.

I said, "It's just like Mamma to pitch a fit about having four refugees from a bawdy house for Christmas dinner, but then make sure they each have a gift under the tree."

"Yep," said Merry. "Let me have that. I wrap better than you. You have no patience."

I handed her the gift set.

"Are you okay?" she asked.

"I'm fine," I said. "I just have to find something Sonny can use for evidence against the much-more-likely killer."

"And you think you know who that is?"

"I have a few ideas."

I watched Merry measure paper for the gift.

Gifts. Bridesmaid's gifts. "*Sonavabitch*," I said.

"What?" Merry's eyes widened with alarm.

"I'm such a poor excuse for a bride."

"What on earth are you babbling about?"

"*Girls*," Mamma called from downstairs. "Dinner."

Mamma prayed extra that night. Blake stirred beside me, impatient to fix his plate. Finally, the buffet was open. We all piled our plates high with turkey and dressing, ham, and a dozen of Mamma's favorite casseroles and side dishes. And yeast rolls. We went outside to the tables Daddy, Blake, and Joe had arranged for Christmas dinner. Mamma wouldn't hear of us eating at two separate tables.

The entire backyard had been covered that afternoon with a series of tents that formed one massive tent. The tent opening overlapped the side of the house, and propane heaters took the chill off the air. Tomorrow, Nicolette and a small army would begin decorating it for the wedding reception. Tonight, it was all about Christmas.

We ate until we couldn't move, then went inside and crowded around the Christmas tree to open presents. This takes longer in our family than most, as Merry demands what she calls "present respect." We all have to watch as each gift is unwrapped and admire the contents before the next package can be handed out.

Amber, Dana, Heather, and Lori seemed touched to have gifts under the tree, modest and somewhat generic though they may have been. They got into the spirit of things, teasing Daddy occasionally under Mamma's watchful eye. But it was clear they were all thinking of their own families. I wished so hard that night that by Christmas Eve they'd all be home and safe.

"What is this thing?" Daddy said when he opened his gift. "It's a hound dog. But what is that, his dish?"

"No, Daddy, that is your own personal salt dish and spoon," I said.

"Well, that's something, isn't it?" He grinned with pleasure. "Look here, Chumley."

Chumley woofed his approval. Mamma rolled her eyes.

We continued opening, oohing and ahhing. Nate loved the leather desk set I'd found, and the desk to be delivered. He'd been working off his lap for a while. Mamma and Merry loved the spa day packages.

Merry, as the youngest, was playing Santa Claus. She handed me a small package. "This is to Liz, from Nate."

It was too big for jewelry, but too small for anything else I could think of. I smiled at him. "What have you done?" I unwrapped the package. It was a Slinky box—the children's toy. I laughed. "What?"

"I wanted to get you something slinky," he said.

Blake, Joe, and Daddy laughed like fools, likely in part due to the look I must've had on my face. No one appreciates a gag gift more than my daddy. Our guests also appreciated the joke. Chumley gave it three woofs.

But this was our first Christmas...I turned the box over in my hands.

"Open it," said Nate.

Inside the coiled wire toy was a Tiffany blue velvet bag. I pulled it out and emptied it into my palm. A stunning emerald ring with side diamonds glimmered in the soft light. "*Ohh*, Nate. You shouldn't have."

"You didn't think I was going to let that family piece be your real engagement jewelry, did you? This ring is for your right hand. I want both of them."

I hugged him tight. "I love you so much," I whispered in his ear.

Despite our best efforts, we were all a bit subdued that evening. After dessert—Mamma's Christmas trifle—we called it a night. Nate and I took our guests back to our house. No one was much in the mood to go to bed, so we settled into the sunroom with the Christmas tree.

I went into the kitchen to get some tea, and motioned for Amber to come with me.

"Is everything okay," she asked.

"Honestly, no," I said. "I was wondering if you could help me out with something."

"Sure."

"I've been told William Calhoun has a type."

"I think that's true," she said.

"How long have the two of you been together?"

"Right at three years."

"Is he good to you?"

"Very."

"Do you know who he was with before you? I think it may have been another College of Charleston student. Possibly also a business or finance major—something in the same field."

Amber's eyes grew. "Yes. Her name is Victoria Baker. She was a year ahead of me. She dropped out of school when she and William broke up. I think she took it really hard."

"How well did you know her?"

"Pretty well. We were friends. I guess that sounds weird."

"Have you stayed in touch?"

"Honestly, no. I think she's mad at me because I'm with William now. It's not like that with his other exes. There's almost a sorority. You go into it knowing it isn't going to last. At least I did."

"But maybe Victoria didn't?"

"Maybe."

"Do you know where she was from?"

"A small town in Virginia. Abingdon."

"So you never spoke with her again?" I asked.

"I tried to call her once. The woman who answered the phone told me she wasn't there and hung up. I took that to mean she didn't want to talk to me."

"Think back. When was the last time you saw her?"

"Gosh. That was more than three years ago. I was a freshman. It was before Thanksgiving break. Maybe a month before? We went to a football game with a group of friends."

"And you never saw her again? Who told you she was dropping out of school?"

"Her roommate. She said someone in the family came by to get her things and said she wouldn't be back."

"And you never saw or spoke to her again?"

"No." She shook her head.

"Thanks, Amber. You've been a big help."

I needed to get to my computer.

She started out of the room.

"Amber?"

"Yeah?"

"I know you said William treats you well, but there's another side to him. I barely know him and I made him angry and he almost ran me down in his car. Don't go anywhere near him. Promise me."

She looked at me like maybe I wasn't quite right, but she nodded. "Okay."

I went about the business of making tea. Amber went back into the sunroom. After a moment, Heather came into the kitchen. "Got a minute?"

"Sure. What's up?" I said.

"I've been thinking about all the things we talked about the first night we were here."

"Okay."

"You asked us if we'd ever heard the name Thurston Middleton. And I told you Henry had asked me about him—if he'd been bothering me."

"Right."

"That's the way I remembered it. But I was shook up, and I think I misremembered."

"What do you mean?"

"Henry didn't ask me if Thurston had been bothering me until after I mentioned that he'd approached Lori near her car."

"So you told Henry that Thurston was asking questions about the house?" I'd wondered how he'd known.

"That's right."

"Thanks, Heather. I appreciate you telling me."

"There's one other thing."

"What's that?"

"It's probably nothing, but I was expecting Henry the Monday night when Thurston Middleton was killed. He never showed up, and when I asked him about it, he acted like he'd never told me he was coming. But he comes every Monday night, usually around six. Any other night it's much later—anywhere between nine and eleven."

Something tightened inside me. "Heather, no matter what happens, stay away from Henry. He may be very dangerous."

"Henry?" She screwed up her face.

"I could be wrong. But please don't bet your life on it. Would you take tea in to the others?"

"Sure."

I took my cup into my office. Nate lounged on the sofa, away from all the estrogen in the sunroom. I filled him in on my latest information while my laptop powered on.

Then I logged into a subscription database and started looking for Victoria Baker. Her digital footprint ended in October 2011. The closest living family I could find were an aunt and uncle and a few cousins. It was late. I'd call them tomorrow.

Next, I opened my photo stream folder and pulled up the photos I'd taken in the parking lot at Rut's the afternoon before. I logged into another database and ran every plate. Many of them belonged to Prioleaus, including Henry's Ducati. Rut's New South Cuisine was truly a family business. But the 2005 Honda Accord belonged to Tyler O'Sullivan. With any luck, this was our waiter from Wednesday night. It had been after three when we'd left that afternoon. Did waiters come in that early?

I started a profile on Tyler O'Sullivan. The address on the tag was on Bonieta Harrold Drive, which turned out to be in an apartment complex, Woodfield South Point, in West Ashley. Within a few minutes, I knew Tyler was driving on a suspended driver's license owing to a year-old DUI. While he was allowed to drive to work, the provision was that he had to be at home by eight p.m. He also had a few possession charges the Prioleau family may or may not have known about. I had leverage.

TWENTY-SIX

Friday morning, Mamma was on my phone first thing. Nicolette and her crew had shown up at dawn and Mamma wanted me to come watch with her and offer input. She wanted to spend the day with me, and I wanted so badly to go. I was getting married the next day. Tonight was the rehearsal dinner, followed by my bachelorette party. But Olivia was in jail, and I had to get her out. I hadn't seen Colleen since before my lunch with Sonny. I took comfort in knowing she'd told me she'd be there when Olivia needed her.

Before I headed to Charleston, I had to call Victoria Baker's family in Abingdon, Virginia. I took a deep breath and typed in the phone number I'd found the night before.

"Hello?" The woman sounded older, or perhaps weary.

"Mrs. Hawkins?"

"Yes. But I don't need a credit card nor an extended warranty, either."

"Ma'am, I'm not selling anything," I said. "My name is Liz Talbot. I'm calling about your niece, Victoria Baker."

"Vicki?" Her tone seemed skeptical.

"Yes, ma'am. Your sister's daughter, right?"

"Well, yes, but we haven't seen that girl in...I guess it's been four years. She's in Charleston. It hurts me I can't see her. But my husband doesn't hold with the way she's living."

"Did you know she stopped going to school at the College of Charleston in October of 2011?"

"Why, no. I don't understand. We paid for her first semester. She had a job to help out. Then that man...he was paying for her school. He was paying for everything. William Calhoun. My husband looked into him. Saw he was married. He told Vicki she had to stop seeing him or never come home. It like to broke my heart. She's all I have left of my only sister. She and her husband died in a car wreck more than ten years ago. Vicki's like mine. Why would she quit school?"

Tears ran down my face. I hurt so badly for this poor woman. I took a deep breath. "Ma'am, I don't know for sure. I wanted to make sure she wasn't there with you. Her friends here haven't seen her in a while. Is there any other family she could be living with? Any friends that you know of?"

"No." She started speaking faster, her voice rising. "The last we heard she was living in a big house with some other girls in Charleston. She doesn't have any other family. Just me, my husband, and our children. They all live around here. None of us have seen or heard from her."

"Mrs. Hawkins, I think you should report her missing. Please contact the Charleston Police Department."

"Let me talk to my husband." Her voice broke with a sob.

I gave her my number in case she needed to reach me. Then I pulled myself together.

Nate held down the fort, watching over our guests. I was on the nine o'clock ferry to Isle of Palms, and in West Ashley by ten fifteen. The apartment complex was off Savannah Highway, behind the Jehovah's Witness hall. It was a typical three-story, multi-building complex with a pool, fitness center, et cetera. I drove around back to Tyler's building.

His apartment was on the third floor. This was good news, as there was only one way in and out, unless he cared to jump off a balcony. I knocked on the door and waited. He'd likely gotten in late and was sleeping. Restaurant hours were notoriously bad, and many of the food and beverage crowd went out afterwards, so I was told. I knocked again, harder.

"Okay, okay." A voice came from inside.

The door swung open. A young man who wasn't Tyler opened the door. "What?" He was half-asleep and highly agitated. Likely a roommate.

"I need to speak with Tyler." I held up my PI license. Fifty percent of the time, folks don't even look to see what it says. If you flash an ID and look stern, they assume you're law enforcement of some sort. People really should be more careful.

"Hang on." The roommate closed the door, which was a mercy. From what I could see, I didn't want to go inside.

Moments later the door swung open again. Tyler wore baggy jeans, a ratty t-shirt, and a bad case of bed-head. "What do *you* want?"

"I need to ask you some questions."

"What? Look, I know you people were in a foul mood last night, but you can't stalk me. If you have a complaint, you need to talk to the restaurant manager."

"Who is that, exactly? Who's in charge?"

"Mr. Prioleau."

"Which one?"

"Rut Junior. But look, I did my best. I really don't need trouble. Can't you just let it go? Karma and all that, dude."

"Rut Junior, is he one of the men who wanders tables talking to people?"

Tyler screwed up his face. "He works the floor downstairs. Mrs. Prioleau is in charge upstairs."

"She's the woman who stands at the upstairs hostess station and greets people?"

"Right. And she works the room, like all the rest of them."

"All the rest of who—the family?"

"Yeah. Lady, I haven't had much sleep. What do you want from me? The old man gave me a nice tip. Do you want it back?"

"No. I don't want your money. I have a few simple questions. I want answers. But first, I want your word that you will not mention I came here to anyone, especially anyone connected with the restaurant."

His scowl deepened. "No way. I'm not talking about the Prioleaus. You don't know these people. They are crazy protective about the restaurant's reputation, their 'brand.'" He made air quotes. "I've seen Henry chase people down the street if they looked unhappy coming out the door."

"I'm not going to tell them anything you say. But you're going to want to talk to me."

"Why is that?"

"Because I know you're not supposed to be driving past eight p.m. And about the possession charges. Out of curiosity, are the Prioleaus aware of your legal troubles? As protective as they are of their reputation, I somehow doubt it."

He looked away.

"Aw, man. Look, I need this job. I have bills to pay. Child support."

"I have no desire to make trouble for you. Honestly."

"What do you want to know?"

"Does Henry normally work on Monday nights?"

"No. The restaurant is usually closed on Mondays. Between Thanksgiving and Christmas they're open seven days a week."

I nodded. "But when the restaurant is open, he's there on Monday nights?"

"Yes."

"Was he there this past Monday night?"

"Yes."

"Do you always work upstairs?"

"Yes."

"Does Henry always work upstairs?"

"Yes—except he works the door from five 'til seven. Then Rut Junior takes over," he said.

"Now think back to this past Monday. Was the restaurant busy?"

"Yeah—like insanely busy. It's been that way all week. People going out for holiday dinners."

"Did Henry come upstairs at seven like usual?"

Tyler thought for a minute. "I remember seeing him come up. It was probably around seven."

"How many of the Prioleaus were working the floor, going around talking to people, Monday night?"

"All of them. Three downstairs, four upstairs."

"Is it possible Henry could've left for a while and no one would've noticed?"

Tyler blinked at me.

"Think about it," I said.

"That would've taken real balls. His mamma would've eaten him alive. She's serious about making folks feel welcome. That's one mean woman."

"But *could* he have slipped out of the rotation, gone down the elevator and left for thirty minutes, came back, slipped back in, and she wouldn't've noticed?" The folks having dinner would've no doubt been grateful for the break.

"I don't know..."

"All I want to know is was it possible, not if you think he did that. I'm not asking you to accuse him of anything."

"Yeah, it's possible." He looked at the deck flooring, then off to the left.

"Is there something else you want to tell me?"

"No."

"Think carefully. This is important. You really don't want me to come back, do you?"

He ran a hand through his hair. "Look, all those people are a little crazy."

"I get that." Boy howdy, as Colleen would say.

"Mrs. Prioleau did ask me once if I'd seen Henry. She was looking for him. I don't know why."

"What time was that?"

"It would've had to've been after seven, or she wouldn't've been looking upstairs. But it was early. Maybe seven thirty? I'd seen him, but I didn't know where he was right then. It was a madhouse up there. Between people being seated, the waitstaff, and the family, it was wall-to-wall people. It was hard to get back and forth to my tables."

"One more question. What does Henry usually wear?"

"A sport coat, khakis, usually a solid colored shirt. Expensive loafers."

"Thanks, Tyler," I said.

"Don't thank me. I didn't say a freakin' word."

From the car, I called Sonny.

"Lookit, I am still mad as fire at you. But I have some things for you."

"I'm listening." His tone was even.

"First, I think the girl buried behind the garage is Victoria Baker. She's from Abingdon, Virginia. Parents deceased. She has an aunt and uncle and a few cousins still in Abingdon, but they're estranged. Victoria's uncle didn't approve of the older man she was seeing. He was giving her money. Sound familiar? Victoria was one of William Calhoun's lady friends. Miss Dean told me she left in the middle of the night about three years back. You can connect the dots. The family's name is Hawkins. Mrs. Hawkins is Victoria's mother's sister. I'm sending you the phone number."

"I appreciate you doing my job for me. Makes my days so much easier."

"Sarcasm isn't becoming. A simple thank you would suffice. Never mind. This is important. Promise me you'll get right on this."

"Yes, ma'am."

I ignored his attitude. "Henry Prioleau was expected at the bordello Monday night. Monday is one of his normal nights. He works for his family's restaurant group, Rut's over on East Bay."

"I know the place. I'm aware of his connection."

"I think he slipped out and went over to see his girlfriend, Heather. But when he arrived, he saw Thurston in the parlor, looking for the rent ledger. Heather told him Thurston was asking questions. He didn't want his apple cart upset, but more than that, he couldn't have his involvement become public. The Prioleaus are insanely protective of their image."

"You have my attention. But this is just a theory."

"Which is why you need to get over to Miss Dean's right this very minute. If he was the person Raylan saw slipping over the fence, his very nice loafers would've likely left footprints in the yard. And he was wearing a sport coat, which could possibly have snagged on the brick wall, or a bush. And he wouldn't have been wearing gloves. He didn't plan on committing a murder. He didn't know he'd run into Thurston. There could be fingerprints somewhere along his trail."

Sonny sighed. "Liz, the solicitor is moving forward with a case against Olivia. My lieutenant considers this case closed."

"*Which is why you need to hurry.* This is Olivia. What is wrong with you?" I may have been verging on hysteria, or sounding like it.

"You know me. You have to know how much I want to help Olivia. But I'm accountable to my lieutenant. I can't just go running around doing whatever the hell I please. That's where my job is different from yours."

I hung up on him. I called James Huger on his private cell.

"Miss Talbot. What can I do for you?"

"Mr. Huger, I take you for a romantic. Would I be right?"

"Absolutely."

"Nate and I are getting married tomorrow."

"Congratulations. I had no idea. I wish you both all the happiness Beatrice and I have found."

I stumbled over that—couldn't quite get the toys out of my mind. "Here's the thing. Olivia Pearson has been arrested for Thurston Middleton's murder."

"Yes," he said. "I heard about that. Utterly ridiculous, of course. I'm certain it will be straightened out very soon."

"Olivia is one of my bridesmaids—one of my oldest friends. The wedding rehearsal starts at six p.m. this evening. I was wondering...do you perhaps know the solicitor?"

"In fact, I do. You would like me to expedite Olivia's release on these frivolous charges?"

"Could you?"

"I believe I can."

I took a deep breath. "It would mean so much to me. Thank you."

"You're most welcome. Call me any time, for any reason."

My instincts were rarely wrong. They told me I could trust him, mostly because he was trusting me. "Mr. Huger?"

"Yes?"

"I'm almost certain it was Henry Prioleau. It might've been William Calhoun, but my money's on Prioleau."

"Do you have evidence against either of them?"

I shared with him my theory of the crime—the one I'd just shared with Sonny. I also told him about Victoria Baker.

"That is sad news, indeed," he said.

"Of course, the autopsy hasn't been done. There's no proof it's her. But..."

"But she's unaccounted for."

"That's right."

"Very well. I'll see what I can do for Olivia and encourage the authorities to scrutinize Henry Prioleau and William Calhoun. As you know, Thurston was a close personal friend. I don't believe for a second Olivia killed him, and I would consider it a privilege to play a small role in bringing his killer to justice."

It was almost eleven o'clock. I could check on Miss Dean, catch the twelve-thirty ferry, and still be at Mamma's by one. On the drive from West Ashley into Charleston, I called and updated Nate.

"Well done, Slugger. Are you on your way home?"

"As soon as I check on Miss Dean. And buy bridesmaids' gifts." Holy shit. "And pick up my dress." How had I almost forgotten that?

"See you soon."

I took a few deep breaths, then called Robert, who was frazzled but holding it together for the kids. I shared with him everything except my conversation with James Huger.

He said, "I'll call Charlie Condon and give him all of this. He should be able to make a case for the solicitor that there's a better suspect than Olivia."

That would be perfect. Two powerful men lobbying for the same thing. "I'll be praying hard on that," I said. "With any luck, I'll see you both tonight. I'm going to stop and check on Miss Dean before I head back."

"Thanks, Liz. I know Olivia will appreciate that."

I parked right in front of 12 Church Street. The door to the porch was unlocked. I walked up the steps and rang the bell.

William Calhoun opened the door, a satisfied smile on his face.

I stepped backwards. "Where is Miss Dean?"

Like an alligator snatching his dinner from the riverbank, he grabbed me, pulled me in the door, and slammed it closed.

I swung my tote at his head.

He ducked, grabbed my arm, turned me around.

He wrapped me in his arms from behind.

I threw one elbow punch before the handkerchief descended over my face.

Chloroform. I held my breath and stomped the top of his foot.

"Bitch." He held the handkerchief tighter over my face.

The struggle left me winded. I had to breathe. My limbs went numb.

Blackness.

TWENTY-SEVEN

When I woke, I was in a chair in the Hugers' playroom over the garage, my hands cuffed behind the chair. My head pounded with a horrible migraine.

William sat on the sofa in the sitting area, directly across from me. He was going through my phone. My tote was beside him, my iPad on his lap. A picture frame also lay on the sofa, one of the five-by-sevens on the bedside tables in all the rooms. He'd come to get the photo of him with Amber, maybe other things that tied him to this place. He wouldn't be worried about fingerprints. He had no arrest record I'd found. His prints weren't on file anywhere. Why hadn't the police taken that photo? Maybe they'd done the same thing I did and photographed it.

"Good," he said. "You're awake. You saved me a lot of trouble showing up here. I was going to have to hunt you down. Or perhaps lure you out."

I had nothing to say to him.

"Why do you have James Huger's private number?" He laid my phone on the sofa.

I shrugged.

"What did the two of you have to chat about for fifteen minutes?"

"I'm getting married tomorrow. I invited him and his wife to the wedding."

He was on his feet and across the room in a flash.

He slapped me hard across the face. My head swung sharply over my right shoulder. My ears rang. Dizzy. My cheek was on fire.

"What. Did. You. Talk. To. James. About?"

He ground out the words through his teeth.

"I'm investigating this place," I said. "You know that. He has a mistress here. I was asking questions. That's what I do."

He stepped back, glared at me, measuring whether he believed me or not. "You mentioned you had photographs of me coming and going from here. They're not in your phone or on your iPad. They're not in your cloud. Where are they? I want them. All of them."

He must've used my fingerprint to access my devices. "Where's Miss Dean?" Lord, my throat hurt.

"She's napping in her room. We had tea together this morning. She's worried about the girls who live here. They seem to have disappeared Tuesday in the middle of the night. What do you know about that?"

He'd drugged Miss Dean. Please, God, she was only napping. That's why he'd had chloroform at the ready, in case she woke up. "How would I know where they went? I need to interview them. If you find them, let me know."

He got in my face.

"Here's how this is going to go. You're going to tell me where I can find all the photos. After I find them and destroy whatever they were taken with, then I'll let you go. But only if you can convince me I have *all* the photographs."

He didn't fool me for a second. There were no circumstances whatsoever under which this psycho planned to release me. He'd killed before, likely for less. I knew too much. And there was the matter of him chloroforming me and handcuffing me to a chair. No way he'd believe I'd let that go.

"You need a breath mint," I said.

He started that foaming at the mouth thing again.

"You do not want to antagonize me further."

I was pretty sure he was right about that. "I lied about the photos. I wanted to see your reaction. It was impressive."

"I don't believe you."

I shrugged.

"How can I convince you? You've checked my electronics."

"Your partner has electronics, too. And maybe a camera. We're going to call and get him to bring the photos to us."

I really liked that idea. I tried to look concerned. "What's the big deal anyway? Didn't you read this morning's paper? Everything about this place is in the news." I needed to stall, but not convince him he was doomed. I didn't mention how the police would've documented that photo he had on the sofa. He was likely thinking they'd missed it. Once he thought his life as he knew it was over, he'd kill me and head straight to the airport and buy a one-way ticket somewhere else.

"But they don't have names," he said. "And they have no proof of who has been patronizing this establishment."

In his dreams. "I suppose that's true. James and I were just discussing that very thing. It's entirely possible none of you will be implicated. The girls are all gone. No one can question them. Miss Dean certainly won't be naming names. James trusts me to be discreet."

He backed off, went to pacing. "I don't believe a thing you say."

That was mutual. "Call James Huger. Ask him."

"You'd like that, wouldn't you? What? You thought you'd yell and he'd hear you? James has as much at risk here as I do. He's not coming to your rescue."

I shrugged. "Then call him."

"I want those photographs. But I think maybe it's a better idea for me to go find them than to bring your partner to our party. Things could get messy. Messier. Suppose you tell me where I can find them."

"I don't think so." He wanted to deal with Nate and me separately. But he would no doubt kill us both if he could.

"Tell me *now*, and I'll not give Miss Dean any more sedatives."

"I'd bet good money you've already killed her," I said.

He walked behind the chair and reached under my armpit. "Stand up." He yanked me out of the chair. My hands were still cuffed behind my back. I struggled for balance.

He pulled me down the short hall towards the door, then into the main part of the house. He dragged me to Miss Dean's bedroom door. "Be quiet. I don't know how far under she is. But I can easily fix that."

He walked over to the bed, dragging me behind him. Miss Dean was lying on her back on her bed. I watched for a moment. Her chest rose and fell. Thank God, she was breathing. Why hadn't he killed her? Maybe he was keeping her alive to lure Amber back—and me. His plan had been to lure me back, he'd said. But what about Olivia? She was in jail. He likely farmed out some of his dirty work—like the "family member" he'd sent to get Victoria Baker's things and notify the College of Charleston she wouldn't be back.

Calhoun dragged me out of the room. He pulled the door closed, then moved in front of me.

I brought up my right knee, twisted left, and slammed my foot into the back of his right knee for all I was worth.

He stumbled, let go of me.

He spun around, raging mad.

I kicked him in the groin.

He roared and doubled over.

I brought my knee up hard and slammed it into his head.

He went down.

He could only be dazed for a moment. I stepped over him and ran for my phone.

Out the double windows behind the sofa, I saw Sonny in the yard with a forensics tech. *Oh thank God.* I turned around and ran for the door leading to the parking area.

Calhoun was on his feet.

I yanked the door open and screamed, "*Sonny!*"

Calhoun slammed the door closed.

He charged me.

I aimed a roundhouse kick at his chest.

He fell back.

Sonny burst through the door, weapon drawn. "Charleston PD. On the floor, now."

Calhoun hesitated for a moment, then complied.

"I want a lawyer."

Sonny cuffed him, then looked up at me. "Miss Dean?"

"He drugged her. She needs to be checked out."

Sonny called for an ambulance.

"You okay?"

"I'm good. Can you help me out of these handcuffs?"

"Will that get me off your shit list?"

"It's a start. I thought you weren't coming over here to check for evidence. You have your suspect."

"Yeah, well. Maybe I don't always do what I'm supposed to either. I know Olivia's innocent. Proving that's what matters. You were right." He unlocked the cuffs. "What happened here?"

I rubbed my wrists and stretched out my arms as I filled him in. "And I think odds are good this is the two a.m. Wednesday visitor Nate ran off—the one with the big knife. Mr. Calhoun seems eager to erase his ties to this place."

"Your face is red as fire. We can't have you walking down the aisle with a bruise," he said. "We need to get you some ice."

"Did you find anything outside?"

"We're not finished, but there's evidence someone's been over that fence recently. Two different people. But one set of footprints are definitely men's dress shoes, size eleven. The others are much smaller. Women's size six."

Heather. "Thank God." I explained about her sneaking out leaving over the fence. "But that was Tuesday evening. I watched her do it."

"We still need more to prove who the men's prints belong to. I've got to try to get a warrant for a comparison."

"But maybe it's enough to get Olivia out of jail."

"I wouldn't get my hopes up."

William Calhoun piped up.

"You want Henry Prioleau hopping over a fence Monday night? I can give you that. Saw it myself out the window as I lowered the shades. But I want my name kept out of all of this."

Sonny looked at him. "Let's you and me go back to the station and have a talk. Maybe you can convince me why I should believe anything that comes out of your mouth. You've just committed your own personal crime wave. Maybe you killed Thurston Middleton. Right now you're looking like my best suspect."

"Lawyer," Calhoun said through bared teeth.

With James Huger's influence, Charlie Condon's legal expertise, and by the grace of God, Charleston PD released Olivia at two. I was waiting for her when she came out, bracelets and charms from the Pandora store for my bridesmaids wrapped and in the back of the car. Colleen escorted her to the car, though Olivia couldn't see her. Olivia climbed into the car. She had a broken look on her face.

"Olivia? Honey are you all right?"

She nodded, looked out the window.

"No one hurt you, did they?"

"No," she said. "But I saw some things I can't explain."

Colleen smirked. She popped out and in to the middle of the backseat.

I said, "I'm sure it was a very traumatic experience. But you're through it now—out the other side. Your Aunt Dean's been taken to the hospital." I explained what had happened. "She's going to be fine. I just left there. But they want to keep her overnight for observation due to her age. She'll likely sleep most of the time she's there."

"I should've made her leave."

"You tried. We both did. This was not your fault." She looked at her lap. "Olivia Tess Beauthorpe Pearson," I said. "Beauthorpe women hold their heads high, no matter what."

She straightened a bit, looked at me. "Why, you're absolutely right. We have a wedding rehearsal to get to. What in the devil are we hanging around here for?"

"That's my girl." I smiled. "Hey, we have to stop and pick up my dress on the way. Then we have a ferry to catch."

Colleen whooped as we pulled out of the parking lot.

TWENTY-EIGHT

Nicolette managed the rehearsal like a drill sergeant in Manolo Blahniks. I'm not sure Father Henry Sullivan knew what to make of her. The first time I'd gotten married at St. Francis Episcopal, Mamma and my godmother, Grace Sullivan, had handled everything. This time, Mamma had decided she needed help.

We were all seated in the first few rows of the church receiving our marching orders. Amber, Dana, Heather, and Lori sat in the row behind us. Until I got the all-clear from Colleen, I was keeping them close.

"All right," said Nicolette. "Places, everyone. We'll run through it twice."

Glyn eyed Nicolette like she'd enjoy watching an alligator have her for lunch. But she stood and moved to the back of the church when Zach urged her up.

"Ushers. I need the ushers right here," said Nicolette from the door to the narthex.

Two of Nate's friends from Greenville were ushers, along with Sonny and Robert. Nicolette huddled with them for a moment. I heard the words "Bride's side" come out of her mouth.

I strolled over. "Nicolette, could I have a word?"

She squared her shoulders and followed me a few feet away.

"We're not segregating sides," I said. I didn't want Nate to feel bad because my family was bigger.

"You have made that abundantly clear," she said. "Would it be all right if I have the ushers seat Nate's parents on the right and yours on the left?"

"That would be my preference."

"That's all I was doing." She gave me a saccharine smile and returned to the usher huddle.

I rolled my eyes and returned to the bridesmaid huddle.

Merry, of course, was my maid of honor. "I'm so eloping. Someplace far, far away."

"You say that now." I eyed Joe, who was in the groomsman huddle along with Blake, two of Nate's friends from Greenville, and his best friend and best man, Marshall Hughes, who'd come in that morning from Greenville. Marshall was eye-candy—six-three, fit, black hair, and green eyes. Every woman in the room had given him an appreciative look or two.

Merry said, "I'm pretty sure I'll be sticking to it. But I'm in no hurry."

"We'll see, baby sister." I smiled. She looked at Joe the way I looked at Nate.

My bridesmaids—Calista McQueen, Moon Unit, Olivia, and Sarabeth Simmons, my friend and also my cousin's widow—smothered giggles.

Calista said, "Is Marshall attached?" Calista was a former client, and a dead ringer for Marilyn Monroe. Everything she said sounded like bedroom talk. If she set her sights on Marshall, he was in serious trouble.

"No," I said. "I thought you were seeing someone." I searched her eyes. She and Blake had been dating off and on.

She shrugged. "Some men aren't ready to commit. I'm tired of sampling appetizers. I'm looking for a main course." The way she looked at Marshall made me think she'd chosen an entrée. My brother was an idiot.

Nicolette moved from the usher huddle to the groomsman huddle. I took the opportunity to grab a word with Sonny. I took his arm and pulled him away from the crowd.

"Glad to see your face didn't bruise," he said. "I'm sorry I didn't react the way I should have when you first called me. It's just—"

"Sonny, it's good. We're good. Tell me about Henry Prioleau."

"Can't you take tonight off? And tomorrow?"

"Sonny."

He sighed. "The footprints were a match. We found some threads that match one of his sport coats. He went over that fence. Calhoun told the solicitor he saw him do just that Monday night. William Calhoun's attorney is working hard to save his life right now. Victoria Baker was identified from her dental records. There's more evidence, but the net of it is, he killed her and we can prove it.

"I talked to Tyler O'Sullivan, and several other people at the restaurant. That was interesting. They aren't being forthcoming to say the least, but Henry is missing, and that speaks volumes."

"He's skipped town?"

"It looks that way. We have an APB out. We'll find him. You need to focus on being a bride."

Nicolette shouted, "Bride. I need the bride. Places, people. The first time we'll do this without music."

The Pirates' Den served double duty that evening. First, we had a casual Lowcountry Boil for our rehearsal dinner. My bachelorette party would be the second act, while the guys retired to Blake's houseboat.

John and Alma Glendawn, the owners and also Moon Unit's parents, had outdone themselves. In addition to the colorful platters of Lowcountry Boil, the long buffet tables with blue and white checkered cloths were piled with side dishes—slaw, fruit salad, fried green tomatoes, hushpuppies, fried okra, black-eyed pea salad—it rivaled one of Mamma's spreads. John laughed out loud when I asked him if four more guests would be a problem. "Eh law. Lizzie, you know we always fix plenty extra."

To Mamma's chagrin, we were at multiple tables. John and Alma couldn't possibly seat a hundred at one table. No one seemed to mind having Amber, Dana, Heather, and Lori join our group except Glyn, who could barely control her outrage. I'd already parried several barbs about the casual menu compared to what they'd done when Scott and I got married. I ignored her.

Before we started down the buffet line, we all gathered for the toasts around the stage used for bands on typical Friday nights. I had champagne in my glass and planned to drink it all weekend. Nate, his dad, and mine were sipping on their respective favorite brands of bourbon, debating the merits of each. Margaritas flowed. And of course, Glyn had her cosmopolitans.

Mamma kept a close eye on Glyn.

Zach, determined to play his role, even though he and Glyn weren't technically hosting the event, stepped to the microphone and offered the first toast. "To Nate and Liz, may they always be as happy as they are today."

Next up was Marshall, who seemed to enjoy the catcalls when he stepped onto the stage. He offered a few jokes at Nate's expense, then said, "To Liz, the woman who makes my best friend happier than I've ever seen him. Buddy, I don't know what took you so long. And to Nate. Liz, you'll never find a man who loves you more."

That brought tears to my eyes. I knew the truth of it.

There were more toasts, more laughing, and we all descended on the buffet like a swarm of locusts. Everyone was having a good time. John and Alma had Jimmy Buffett and Kenny Chesney playing in the background. I was talking with Calista, and Nate came up from behind and put his arms around me. "Want to step out onto the deck? I could use some fresh air."

"Sure." I smiled up at him.

He took my hand and we made our way through the crowd and out the french doors onto the deck overlooking the Atlantic. It was a lovely night. Chilly, but a million stars dotted the night sky.

Nate said, "I just wanted a few moments alone with you before I have to leave you with that wild bunch of women. I understand custom dictates I won't see you again until I meet you at the altar tomorrow evening."

"That would be correct. I'm an old-fashioned girl."

"In some respects," he said.

We held each other close for a few minutes.

Movement in my left peripheral vison caused me to turn. A woman walked serpentine from ground level towards the top of the sand dunes. The deck was elevated, so we were looking down at her as she climbed the dune.

"Nate," I said. "Is that..." No, it couldn't be.

"Oh my God," said Nate. "Mother."

"What on earth is she doing?"

"I'd say she wanted fresh air and went out the wrong way. I should go check on her."

A man appeared behind her, walking in a straight line towards her. Daddy. "It looks like Daddy has it."

"Still." Nate pulled away a bit.

I pulled him back. "Daddy can be remarkably sensitive. It will be fine. If you go down there, she'll just say something to hurt you."

"Glyn?" Over the breeze and the surf, we heard Daddy call to her.

She climbed to the top of the dune, and was roughly level to us. She stood there for a moment, seemed to get her balance. No one was supposed to be on the dunes, but I wasn't going to give her a lecture on beach erosion just then.

Daddy stopped, seemed undecided if he should follow her further or not.

Glyn lifted the skirt of her cocktail dress.

"What is she—" Nate's face went white.

She lowered her underpants.

"Is she mooning us?" I asked.

"She can't see us. I need to find Dad."

Glyn squatted.

"She's...powdering her nose," I said.

"God in heaven, how much has she had to drink?" Nate stood there, stupefied.

Daddy turned the other way, but didn't retreat.

Then Glyn lost her balance. She cried out as she tipped

forward and went ass over teakettle, rolling down the front of the sand dune, which was covered in sea grass, sea grapes, several members of the cactus family, and other erosion resistant plants.

"Oh my God," Nate said. He took a step towards the walkway to the beach.

But Daddy was closer. He'd turned around when she hollered and he was already on top of the sand dune.

"Nate, it will just embarrass her more if she knows you saw that."

Daddy walked sideways down the other side of the dune. "Hold on, Glyn. I'm coming."

After a minute, we heard him say, "Here, take my hand. Let's get you up." We couldn't see either of them, but the breeze carried their voices in our direction.

Daddy said. "It'll be easier if we walk down the beach a ways and go over the walkway back inside."

"No, no," said Glyn. "I prefer to go back indoors the way I came. I need to go to the ladies room."

"We shoulda done that before we came out here, shouldn't we?" asked Daddy.

"If you could just help me back up that hill, I'd be in your debt."

They argued for a few minutes.

"All those plants will just scratch you again. You're already scraped up pretty bad," Daddy said.

"Very well," said Glyn, her words slurring. "I can climb this hill the same way I came down it. By myself."

"Here, here. Let me help you, then."

"I don't freakin' believe this," Nate said.

There was relative silence for a few minutes. Then Daddy said, "We're never going to get up to the top of this sand dune like this. We've got to get your britches up."

Nate sat in a deck chair and dropped his head into his hands.

Glyn said, "I'll lose my balance again if I bend over."

Daddy said, "Here. Put your hands on my shoulders."

A few minutes later he said, "There, that's got it."

Presently, the tops of their heads came into view.

"They're up. She's fine," I said.

"Does she have all of her clothes on?" Nate asked.

"Well, I don't know what happened to her shoes. Let's go find your dad and let him know he may need to get her back to the hotel."

"I..." Nate was speechless.

"Sweetheart, it's going to be fine," I said. "No one but us saw that. She'll have a few scratches, but she's okay."

"I don't think I can ever look her in the eye again."

"Yes, you will. Family is family."

"Well, if you didn't know before what you were getting into, you sure as hell know now."

"Oh, I had a pretty good idea."

"I hope Blake has a lot of bourbon on that houseboat."

"I'm sure he does." I gentled him back into the restaurant.

TWENTY-NINE

Saturday dawned sunny and mild. I'd stayed in my room at my parents' house after the bachelorette party. Mamma, Merry, and I met Olivia, Moon Unit, Calista, and Sarabeth at Dori's Day Spa for all day pre-wedding primping. Brunch, complete with mimosas, was catered in. We had the run of the place. At Mamma's insistence, the photographer started at nine that morning and tailed us all day.

I slipped into the ladies room to check in with Sonny only once, in the early afternoon. Still no sign of Henry Prioleau, but they'd found a large knife with a leg sheath, some dark athletic clothes, and a ski mask when they searched William Calhoun's house.

We all dressed at St. Francis Episcopal, ladies in the bride's room. Mamma adjusted the brooch in my hair and stepped back. In the background, we could hear the string quartet playing "Jesu, Joy of Man's Desiring."

Mamma had tears in her eyes. "It's almost time. I never told you this. Maybe I should've. I knew Scott was a mistake from the first moment you brought him home. It tore me up inside to see you marry him. But you had your heart set."

"Mamma—"

"Hush now," she said. "Just as I knew he was wrong, I know Nate is the right one. You could've looked the world over and not found a better man."

I teared up. "I know."

"Here now, don't be messing up your makeup. And don't forget to touch up your lipstick after the ceremony. Your wedding photos are forever. You don't want to look pale in them." We'd decided on candid shots before the wedding, non-flash photos from the choir loft during, and posed group photos afterwards.

I laughed. "I will, Mamma."

Nicolette opened the door. "Grandmothers. I need grandmothers."

Grandmamma Moore, Mamma's mother, gave me a hug. "You look so pretty," she said. She and Nate's grandmothers followed Nicolette out the door.

I thought about Gram and how much I missed her.

"Mothers, you're up next," Nicolette said.

Mamma looked around. "I can't believe Glyn wouldn't join us."

I said, "She wanted her privacy. The ladies room is very nice."

"She had entirely too much to drink last night," Mamma said.

Oh, you have no idea. Daddy wouldn't've told her, though his favorite pastime was getting a rise out of Mamma any way he could. On any other occasion, he would've had a field day with the stunt Glynneth Andrews pulled the night before. But not on my wedding day. He would've known that would just create more tension. But you could bet your mamma's pearls he'd trot that story out next week.

"Mothers," Nicolette called. She looked around, confused.

Mamma said, "Come along, Nicolette. We'll find Glyn."

Nicolette called over her shoulder, "Flower girls, you're next."

Colleen's nieces, her sister Deanna's girls, Holly and Isabella, were my flower girls. Holly looked so much like Colleen it broke my heart.

The music changed to "Canon in D."

Nicolette opened the door again. "Okay, line up, flower girls, then the bridesmaids. Just like we rehearsed. It's show time!"

Daddy took my right arm in the narthex. "You look beautiful."

"Thank you, Daddy. You look mighty handsome yourself."

"Well, thank you, Tuti."

"Daddy, could you call me by my name, just for today?"

The music changed to "Trumpet Voluntary." It was time.

"I'll make a deal with you," Daddy said as we stepped towards the door to the nave. "I'll call you anything you like if this is the last time we do this."

Everyone in the church stood and turned towards us. At the front, Nate waited for me. My heart was so full of love for him. "Deal."

Daddy and I were still in the narthex just outside the nave. But I could see everything. I'd always loved this old church, decorated now all in white. I'd spent many a Sunday staring at the massive stained glass windows. Vases of white flowers, my favorites—magnolias and hydrangeas—mixed with gardenias, ranunculus, and roses—stood behind the altar. Our bouquets were hydrangeas and roses with cream and gold ribbon. Bows made from the same ribbon adorned the family pews.

Marshall stood by Nate, and Merry waited for me at the bottom of the steps to the altar. The bridesmaids and groomsmen lined up, half on each side of the altar, with Father Henry to the left.

I heard the front door to the church open, felt air. I turned my head just in time to catch a glimpse of Henry Prioleau as he stole in behind us. He pressed something metal against my right temple.

A gun.

Henry said, "Daddy, you stay real still, and maybe you won't get your daughter's brains all over your tuxedo."

"Okay, friend," Daddy said. "No need to get excited." He tightened his grip on my arm.

Henry said, "We're going to stand here for a minute, until the wedding coordinator comes to see why the bride isn't walking down the aisle. When she brings me Heather, we'll be on our way. If no one follows us, Heather gets to live. No one dies today."

"What if Heather doesn't want to go?" I asked.

"Oh, Heather wants to go. She's my soulmate. We're going to have a wedding that will make this look like a hog-hollering contest. Just as soon as I get her someplace safe."

"But you'll kill her if we come after you?" I asked. "Doesn't sound like love to me."

"You got me there, bitch. We're going to have to take a hostage. I figure you'll do fine."

"Look here, now," said Daddy. "You and your young lady can just leave us in peace and we'll do the same. There's no need for you to be taking anybody hostage."

"I'd be arrested before I got a block away and we all know it. Nice try, old man."

Over heads and between guests, I spotted Nicolette making her way down the side aisle. She stared towards me, but I wasn't sure could see me, still in the shadows of the narthex. There was no way she'd spot Henry behind Daddy and my dress. The angle was wrong. In a minute, she'd be in front of us.

For the first time, I wished I'd worn the heels Mamma and Nicolette wanted me to wear. A spiked heel in the top of his foot would've made Henry lower the gun just enough.

I patted Daddy's arm and slid mine out of it. I dropped my bouquet.

Guests in the back few rows whispered to one another.

"No moving," said Henry.

The expression on Nate's face changed. He knew something was wrong. None of the wedding party was armed, but all of the Stella Maris Police Department was inside this church. Every one of them except Blake carried a gun. None of them would risk getting me shot.

Dammit to hell, Henry Prioleau wasn't leaving here with Heather. He'd kill her when he learned she wasn't obsessed with him like he was with her.

He'd kill me first.

He wasn't going to hurt either of us, and he damn sure was not going to ruin my wedding.

I'd practiced this move hundreds of times in class. I'd never done it with a loaded gun to my head.

With my left hand, I reached up and grabbed the gun.

Simultaneously, I dropped my right knee forward and brought

my right arm up behind me hard, slamming Henry under his right arm.

I twisted right, redirecting the gun towards Henry.

He let go and stared at me in shock for a heartbeat.

Then he bolted for the door.

Daddy had stepped forwards and turned, ready to pounce. He was hot on Henry's heels.

I picked up my bouquet just before Nate, Blake, and Sonny blew by me.

"Henry Prioleau," I said.

"I saw," said Nate.

Clay Cooper, Sam Manigault, and Rodney Murphy, Blake's officers, scrambled from different corners of the church and sprinted by in the next wave.

Nicolette stared at me slack-jawed. She had no plan for this.

The music stopped. A roar of shock rippled through the church. Mamma, Merry, Olivia, and the other bridesmaids gathered around me.

"*E-liz-a-beth.*" Mamma pulled me into a hug.

Merry said, "I can't believe you did that. He could've shot you in the head."

"That was his intention," I said. "I had to do something. Could you see what was going on?"

"Not until you went all Kung Fu," said Moon Unit. "We could see you and your daddy."

Calista said, "That was amazing. You're so brave."

"Not really," I said. "I knew if I didn't do something he'd kill me. I had way too much to lose. Krav Maga. It comes in handy."

Tears rolled down Olivia's face. Sarabeth and Heather each had an arm around her. Heather spoke softly. I couldn't make out what she was saying.

"Olivia." I moved towards her. "Everything's fine. Why are you crying?"

"My big ole mess just ruined your beautiful wedding," she said.

"That's nonsense," I said. "Nothing's ruined at all. Trust me. I'm getting married in just a few minutes. Heather..." I didn't know what to say to her. Did she love Henry Prioleau?

"I'm so, so sorry," she said. "I—I had no idea he would ever do such a terrible thing."

"You have nothing to apologize for," I said.

The church doors opened. Nate rushed to my side, looked me up and down. "Are you all right?"

We made eye contact. "I'm fine."

My daddy dragged Henry Prioleau back inside the church in handcuffs. "Well?"

Henry looked at Daddy like he'd lost his mind. Then he saw Heather. "Heather. I love you so much. Heather. I'm going to fix this, I promise."

Heather shook her head, her eyes wide in horror. She backed away.

"Heather!" Henry said. "Heather..." The starch went out of him. He looked like a wounded puppy.

"I'm not a patient man," Daddy said. He shook Henry good.

Henry said, "Miss Talbot, I apologize for intruding on your wedding and threatening your life."

Daddy shook him again.

"And for the despicable and counterfactual name I called you."

Daddy turned to Blake. "Who do you want me to give this to?"

Blake said, "Rodney, Sam, would you escort Mr. Prioleau to jail? Sonny, will you call someone to come get him?"

"Already taken care of," said Sonny. Rodney and Sam each took one of Henry's arms and took him away.

I turned to Nicolette. "Where were we?"

In her outside voice, Nicolette said, "Everyone, where you were, please." For a few seconds, no one moved. Merry looked at me.

Mamma said, "You heard her. Everyone back where you were before we were so rudely interrupted."

Then everyone hustled.

Within moments, "Trumpet Voluntary" had resumed. The church looked exactly as it had moments before, everyone in place.

Daddy and I stepped into the nave, and my eyes locked on Nate's.

As he walked me down the aisle, Daddy said, "I should never've agreed to leave all my guns at home."

There was still a bit of chatter among the pews. If I'd looked left or right, I would no doubt have seen wide eyes. But mine were only for Nate.

"Smile, Daddy," I said. "Our guests seem nervous."

We reached the front of the church and Nate, Marshall, and Merry turned to face Father Henry.

Father Henry smiled at me, his eyes twinkling. "Dearly beloved: We have come together in the presence of God to witness the joining together of this man and this woman in Holy Matrimony..."

I confess I held my breath when he got to the "speak now, or else forever hold your peace," part. A part of me harbored a suspicion Scott would show up just to spite us all.

But we sailed into the Declaration of Consent, our "I wills," without incident.

Father Henry asked, "Who gives this woman to be married to this man?"

Daddy turned to Nate and gave him a long, level look. Then he looked at Father Henry, nodded, and said, "I do." He stepped back from between us and went to sit by Mamma.

Nate and I, along with Merry and Marshall, climbed the three steps to the level where Father Henry stood.

Next came the lessons, followed by the hymns, the Gospel, and the homily. Then we turned to face each other. Through our eyes, something mysterious and profound from deep inside connected.

Tears slipped down my cheeks as Nate took my right hand and spoke: "In the name of God, I Nathan Thomas Andrews, take you, Elizabeth Suzanne Talbot, to be my wife..."

Saying our vows was the most intimate moment of my life, and yet the communal bond with everyone standing witness was profound. I was left breathless and weak-kneed, feeling that I radiated boundless joy.

After the prayers, the blessing, and the peace, came the Holy Communion. Episcopal weddings often include a Mass, and you'd better believe Mamma saw to it we had one. It was a longer than average service.

When the recessional finally started, I noticed tiny sparkles, like fireflies, all through the church.

Colleen.

And then, she faded in and marched down the aisle right between Olivia and Merry. Her dress matched the ones the other bridesmaids wore. I smiled and shook my head.

"Who is that?" murmured Nate.

I knew he couldn't see Colleen. I glanced around to see who he was talking about. "Who?"

"The redhead who has on a dress just like the other bridesmaids. I've never heard of someone crashing a bridesmaid lineup before."

I froze. What was she up to now?

Above the music, I heard her say, "And the two shall become one flesh..."

I can tell him now?

She bray-snorted exuberantly. "Yep. But you may need my help explaining."

"You are so not coming with us to St. John," I said.

"What?" Nate stared at me. We continued smiling down the aisle.

"I have so much to tell you," I said.

Nicolette earned her paycheck. Mamma and Daddy's tented backyard was transformed into a fairyland, with tulle, white lights, flowers, and candles. A black and white checkered dance floor sprawled in front of a bandstand. Round tables—eight tops with gold chairs skirted in tulle—formed a semi-circle around the dance floor.

At the perimeter, buffet tables and food stations were piled high with everything from beef tenderloin to shrimp and grits to crab cakes to a macaroni and cheese station. Even Mamma had never put on such as spread as Cru Catering did that night.

For our first dance, Big Ray and the Kool Kats played "With This Ring," and Nate and I shagged. You don't grow up in South Carolina and not learn the state dance.

"That sure is some fancy footwork, Mr. Andrews." I smiled at my brand-new handsome husband.

He smiled back at me. "You're not half-bad yourself, Ms. Talbot."

"I think I'd like it quite a lot if you called me Mrs. Andrews."

"Then I'll do it often, Mrs. Andrews." He spun me around, dipped me, and kissed me soundly as our dance ended.

Big Ray and the Kool Cats transitioned straight into "The Way You Look Tonight." Daddy and I slow danced. He needed a drink or two of Jack Daniels before he'd be willing to shag.

I watched Blake watching Calista flirt with Marshall. My brother wore a thoughtful look. Moon Unit handed him a glass of champagne and commenced to distracting him. I smiled.

Daddy said, "Are you happy, sunshine?"

"I'm happier than I've ever been in my entire life."

"That's what I wanted to hear."

Then the band played "Something to Talk About."

And we all danced.

AUTHOR'S NOTE

Parts of the Liz Talbot series take place on the fictional island of Stella Maris, which resides just north of Isle of Palms, SC—roughly where Dewees Island resides on ordinary maps. Everything on Stella Maris is a figment of my imagination.

Once my characters travel off their island home into the greater Charleston area and off to other South Carolina cities, with very few exceptions, the locations are real, while used fictitiously. In this book, one such location is the house at 12 Church Street, Charleston, SC.

When I began writing this book, the house belonged to my cousin, who thought it a great hoot to use her home as a "grand ole whorehouse." Regrettably, she sold it before this book was published. I'm certain the folks who purchased it are lovely people, and I want to reassure them that, to the best of my knowledge, the house has never been a bordello. Dearest readers, please don't drive slowly by in an attempt to get a glimpse of the floozies. They are fictional. Also I should mention I took liberties with the floorplan of that historic home to suit the needs of my novel.

I also needed a certain kind of restaurant for this book, one about which unflattering things might be said. I've never found such a restaurant in Charleston, so I had to make one up. Rut's New South Cuisine and all affiliated restaurants are figments of my imagination.

Susan M. Boyer

Susan M. Boyer is the author of the USA TODAY bestselling Liz Talbot mystery series. Her debut novel, *Lowcountry Boil*, won the 2012 Agatha Award for Best First Novel, the Daphne du Maurier Award for Excellence in Mystery/Suspense, and garnered several other award nominations, including the Macavity. *Lowcountry Boneyard*, the third Liz Talbot mystery, was a Spring 2015 Southern Independent Booksellers Alliance Okra Pick. Susan loves beaches, Southern food, and small towns where everyone knows everyone, and everyone has crazy relatives. You'll find all of the above in her novels. She lives in Greenville, SC, with her husband and an inordinate number of houseplants. You can visit her anytime at susanmboyerbooks.com.

In Case You Missed the 2nd Book in the Series

LOWCOUNTRY BOMBSHELL

Susan M. Boyer

A Liz Talbot Mystery (#2)

Liz Talbot thinks she's seen another ghost when she meets Calista McQueen. She's the spitting image of Marilyn Monroe. Born precisely fifty years after the ill-fated star, Calista's life has eerily mirrored the late starlet's—and she fears the looming anniversary of Marilyn's death will also be hers.

Before Liz can open a case file, Calista's life coach is executed. Suspicious characters swarm around Calista like mosquitoes on a sultry lowcountry evening: her certifiable mother, a fake aunt, her control-freak psychoanalyst, a private yoga instructor, her peculiar housekeeper, and an obsessed ex-husband. Liz digs in to find a motive for murder, but she's besieged with distractions. Her ex has marriage and babies on his mind. Her too-sexy partner engages in a campaign of repeat seduction. Mamma needs help with Daddy's devotion to bad habits. And a gang of wild hogs is running loose on Stella Maris.

With the heat index approaching triple digits, Liz races to uncover a diabolical murder plot in time to save not only Calista's life, but also her own.

Available at booksellers nationwide and online

Visit www.henerypress.com for details

Henery Press Mystery Books

And finally, before you go...
Here are a few other mysteries
you might enjoy:

BOARD STIFF

Kendel Lynn

An Elliott Lisbon Mystery (#1)

As director of the Ballantyne Foundation on Sea Pine Island, SC, Elliott Lisbon scratches her detective itch by performing discreet inquiries for Foundation donors. Usually nothing more serious than retrieving a pilfered Pomeranian. Until Jane Hatting, Ballantyne board chair, is accused of murder. The Ballantyne's reputation tanks, Jane's headed to a jail cell, and Elliott's sexy ex is the new lieutenant in town.

Armed with moxie and her Mini Coop, Elliott uncovers a trail of blackmail schemes, gambling debts, illicit affairs, and investment scams. But the deeper she digs to clear Jane's name, the guiltier Jane looks. The closer she gets to the truth, the more treacherous her investigation becomes. With victims piling up faster than shells at a clambake, Elliott realizes she's next on the killer's list.

Available at booksellers nationwide and online

Visit www.henerypress.com for details

PILLOW STALK

Diane Vallere

A Madison Night Mystery (#1)

Interior Decorator Madison Night might look like a throwback to the sixties, but as business owner and landlord, she proves that independent women can have it all. But when a killer targets women dressed in her signature style—estate sale vintage to play up her resemblance to fave actress Doris Day—what makes her unique might make her dead.

The local detective connects the new crime to a twenty-year old cold case, and Madison's long-trusted contractor emerges as the leading suspect. As the body count piles up, Madison uncovers a Soviet spy, a campaign to destroy all Doris Day movies, and six minutes of film that will change her life forever.

Available at booksellers nationwide and online

Visit www.henerypress.com for details

DOUBLE WHAMMY

Gretchen Archer

A Davis Way Crime Caper (#1)

Davis Way thinks she's hit the jackpot when she lands a job as the fifth wheel on an elite security team at the fabulous Bellissimo Resort and Casino in Biloxi, Mississippi. But once there, she runs straight into her ex-ex husband, a rigged slot machine, her evil twin, and a trail of dead bodies. Davis learns the truth and it does not set her free—in fact, it lands her in the pokey.

Buried under a mistaken identity, unable to seek help from her family, her hot streak runs cold until her landlord Bradley Cole steps in. Make that her landlord, lawyer, and love interest. With his help, Davis must win this high stakes game before her luck runs out.

Available at booksellers nationwide and online

Visit www.henerypress.com for details

PRACTICAL SINS
FOR COLD CLIMATES
Shelley Costa

A Mystery

When Val Cameron, a Senior Editor with a New York publishing company, is sent to the Canadian Northwoods to sign a reclusive bestselling author to a contract, she soon discovers she is definitely out of her element. Val is convinced she can persuade the author of that blockbuster, The Nebula Covenant, to sign with her, but first she has to find him.

Aided by a float plane pilot whose wife was murdered two years ago in a case gone cold, Val's hunt for the recluse takes on new meaning: can she clear him of suspicion in that murder before she links her own professional fortunes to the publication of his new book?

When she finds herself thrown into a wilderness lake community where livelihoods collide, Val wonders whether the prospect of running into a bear might be the least of her problems.

Available at booksellers nationwide and online

Visit www.henerypress.com for details

NUN TOO SOON

Alice Loweecey

A Giulia Driscoll Mystery (#1)

Giulia Driscoll has just taken on her first impossible client: The Silk Tie Killer. He's hired Driscoll Investigations to prove his innocence and they have only thirteen days to accomplish it. Talk about being tried in the media. Everyone in town is sure Roger Fitch strangled his girlfriend with one of his silk neckties. And then there's the local TMZ wannabes stalking Giulia and her client for sleazy sound bites.

On top of all that, her assistant's first baby is due any second, her scary smart admin still doesn't relate well to humans, and her police detective husband insists her client is guilty. About this marriage thing—it's unknown territory, but it sure beats ten years of living with 150 nuns.

Giulia's ownership of Driscoll Investigations hasn't changed her passion for justice from her convent years. But the more dirt she digs up, the more she's worried her efforts will help a murderer escape. As the client accuses DI of dragging its heels on purpose, Giulia thinks The Silk Tie Killer might be choosing one of his ties for her own neck.

Available at booksellers nationwide and online

Visit www.henerypress.com for details

29612485R00149

Made in the USA
Middletown, DE
25 February 2016